ACQUAINTANCE

Book 1:
MEDICINE FOR THE BLUES
trilogy

by
Jeff Stookey

PictoGraph Publishing
Portland, Oregon 2018

Medicine for the Blues trilogy
Book 1: Acquaintance

PictoGraph Publishing
©2017, 2018 by Jeff Stookey

Book and Cover Design
Amy Livingstone, Sacred Art Studio
sacredartstudio.net

ISBN: 978-1-7326036-0-8

Library of Congress Control Number:
2018908711

PERMISSIONS PAGE

DEDICATION

from "For the young who want to,"

Talent is what they say
you have after the novel
is published and favorably
reviewed. Beforehand what
you have is a tedious
delusion, a hobby like knitting.

—Marge Piercy

For Ken:
When you first began learning to knit, you unraveled
the yarn of that sweater over and over, only to start again.
Where would I be without your fine example?
If the sweater fits, wear it.

After his death in 1983, Dr. Carl Holman's memoirs were found in a desk drawer. The estate sale manager donated the document to the local historical society. This quotation was paper clipped to the front of the manuscript:

"I've held nothing back of the bad, added nothing extra of the good, and if it happens that I've used some small embellishment, it's only because of the gap in my memory; I may have supposed something to be true that could well have been so but never something that I knew to be false."

—Jean-Jacques Rousseau, *Confessions*

Facsimile of the title page from Carl Holman's manuscript.

Memories of Jimmy

by Carl Travis Holman, MD

completed 1981

"Oh, let me, true in love, but truly write."
-William Shakespeare, Sonnet 21

How oft, when thou, my music, music playst,
Upon that blessed wood whose motion sounds
With thy sweet fingers when thou gently swayst
The wiry concord that mine ear confounds,
Do I envy those jacks that nimble leap
To kiss the tender inward of thy hand,
Whilst my poor lips, which should that harvest reap,
At the wood's boldness by thee blushing stand.
To be so tickled they would change their state
And situation with those dancing chips,
O'er whom thy fingers walk with gentle gait,
Making dead wood more blest than living lips.
    Since saucy jacks so happy are in this,
    Give them thy fingers, me thy lips, to kiss.

—William Shakespeare, Sonnet 128

ONE

May 1923

The first time I saw Jimmy, he was playing the piano.

Even before I laid eyes on him, I could hear him playing. Jimmy's music mingled with the buzz of voices from the Iverson wedding reception as I walked along the Chandler Hotel's wood-paneled mezzanine toward the Grand Ballroom.

From his precise phrasing the rippling passages of a Mozart piano invention flowed, clear and fresh. The spontaneous enthusiasm of a trout darting along a rivulet ran through the light, lyrical performance, yet something lingered that I couldn't quite put into words.

When I entered, I saw Jimmy sitting at a grand piano next to a polished wooden column and a potted palm. He was engrossed in his playing, bathed in light from a stained-glass skylight.

Everything about him looked crisp and clean, from his sandy hair parted neatly down the middle and slicked back movie-star fashion, to the white tie, the starched dress shirt, the fit of the tail coat hugging his trim body. His right foot worked the piano pedals while his left was planted firmly beneath the bench as his torso swayed with the rhythm.

I'm not a musician and I have none of Jimmy's technical background or understanding. But I love music. And I know when music moves my emotions. Jimmy's music stirred my heart. Maybe it was only my imagination, but I now found words for the quality I couldn't at first express. My ear caught the song of a distant satyr's panpipe twined up inside Jimmy's playing. His intensity drew me in. I moved through the crowd to position myself closer to the piano.

I watched for a time, pretending to be more seduced by the music than the maker, then at last turned away before I appeared to show too much interest in him.

The music continued to fill the room as I made my way through the men in morning dress and the women in fashionable spring frocks. The crowd was still sparse since most of the wedding guests had not yet arrived from the church across the river. A few sat at tables, but most stood talking in small, scattered groups. As I passed by, I recognized a gaunt man with sharp features, a fellow surgeon with a less-than-praiseworthy reputation who owned a small private hospital.

"Good afternoon, Dr. Adrian," I said as I caught his eye. I may have misread him, but I thought he gave me a cold look before making a slight nod and turning back toward the Police Commissioner who stood beside him saying, "...and then Ruth belted one right out of the ballpark. I couldn't believe my eyes."

A large party of guests entered the ballroom, talking excitedly, and I wandered across the room toward the tables. A roving white-coated waiter carrying a silver tray offered me a glass of prohibition punch. The scent of lemon rose as I took a sip, but the taste was overpoweringly sweet. I scanned the faces in the crowd. My colleagues, Gowan and Bleeker, stood with their wives toward the side of the room, talking with a tall gentleman I didn't recognize. Dr. Gowan was an imposing figure, tall and bulky, his gold spectacles and bald head glinting in the sunlight from a nearby window. His charming smile and jovial manner dominated the group, but he looked uncomfortable in his wedding garb. Dr. Bleeker, grey-haired and slight, appeared, as usual, the very picture of East Coast propriety, his wife a perfect match in her stiff little dress. Gowan spotted me and made a small upward gesture inviting me over. I went to meet them.

The group exchanged greetings with me, and the man I didn't know eyed me with curiosity. As I took Mrs. Gowan's gloved hand, I caught the scent of her perfume. Her smile and demeanor were civil, but she seemed decidedly cool toward me, as was often the case. Maybe it was something to do with my relationship to her husband. Or could it be some quality she sensed about me that she disliked?

"I'm glad you were able to get away from the hospital," Gowan said. "I thought it was important for you to join us today. I don't believe you've met Jack Iverson, father of the bride." He presented the tall gentleman. "Jack, Dr. Carl Holman." So that was it. The new hospital.

"It's a pleasure, Mr. Iverson," I said as I shook his hand.

In the last few months, there had been considerable discussion, planning, and newspaper ink devoted to the building of a new hospital. Iverson was donating the land for the project and the Gowans were instrumental in promoting it along with the Masonic Lodge and a Lutheran church group.

"Hello, Dr. Holman. Happy to meet you at last." Iverson placed his hand on my shoulder and the aroma of cigar wafted up. "Younger fellow than I expected, Bob," he said turning to Gowan, "to have such a fine reputation as a surgeon." He laughed and turned back to me.

"I'm flattered," I said, "but I think you exaggerate."

"Now don't be so modest, Dr. Holman. I've heard all about your medals and awards. I expect your experience during the War was a good education."

"A lot of cases I would never have seen in medical school," I said.

"Well, son, a brand new modern hospital would provide you with a real opportunity to demonstrate your skills, wouldn't it? That's what I hope to provide for this great community."

"You're right, Jack," Gowan said. "A modern facility would be a boon to any community,"

"All of the latest techniques and equipment," Iverson said. "Science is our future, eh, Dr. Holman?"

"Yes, basing our medical practice on sound science is essential,"

I said, "but there is still an element of art to it." I had been reading Shakespeare the day before and Hamlet's admonition to Horatio came to mind. *There are more things in heaven and earth, Horatio, than are dreamt of in your philosophy.* But this was not the place or time to be spouting Shakespeare, and I kept my thoughts to myself.

"Take the radio, for instance. Or the automobile industry," Iverson said. "New scientific innovations every year."

"There's no doubt about it," Gowan said.

I suppose it is necessary, but I'd never liked this kind of boosterism. I was unsure what role Gowan and Iverson expected me to play in their venture, and I felt uncomfortable being the center of attention. I took advantage of a remark I'd heard from Irene Iverson, one of my patients, to divert the conversation.

"Mr. Iverson, I hear from your sister that you're interested in thoroughbred horses."

"Why, yes. It's a hobby of mine. Magnificent animals, aren't they?

"The most beautiful creatures in the world," Mrs. Gowan said. "You were so smart to include equestrian facilities at Greenwood Estates."

"Jack, that reminds me," Gowan said, "I've been meaning to ask if that boundary dispute has been settled out there?"

"The attorneys tell me that the real estate boundaries are clearly spelled out in the original papers," Iverson said. "There is nothing to dispute. I don't care if that old farmer has been there for fifty years. He simply doesn't want to admit that he's wrong." Then he changed the subject. "You know, this city could use a first-class race track."

"I'm afraid you'd have to build it indoors, Jack," Bleeker said, "if you wanted to attract a crowd during the winters here."

"Now, Harold, there's an enterprise worth considering," Iverson replied, laughing.

The murmur of voices rose as another wave of guests arrived. Underneath it all was the music. I restrained my desire to glance over at the piano player.

A lady approached with a middle-aged couple in tow.

"Jack," she called out. "You must meet some friends of mine.

They're just up from California. This gentleman is in banking and wants to talk to you about opportunities in Portland."

After introductions, the Californian mentioned that he was an old friend of a wealthy Portland lumberman, and Iverson seemed favorably impressed.

"My, but you've arrived for some lovely weather," Mrs. Gowan said.

"Yes," Mrs. Bleeker chimed in. "The rest of the country thinks it rains all the time in Oregon, but we have one of the best climates you could ask for here in Portland."

As I watched the women talk, I wondered if, now that they had the vote nationwide, they would vote according to their own thinking, or if they would simply followed their husbands' preferences.

The three women began discussing the food and the caterers and went off to examine the fare. Bleeker followed his wife, while Gowan patted his paunch and said he was dieting and didn't want to be tempted. His self-control often impressed me. The Californian insisted that Iverson come talk with his old friend the lumberman, and they disappeared into the growing crowd.

When Gowan and I were alone, he turned to me. "You remember me telling you about Greenwood Estates—Jack's development out on Wilcox Road?"

I sensed what was coming.

"You seriously ought to consider investing some money out there."

"I just bought my bungalow in Sunny Grove a while back. I believe I should stay put for a while."

"Yes, but this is going to be first class all the way. It even includes tennis courts and, as my wife mentioned, stables for horses with bridle trails through the forest. Luxury living in a country setting—within easy reach of downtown, just like the advertising says."

"But I'm only now settling in."

"At least drive out there with me sometime. You'll need a bigger place once you have a wife and family."

"I'm afraid you're talking to a confirmed bachelor."

"Oh, give it time, Carl. Give it time. Anyway, it won't do any harm to let me show you around out there."

"I'll give it some thought."

"Remember, it's not just a good investment. It will be a quality residential neighborhood with quality people. Marge and I plan to build out there. I've already got my eye on a couple of prime lots right near the country club. Bleeker is thinking about it. And I know Dr. Adrian has already bought one of the lots."

"You don't say. You know, I said hello to Dr. Adrian earlier, just after I got here. He didn't seem too pleased to see me."

"He's worried about possible competition from this new venture of ours. But this city needs a new hospital. Portland is growing."

"It certainly is. But I guess I can understand his concern."

"Besides, you know he's not too happy about the work you're doing with the American College of Surgeons—and with that Catholic hospital organization to boot."

"But surely he recognizes the value of modern standards and patient histories for proper medical care." I wanted to avoid the subject of Catholicism and St. Mary's Hospital.

"Look, Carl, I know you served in the War, and you're used to following orders. And I know that a lot of those East Coast medical school doctors who were in the service want to shake things up a bit now. But you've got to understand that after a man's been practicing medicine for more than thirty years in his own private hospital like Dr. Adrian has, he knows what he's doing and he doesn't like to change his ways."

"But, Dr. Gowan, we all have to work together to bring medicine into the 20th century."

"By golly, Carl, when your father told me he had a son who was a doctor and served in the War, we were excited to bring a veteran into our business—because we're proud Americans. But I should have known that you would bring a head full of new ideas with you.

Just like all these low-class immigrants crowding into our city with their foreign ways." His voice had taken on considerable emotional energy. He took a deep breath and I could see his face soften as he regained control of his emotions. He continued in a measured tone. "There are some things that have stood the test of time, and they shouldn't be changed. Let me give you a piece of advice, Carl. Don't push things. Take it slow."

We fell into an awkward silence and turned to watch as more reception guests entered. "My, but the place is certainly filling up," Gowan said, taking on his jovial manner again.

A loud crash drew our attention to the buffet tables where a gentleman had just dropped a plateful of food. One of the white-coated serving staff hurried to clean it up. Bleeker and his wife were squeezing through to the buffet line as a robust blonde with a majestic gait sauntered away from the food tables. Before her generous bosom, she carried a plate filled with an abundant portion. Her formidable hips accentuated her stately progress past the end of the punch bowl table. She crossed to the side of the room not far from us and took up a position next to a portly silver-haired fellow, giving him an affable greeting. He returned the greeting in a way that indicated they were more than casual friends and he smiled as he eyed her plentiful form. I never truly understood the appeal of such voluptuous fleshiness, the current fashion toward boyish figures being more to my taste. *De gustibus non est disputandum.* There's no accounting for taste—that old saw from college Latin.

"A real armful, isn't she?" Gowan said, following my gaze.

Chewing leisurely, the woman appeared to savor the tastes, her moon-shaped face radiating pleasure. At last, she swallowed with satisfaction and turned to her companion, gesturing toward the plate with her fork. Eating is definitely the fashionable real estate at the front end of the alimentary canal, I thought. I always carried in my mind a map of the human body, and after operating on an incarcerated bowel at the hospital early that morning, I couldn't help thinking of the gut course as I watched her ingesting.

"I hear she and her second husband have what is now being

called an open marriage," Gowan said.

"Is that so?" I took a sip from my punch cup.

"She's said to be inclined toward illicit affairs. Several years back it was rumored that she had a torrid affair with a local attorney."

In my mind's eye, I saw the medical illustrations of the microvilli that multiply the surface area of the small bowel like millions of tiny fingers.

"I guess she and the attorney carried on like that for about six months. Hotter than a bitch in heat. When he divorced his wife to marry her, she dropped him like an old rag."

Beyond the small intestine, only useless waste is left, sapped of vitality, budged along the colon as the last of its fluids are absorbed. But in spite of the fact that its workings are one of the first signs of a healthy body, that dark lower end of the intestinal tract is deemed unmentionable in polite society. The site of shame.

"Being a bachelor, Carl, you wouldn't be one to take up with married women."

I wondered if this lady and her various paramours ever engaged in anal intercourse, as I had.

"Not a chance," I said.

"It never looks good, should word leak out."

I smelled an unpleasant odor. Had Gowan passed flatus? A lapse of self-control? Or was it that because there were no ladies present in our immediate company he had relaxed his guard?

The blonde's companion leaned in close to say something and she let out a small giggle.

"She seems to have a penchant for older men," Gowan said.

She speared a sardine with the tines of her fork and consumed it. I had to smile remembering Hamlet's speech: "A man may fish with the worm that hath eat of a king, and eat the fish that hath fed of that worm….to show you how a king may go a progress through the guts of a beggar." *The eviscerated guts. That young soldier. The German artillery barrage at Meuse-Argonne.* I took a deep breath, and I put the memory out of my thoughts. I focused on the lady eating. Another smile of enjoyment came over her face.

"She seems to have a penchant for good food, too," I said. I was reminded of Freud's pleasure principle. He was all the rage now.

A Mozart minuet came to a close. The tumult of voices and laughter seemed to surge up to fill the void left by the music. My attention unconsciously drifted toward the musician. I never felt that the popular press did justice to Freud's distinction between sexual aim and sexual object choice.

Iverson's sister Irene crossed in front of the pianist, as she moved nervously from one group of guests to another, enforcing conviviality.

"Oh, there's Miss Iverson," I said to divert attention in case Gowan had seen me eyeing the pianist.

"Tedious hypochondriac," Gowan said. "No wonder she's never married."

"She's one of my many patients whose gastrointestinal problems seemed to be caused by nervous conditions." Where can one draw the line between the mind and the body? As a physician, it was a question that was always with me.

"I've noticed that same thing in many of my patients over the years," he said.

"She sometimes comes to me complaining of abdominal distention, but on physical exam there is never anything to it. I suspect her mind simply exaggerates some minor physical discomfort."

"My guess is she's just interested in getting a physical exam— and some attention. I appreciate you taking her on as your patient. Relieves me of having to deal with her."

"I've read about East Indian yogis," I said, "who could mentally control their digestion, even their breathing and heart rate. We in the West don't seem to have the knack for that kind of mental control."

Gowan gave me a skeptical glance.

"I'm sorry. This morning I had an incarcerated bowel surgery," I explained, "so the digestive tract has been on my mind. Certainly the case today was one where no amount of psychological control would have helped."

Surgery. Hard steel and soft flesh. Our highly controlled violation of the boundary between the interior and the exterior of the body.

A new piece of music rippled into the air over the increasing babble, and the room seemed to change. My eyes were drawn back to the piano player. Then I recognized Agnes Washburn from the public library, standing near the piano watching him play. His body swayed rhythmically, his face rapt with concentration. I took stock of his profile, the straight nose, the strong jaw line.

"Are you a music fancier?" Gowan asked.

"Oh, as much as the next fellow, I guess." I felt as if I'd been caught. "I just recognized Miss Washburn over there by the piano."

"Oh, yes. Isn't she the girl who's been finding those medical articles for you? A nice-looking young lady."

There's no accounting for taste. I'd always thought of her as rather mousey. And now viewing her standing next to the piano player... "That's right, the librarian. She's quite sharp," I said.

Agnes Washburn's brother had been killed on the battlefield in France, and when she learned that I had served at a dressing station near his regiment, we formed a bond. "You know that her mother has colorectal cancer," I said.

"That's too bad. A lamentable affliction. Cancer's one of our greatest challenges in medicine."

"Yes, isn't it strange how the malignant cells seem to lose all regard for cell boundaries? The sense of the self and the other within the organism seems to break down and the cancer grows out of control."

Gowan gave me a curious look. Then as if not knowing how to respond, he said, "I recall that Dr. Adrian had Mrs. Washburn as a patient at his hospital."

"He apparently misdiagnosed her case. Now the tumor is inoperable."

"Don't judge too harshly, Carl. No doctor is infallible. Once you've lost a few patients, you'll be more forgiving."

"I lost plenty of patients during the War, Dr. Gowan." I glanced at him, remembering the soldier from the Meuse-Argonne.

Gowan turned back toward the reception crowd.

I continued, "According to the pathology report, the resection appeared to have missed part of the tumor. She needed another operation. If that information had been requested at his hospital, Dr. Adrian could have gone after the tumor instead of just sending her home."

"And where did you hear that?"

"From the inspection at St. Mary's. Where they did the first operation." I became aware how much emotion had crept into my voice. I realized I had stepped over a boundary and I immediately regretted it.

"Of course." Gowan's voice was firm and pointed.

"I'm sorry, Dr. Gowan. I've spoken out of turn. Besides this isn't the proper place for me to be discussing such matters. Forgive me. At any rate, I hear they've started Mrs. Washburn on morphine now. She shouldn't be in any pain."

"Yes, Dr. Adrian put her in touch with a young pharmacist we've been working with, Lloyd Haskell. A bright young fellow we know from some of our fraternal associations. His pharmacy is near her home. You mustn't fret about Mrs. Washburn. I'm sure Haskell will take good care of her."

I had suspected that Adrian—and Gowan as well—worked with some local pharmacist to concoct proprietary medicines they could sell to their patients in order to pad their incomes. Now I knew the name.

"That's good to know," I said, trying to keep my tone flat and my eyes diverted in Miss Washburn's direction.

Agnes took a couple of steps closer to the piano, as if to read the title on the sheet music.

"You know, I ought to go say hello to Miss Washburn. If you'll excuse me, Dr. Gowan."

He turned to me with a sly smile as if encouraging me to pursue her and said, "Certainly."

I headed through the crowd, relieved to be away from him.

I recognized a Bach partita I'd heard at a concert in Berlin the year after the armistice. It was around the time Gerald took me to a lecture by a German physics professor named Albert Einstein, who was then teaching at the University of Berlin. I was fascinated by his theories about electromagnetism and ether.

I met Miss Washburn at the public library when I was searching for articles about Einstein's work. She found one about the 1919 British expeditions to Africa and Brazil to observe a solar eclipse, which helped prove Einstein's theory of general relativity. He became famous almost overnight, and the scientific cooperation between England and Germany was hailed as a step toward healing the great animosities of the War.

As I moved through the crowded ballroom in the direction of the piano, I wondered about the relationship between music and electromagnetic waves.

"Hello, Miss Washburn. How good to see you."

"Oh, Dr. Holman."

"I missed you at the wedding."

"Yes, I was delayed. Caring for Mother. So I just came for the reception."

"How is your mother doing?"

"As well as can be expected. And how are you, Doctor?"

After her brother's death, some of Agnes's brotherly affection transferred to me and probably went beyond the platonic. I was not interested beyond a simple friendship.

As we talked, my eyes kept wandering toward the piano player behind her. That certain grace in the way he moved as he played created an electromagnetic field of its own that kept pulling me in.

"I'm doing fine," I said, bringing my attention back to her face. "Just extremely busy."

"I don't mean to add more to your heavy schedule, but I saw a notice for a lecture that you may be interested in."

Closer up, I reexamined the features of the piano player's face, just beyond Miss Washburn's shoulder.

"What's the subject?" I kept glancing back to her face, calculating that I was covering up the distraction.

"Eugenics. I remembered that was the subject of some of the articles you asked me to find."

Facing the pianist in such close proximity while trying to talk with Miss Washburn became unbearable. I moved slightly so that the pianist was hidden behind her.

"It's on Friday evening if you're free."

"Let me check my calendar at the office, and I'll let you know." It was becoming too difficult for me to focus on our conversation, and I wanted to avoid committing myself to a date with her. "Please give your mother my regards." I excused myself to get more punch.

Making my way toward the punchbowl, my path was impeded by the dense crowd and I had to slow directly behind the pianist. I caught the scent of his hair oil, just as his fingers bounded into a lively scherzo. Pretending to be drawn by the music, I seized the chance to turn and look. His hairline in back formed a perfect symmetry at the base of his head, coming to a straight line in the middle and feathering out on each side over the muscles at the back of his neck. His long slender fingers, strong and precise, scampered over the keys with deft confidence. The blue-green veins stood out on the backs of his hands as the fine bones beneath rippled with his playing. The crowd in front of me thinned and I tore myself away.

Near the punchbowl I came across my neighbor, Tom Harris. His wiry hair never quite took to combing, and it stood out here and there in an amusing way. Since I arrived at the reception, his was the first familiar face that I felt genuinely glad to see.

He gave me his friendly, off-handed greeting—the same casual quality that had drawn me to him when we first met.

"I didn't know you covered weddings," I said.

"I don't. I'm in the unfortunate position of being the groom's cousin." His round horn-rimmed glasses caught the reflection from a window, and I took a step sideways to see his eyes behind the thick lenses. "I'd prefer to be out covering murder and mayhem and political corruption."

Tom first introduced himself to me shortly after I moved to town three years before. I had just done surgery for a gunshot wound at St. Mary's Hospital, and Tom was covering the story for one of the local papers.

"I believe I know how you feel," I said. "I'd prefer to be elsewhere myself. But you may find some corrupt politicians at this gathering. I saw the Police Commissioner here earlier."

He laughed. "I'll keep an eye out for him—and give him a wide berth."

Tom and his wife had lived in the Sunny Grove neighborhood for two years when we met. I was renting an apartment then and when the house across the street from them came on the market at a good price, Tom encouraged me to buy it.

"Tell me what's new in the world."

"The Ku Klux Klan. Big recruiting push. Generating a lot of political interest. They aren't too keen on the Catholics. Especially Catholic schools."

"I've heard something about that," I said. "Although, I admit, I don't follow politics as closely as I should."

"I know. That's why I'm telling you. I think this is a story you'll want to keep your eye on. Especially since you've been working with St. Mary's."

"Hmm. I've got so much medical reading to keep up with—it's hard to stay abreast."

"You're probably up on the eugenics issue. The legislature will be voting on it soon. Surely you know about the lecture on Friday."

"I just now heard mention of it."

"That woman doctor—what's her name? Higgle...? Higgenbotham. Dr. Higgenbotham is lecturing at Fitzsimmons Hall. Friday at 8. You ought to take it in. You'll get the whole political scoop."

"It sounds interesting. I'll try to catch it. How're Polly and the kids?" I had delivered their second child, Rachel. Their son William was now 5. Even though they lived right across the street, I was so busy that we seldom got a chance to talk.

"They're all fine. We just got a kitten for the kids—you've probably seen it in the yard. They're driving the poor devil crazy. Rachel has discovered her mother's make-up and we keep finding rouge and powder on her dolls. So now Polly has to keep the dressing table locked. And William has recently taken an interest in pirates. He keeps threatening to make me walk the plank."

"Oh, Mr. Harris." A young woman walked briskly to his side. "How are you?" She extended her hand. "We were so glad that you could come to our fundraiser for the new hospital last week. I'm sure it was your coverage in the *Oregon Register* that made the event so successful. We raised over $5,000 for the Shriners."

"Nice to see you," Tom said addressing her by name. "Have you met Dr. Holman? He's an associate of Dr. Gowan's."

"Oh, my. No, we haven't met. I've heard so much about you. So happy to make your acquaintance, Doctor."

"How do you do," I said.

"I was just telling the mayor's wife about my husband's work drawing up papers for Mr. Iverson's generous donation of property for the new hospital. Dr. Gowan and his wife have played a key role in getting this project off the ground."

"Yes, they are certainly active in the community," I said.

"Do you plan to buy out at Greenwood Estates, Dr. Holman? I know the Gowans are. My husband and I are so excited about the prospects there."

"I've got a small bungalow over in Sunny Grove."

"How nice for you. Sunny Grove is such a charming little neighborhood."

"Nice enough for your mother," Tom Harris said, turning to me. "Maude Williams." The lady gave Tom a haughty side-long glance.

"What a small world," I said. "I live right next door to her. She's such a pleasant person. And what a gardener. She gave me fresh vegetables from her garden several times last year."

"Talents she learned on the farm down near Bayfield, no doubt, wouldn't you say?" Tom said, turning toward her.

"Oh, that was all so long ago, Mr. Harris." She turned from him back to me, and Tom gave me a wink and smiled. "I expect, Dr. Holman, you'll be associating yourself with the new Lutheran Hospital, along with Drs. Gowan and Bleeker?"

"Once there is a building available with modern operating rooms, I would welcome the opportunity to do surgeries there."

A wave from Irene Iverson caught my eye. She stood nearby chatting with a gray-haired couple. "Dr. Holman," she called.

"My goodness, there's Miss Iverson. I must go say hello to her. Excuse me, won't you? Good to meet you. I'll tell your mother we met. See you later, Tom." He gave me a knowing smile.

"There's my handsome young physician" Miss Iverson said, taking my arm. "I do believe you are the most eligible bachelor here today. Watch out when the bride tosses her bouquet."

"Miss Iverson, I just met your brother Jack. We'd never been introduced. My, but there is a family resemblance. And aren't you looking lovely today."

"Why, thank you, Doctor. Now, I want you to meet these people." She introduced me to the couple at her side. "Their daughter is one of the bridesmaids. She's just home from university back East. Have you met her?"

"I don't believe so."

"You must let me introduce you when she gets here with the wedding party." Miss Iverson told me that the older couple were both professors of literature at one of the local colleges in Portland. "He specializes in Shakespeare," she said.

"How interesting," I said. "Something that someone said just reminded me of *Hamlet*."

"I'm not surprised," he said. "So many common expressions come from Shakespeare. For example, 'There's the rub,' and 'Something's rotten in the state of Denmark.'"

"And isn't it interesting," the wife added, "that Hamlet is such a modern character, with all his doubts and ruminations."

"Why, I'd never thought of it that way," I said. "A German friend in Berlin recently wrote to me, raving about *Hamlet*. I was ashamed that I'd never read it, so I went out and bought a set of Shakespeare."

Miss Iverson was making nervous little movements from which I inferred that she wanted more attention. I turned to her. "I take it the blushing bride and groom haven't arrived yet?"

"A lady from my church told me there was an accident right at the east end of the Burton Street Bridge," Miss Iverson said. "A farmer in a model T crashed into a street car and knocked it right off the tracks. The traffic is all in a snarl now and that has delayed the whole wedding party. I don't know why they insisted on having the wedding at that brand new church on the east side—when there are so many lovely old churches on this side of the river."

"It was a beautiful wedding though. And this is a fine place for the reception," I said. Then, before thinking, I found myself asking, "Where did you find the piano player?"

"He's from our church. He plays the organ there. Quite good, isn't he?"

"Yes. He's an excellent musician. I wonder if he plays anywhere else."

"I've been told he plays in a dance band at different venues around town. Why, he's just finished the piece. Let's go ask him." She excused us from the professors and led me across the room.

I couldn't believe my good fortune, yet I wasn't sure I was ready to meet him. My attraction exacerbated my nervousness. And besides, I asked myself, what does one say to a musician?

Miss Iverson wound her way through the clots of reception guests to the piano. The pianist was sorting through sheet music.

"Mr. Harper, hello. Do you remember me? Irene Iverson from St. Michael's Episcopal Church. Your playing is just splendid." She patted the piano with her white-gloved hand. "I was just telling Dr. Holman here I've heard that you play in a dance band. Let me introduce you. Dr. Carl Holman, James Harper."

I extended my hand. His handshake was strong and firm. His

grey eyes glittered and he gave me a slightly crooked smile.

"James…Harker?" I said. It was sheer nervousness that made my tongue stumble over the name.

"Harper," he replied. "Jimmy Harper."

"So you play popular music too?"

"Some other fellows and I are just starting up a small jazz combo. We call it the Diggs Monroe Jazz Orchestra."

Miss Iverson gave a little gasp and glanced away. Jimmy caught her reaction and smiled.

"Where do you perform? I'd enjoy hearing you play—your new sound." I caught myself before using the offensive term "jazz" again.

Jimmy laughed as he placed some of the sheet music on the stand. "It's a bit out of the way, but next Saturday night we'll be playing for a dance near Bisby—east of town—at the Bisby Grange Hall. We're just getting started, as I said, so we've got to take whatever work we can get. We're hoping to line up more dates here in town as we get to be better known."

"I'll try to catch it. That's a week from today?"

He nodded.

A new buzz of excitement arose near the entrance to the ballroom. On tiptoes Miss Iverson craned her neck peering through the crowd.

"Mr. Harper, we'd better let you get back to entertaining the guests," she said. Placing her hand on my arm, she said, "Dr. Holman, some very important guests have just arrived. I must introduce you."

"Good to meet you," I said to Jimmy as Miss Iverson tugged on my arm. Casting an amused glance at her, Jimmy chuckled and winked at me before he turned back to the keyboard. I wondered how much significance I should attach to his wink as I allowed myself to be led away.

An extremely old couple was being escorted with much deference to one of the tables. Miss Iverson pulled me along toward the group that was forming around them.

"They met coming out in a wagon train," I overheard someone say, "just after her brother was killed by Indians." Miss Iverson excused our way through the group which recognized her as part of the family and made an opening.

The ancient woman slowly lowered her spindly frame into a chair with the help of a young army captain in formal dress uniform. I couldn't take my eyes off him.

"That's one of her great-grandsons," a woman's voice whispered behind me. "Isn't he handsome?"

My attention was riveted on the officer. He appeared to be in his early 30s, about my age, and his medals indicated that like me, he had served in the occupation of Germany after the War.

For a moment the wedding reception faded into the background, and I was at that 1919 diplomatic ball in Berlin watching Gerald in his captain's dress uniform, waltzing with a *fraulein*. He moved with such grace and physicality as he danced to the small chamber orchestra that I wanted to be that *fraulein*—not because I felt feminine in any way but because I wanted to be held in Gerald's arms and feel the movement of his body as he waltzed me around that ballroom, gazing into my eyes and laughing.

The officer leaned in and asked the old lady if she was comfortable and then positioned himself behind her chair. To avoid staring at him, I refocused my attention on her. Her strong, angular features bordered on the masculine, accentuated by gauntness. Her white hair was so thin that the scalp showed through. The old gent beside her was plump with round, clean-shaven features and a full head of white hair that had not seen a barber in some time. Steadying himself with his cane, he carefully settled onto the seat next to her.

"Don't make such a fuss over me," the old woman said in a rich, husky voice. She raised a hand, blotched by age spots, and with a bony finger, bent by arthritis, scratched her upper lip, which was scattered with wisps of white hair.

"Where is Matilda?" the old man said. His voice was high and thin.

Except for their clothing, I'm not sure I would have known

which was the husband and which the wife.

"Grandmother," Miss Iverson said. "Grandfather. I want you to meet Dr. Carl Holman."

The old woman looked up. "I'm pleased to meet you, Dr. Holman."

"The pleasure is mine." I gave a little bow of my head.

"He is an excellent physician," Miss Iverson said, "next time you need one."

"We already have a family physician, Irene, as you know. But I will keep your name in mind, Dr. Holman."

The old man had turned to watch a group of young ladies walk by. Then he cocked his head, stuck his little finger in his ear, and twisted it back and forth vigorously.

"Grandfather, can you say hello to Dr. Holman?"

"Who?"

"I want to introduce you to Dr. Holman. He's my doctor."

He turned to me and opened his mouth. "Aaah," he said loudly.

"I don't need to examine you, sir," I said. "I'm just here to meet you. I'm Dr. Holman." I extended my hand.

"Oh," he said. "Hello." He turned back to looking at the young ladies.

The army captain laughed. I glanced up at him and then quickly turned my gaze back to the old woman.

"Grandma," a young man in a morning coat said, stepping up to the old woman. A young lady beside him held a chubby baby dressed in pink.

"You remember Jack Junior," Miss Iverson said.

"Of course, I do," the old woman turned to the young man without looking at Irene. "How are you, Junior?"

"Fine. Just fine. We want you to meet the baby."

"Oh, yes, dear. I heard you had a new little one. Remind me, my memory isn't as good as it used to be, is it a boy or a girl?" Always the first question, I thought, having delivered numerous newborns.

"He's boy. We named him after Great-Grandpa." At that the old man turned back to our group. The young woman holding the baby moved in closer and bent down to show off the infant. The round pink cheeks of the baby contrasted sharply with the sunken and wrinkled cheeks of the old woman.

"Aren't you a sweet little fella," the old woman said, reaching up to take his tiny hand.

How significant, I thought, that in the extremely young and the extremely old the differences between the sexes are so much less pronounced, and yet people have no trouble accepting that fact.

"Imagine," Miss Iverson said, "your great-great-grandson." She turned to the old man and said in a louder tone, "What do you think of that, Grandfather?"

"Another little pooper, eh?"

Later on, after I had disentangled myself from a conversation with the daughter of the college professors, I withdrew from the crowd and stood apart where I could see the piano. I recognized another Bach variation, which Gerald had remarked about at an open-air concert in Berlin. When the piece came to a close, I caught Jimmy's glance. He looked me straight in the eyes for a moment longer than I would have expected from another man. Then we both became aware that the gaze had lasted too long, and I hurriedly cracked a smile to signal that it was all right. Jimmy's expression did not change, and his eyes went back to the piano. I sensed a momentary uneasiness in him as he fidgeted with the sheet music, but then he began to play again and the moment passed and the room changed.

"Carl," I heard a woman's voice behind me. I turned to see Charlene Devereaux strolling gracefully toward me in a stylish sapphire-colored party dress.

"Charlie," I responded. "What a nice surprise to see you here."

"Aunt Inez asked me to drive her. She's such a dear that I couldn't refuse."

"You look beautiful, as always," I said. She was tall and slender—

some would say willowy—with a porcelain complexion and naturally blonde hair worn in a fashionable bob, which now showed only in curls at the rim of her cloche hat. She could easily have been a movie star or a fashion model. Charlie moved with a poise and a fluid elegance that mesmerized on-lookers. I suspect she knew the effect her appearance had on people, especially men, but she gave no sign, which only intensified her charm. Fortunately, I was immune to her allure and we could maintain a casual friendship.

"Gwen isn't with you?" I said. Gwen Cook, one of my oldest and dearest friends, shared an apartment with Charlie.

"She wasn't invited." Charlie gave me a knowing look. "Besides she's working today."

"I expected she would be at the hospital."

"Of course." Charlie sighed. "As you know, St. Mary's only gives nurses one day off a week."

"She's well?" I asked.

"As always. She visited her parents during her day off last week."

I heard a hint of pique. "I guess it was good for her to get away and see family," I said. On a number of occasions, Gwen and I had driven out to her family farm near the mouth of the Columbia River. I was fond of her parents.

Charlie smiled and examined my face. "What brings you here?"

"I wouldn't have come except for Dr. Gowan's insistence. The Iversons, you know."

"The new hospital."

"Precisely. And then I had a chilly run in with Dr. Adrian."

"Oh, yes. Aunt Inez introduced me to him. He seems to have a soul made of ice."

"I wish I knew what he and Gowan said about me behind my back."

Charlie glanced around to make sure no one was within earshot. "I don't know about Dr. Gowan, but I really ought to tell you about a conversation I overheard earlier between Dr. Adrian and that police commissioner."

I was all ears.

"They were talking sports when they spotted Dr. Gowan across the room and the commissioner asked about that new young doctor working with Gowan, obviously referring to you. Adrian said that you fancied yourself the Big Bill Tilden of the operating theater and that you went mincing around the hospital making trouble about modern surgical standards and medical records."

"Mincing?" I said.

"Yes, I was startled to hear him use that expression, too. But it got worse. They were speaking very negatively about Catholic hospitals and suggesting that the Klan should get involved. He said Gowan should pitch in, which made it sound to me like Dr. Gowan is associated with the Klan. But then he went on to imply that there is no love lost between Gowan and himself."

"No, I understand Dr. Adrian is not thrilled about the new hospital. More competition."

"But Carl, what most concerned me was that they were wondering if you were a drinking man, and then they speculated that you might have known some Bolsheviks when you were in Germany. It was as if they were thinking about making some sort of trouble for you."

"Dear God, that's disturbing."

"It is. I didn't want to trouble you, but I felt you should know."

We were silent for a time. I happened to glance over at the piano player. My dark thoughts contrasted with the light-hearted music he was playing.

"Handsome young piano player." Charlie looked at me.

I wondered if Charlie had seen me watching him earlier.

I smiled back. "And an excellent musician, isn't he?"

Charlie nodded. "You wouldn't guess that I play the piano too."

"Why no, Charlie. You never told me." She smiled at me and turned back to watch. In the back of my mind I had an inkling that she might be feeling possessive of our friendship. Maybe she had indeed observed me paying too much attention to Jimmy Harper. "You must play for me sometime."

We listened to the music for a bit.

"Hasn't it been lovely weather recently?" Charlie said. "I'd much rather be home. Or outdoors somewhere." She glanced toward the window. "May is such a beautiful time of year here. When I left our apartment today, the rhododendrons were in full bloom."

"They are at my house, too."

Just then a considerable hubbub arose as the bride and groom arrived. Charlie said she should go find her aunt. She gave me a peck on the cheek and disappeared into the crowd.

During the cutting of the wedding cake, Jimmy took a break from the piano and went to an hors d'oeuvres table. With some trepidation, I made my way there, too. When I approached and he saw me, he again seemed to be overcome with an uneasiness that he struggled to conceal. He quickly looked away, studying the different canapés.

"They've provided quite a spread, haven't they?" I said with a smile, hoping to put him at ease.

"They sure have," he replied. "These little pastries seem to be filled with some kind of salmon concoction. Salmon is one of the foods of the gods." He glanced at me briefly and then popped a puff pastry into his mouth and returned to his perusal of the other delicacies on the table.

I picked up one of the pastries and took a bite. It was filled with a creamy salmon mousse. "Ambrosia," I said.

Jimmy glanced up, gave a little chuckle, and turned back to the food. Once again I was mesmerized by the color of his eyes. I could not stop admiring the shape of his face and the grace of movement of his slender body. Although a working-class he-man with hair on his chest might have had second thoughts about a certain refinement in Jimmy Harper's demeanor, nothing about him could be characterized as effeminate.

The silence between us grew too long, and desperate not to squander the occasion, I blurted out, "The feel of a room certainly changes without music."

Jimmy turned to me with an eagerness in his expression, and his face opened like a book. "Yes, exactly," he said. "Music can change the shape of a room." Our eyes met for a moment. "Not physically," he continued, as he looked away, "I mean, not carpentry. But emotionally. Spiritually. Music affects the soul. But there's a spatial dimension, too." He glanced at me to see if he was making sense.

Obviously, I did not need to remind Jimmy about the "more things in heaven and earth." Here was a fellow with whom I felt I could develop a rapport. I looked into his clear, grey eyes. "I believe what you are saying."

"Now if I were playing jazz here, this room would have a considerably different shape."

"I have no doubt about that." We both laughed. "Where did you pick up jazz?"

"I first started dabbling with it in college. It's been my dream to go to Chicago to take in the Negro jazz scene there."

I was about to ask where he went to college, when Miss Iverson bustled up to Jimmy, burbling about a waltz for the bride and groom, and the two of them disappeared into the crowd.

Before long Jimmy began playing the waltz and again the room changed. The bride and groom began to dance and after a while other couples joined in. Again, I remembered Gerald waltzing at the diplomats ball in Berlin, but now I found my attention focused on Jimmy, his body moving with the sensuous rhythm of the music as he played. My frame of reference had changed.

I thought over what Jimmy had said about the room changing and remembered that Einstein lecture in Berlin. I had trouble completely grasping all of the professor's ideas, but I was impressed by the way he demolished the theory of ether as the medium that carried light rays. By looking from different frames of reference, he demonstrated that our traditional ideas of time and space are not absolute.

After I returned to Portland from Germany, Einstein was awarded the Nobel Prize for physics and completed a triumphal tour of the United States in 1921, appearing on the front pages of newspapers across the country. In one article, I read that Einstein played the violin, and now as I listened to Jimmy's music, it did seem to change the nature of time itself in the ballroom. If time and space truly were interrelated, maybe Jimmy could change the shape of a room.

I listened and watched as he played a few more pieces, but I did not catch his eye again. After a while I checked my pocket watch and saw that it was time to get back to the hospital. As I made my way out of the ballroom, I paused and glanced toward the piano one last time. Jimmy was bent over the keyboard, absorbed in his music. For my part, I knew I'd been hooked.

TWO

It was later than I expected as I crossed the campus green to meet Gwen. I checked my watch and was glad to see that we still had a little time to chat before the lecture. Near the statue of Thomas Jefferson, I spotted Gwen on a park bench beneath the trees. She had removed her hat and laid it next to her handbag. Red highlights shimmered in her auburn hair as it caught the slanting rays of the late-day sun through the leaves. She wore her hair as she always had, done up on top of her head in a loose Gibson-girl arrangement that flattered her wide, attractive face. I wondered why she didn't get her hair bobbed. It seemed to me that for a busy nurse, short hair would be much easier to care for. Maybe she felt that her patients were more at ease with a traditional hairstyle, or maybe it was something related to that doggedly persistent quality in her personality that kept her constant and reliable.

Her head was bent over a book as I approached, and I called out to her. Gwen looked up. "Oh, there you are, Carl dear."

"Sorry to be late." In my hurry to get there, I had worked up something of a sweat. I took off my felt hat and began fanning myself with it.

Gwen closed her book and smiled up at me. "You're a sight for sore eyes."

"And you, as well."

"Do sit down."

I picked up her hat, a piece of straw summer millinery decorated with crepe flowers, and took a seat in its place. "Lovely chapeau." I held her hat in one hand and mine in the other, as if I were weighing their relative merits on a scale. The plain dark hatband against grey felt versus the blue satin ribbon and red crepe petals set off against the light tan of the woven straw. I pantomimed the two hats nodding to each other as if in conversation, and Gwen chuckled and bumped me with her shoulder.

"My mother gave me that hat years ago. A birthday present, I think."

"A nice gift—from a nice woman. She chose well. My, but we haven't seen each other in a while. I think it was when we last drove out to see your folks on the farm. Was that a month ago?"

"It's been a month if it's been a day." She placed her hand on my arm. I set the hats aside and covered her hand with mine.

"I mentioned on the telephone that I saw Charlie at that wedding reception last weekend. Usually it's her I never see."

"Yes, she told me all about it. I guess they had a talented pianist there."

Jimmy Harper. The physical presence of his body as he moved. Jimmy. A pang went through me. Then I remembered the formal dress uniform. Gerald at the embassy ball in Berlin. I squeezed Gwen's hand.

"They did," I said.

She observed my face intently. What more could I possibly tell her?

"I guess we've both been busy lately."

"As usual," she said, continuing to search my face for a moment. I looked away. "I suspected you might be detained at the hospital. It always seems to happen that way, doesn't it, when you have somewhere to get to? What was it this time?"

"Another appendectomy. Nothing interesting."

"I helped with an unusual obstetric case today," she said. "The poor little girl was born with six fingers on one hand."

"Hmm. I've read that polydactyly is not as rare as you might think. Otherwise healthy?"

"Yes, a beautiful baby."

"Who did the delivery?"

"Dr. Fortis."

"Are they planning to operate on the finger?"

"Later on."

"I always wonder," I said. "Maybe it would turn out to be handy—excuse me, no pun intended—having an extra finger. As long as everything functioned properly."

"It does make one think, doesn't it? Unfortunately, in this case, the extra finger sticks out to the side, perpendicular to the pinky finger. Think of it. The child would never be able to wear gloves. I wonder what Dr. Higgenbotham would have to say about this little babe?"

"Me, too. I'm curious to hear her lecture. You're no doubt remembering that Introductory Biology class."

Gwen and I had first met during a heated classroom discussion about eugenics in my freshman year at the state university. It was 1910, before I went to medical school and before she began nurse's training. A "human sterilization" bill had passed the Oregon legislature the previous year and had been vetoed by the governor.

Back before the War, as an impressionable undergraduate, I thought the arguments put forward by eugenicists were reasonable and scientific. I found myself defending eugenic programs in that classroom discussion. The exchange of views became emotional, and Gwen was one of the most passionate and eloquent students to speak in opposition to sterilization.

After that class, she and I continued our debate, and over time, she eventually got me to see the danger for abuse by the institutional practice of sterilization. I slowly came round to her point of view and became a committed opponent of eugenics legislation. Gwen and I were fast friends after that, and we kept in touch all through medical school and during the War. As I slowly got to know myself better during the war years, my interior blindness cleared and I saw that I was one of those moral degenerates at which the sterilization laws were aimed.

"Yes, what a time that was," Gwen said. "I'm glad I was finally able to talk some sense into you or you'd still be arguing for eugenics legislation."

"I agree. I'm grateful for your perseverance—and your clear-sightedness."

"Here it is more than ten years later and eugenics is still an issue in the legislature. And now there's this Compulsory Education law. I hope I'm not going to have to talk you into opposing that."

"No argument there," I said. "What with working around St. Mary's I've been hearing something about that."

"Unfortunately, the new governor signed the bill as soon as he took office. But the Catholic bishops are fighting it in the courts now. In a democratic society, the populace should never have passed such an initiative."

"No. You're right."

"The backers were so clever to describe it as an issue of making children get an education," Gwen said. "Who doesn't want kids to be educated?"

"I've been hearing that the Ku Klux Klan is behind it."

"Yes, the Klan. And this governor is their boy. Why, from the very start the nuns at the hospital saw the initiative as an attack on parochial schools. Now they are afraid that there will be an attempt to close down the Catholic hospitals. But there is such a need, so many sick and indigent, that I just can't see that happening."

"I think you're right."

Gwen let out a deep sigh, signaling that she was ready to let the subject drop. We knew we were in accord.

"What are you reading there?" I asked.

"I thought I should read Bryan's new book."

"Bryan?"

"William Jennings. *In His Image*. Have you read it?"

"No. Any good?"

"I was mainly interested in it because of that Kentucky statute last year," Gwen said, "the one that tried to ban teaching Darwin in the public schools."

"I remember hearing something about that."

"You know it was defeated in their legislature by just one vote. In spite of Bryan's support."

"Is this one more plank in the *return to normalcy* platform?" I asked. "What is *normalcy* anyway? It's not even a real word, is it? For that matter, what is *normal?*"

Gwen looked at me and chuckled. "Harding always has been fond of bloviating," she said. "But you bring up a good point. Normalcy may be exactly why the issue is so popular. So many things changed during the War, I think a lot of people are just tired of change. A number of states are now considering similar laws to ban the teaching of evolution. So I think that's why Bryan's taken the issue on the road right now, to make it a national campaign."

"I've been with him in the past," I said, "on women's suffrage and support for small farmers. My dad voted for him in the presidential election of '08 and I supported him—of course, I was only in high school then and couldn't vote. I especially applauded Bryan for resigning from the Wilson administration when they began to lean toward getting into the War. But this anti-evolution campaign sounds a bit backward for a Progressive."

"But remember, he's always been a man of God," she said. "'You shall not press down upon the brow of labor this crown of thorns, you shall not crucify mankind upon a cross of gold.' What should we expect?"

"I suppose." I checked my watch again. "Shall we head over and see what Dr. Higgenbotham has to say?"

We put on our hats and walked across the lawn toward the lecture hall.

People were already assembling.

"You're lucky to have gotten tickets," Gwen said. "I heard one of the other nurses say it was sold out."

We approached the crowd that was inching its way up toward

the entrance doors beyond the Corinthian columns.

"Miss Washburn at the library arranged for the tickets," I said.

"Oh, Carl, you didn't disappoint her, did you?"

I was uncomfortable discussing the subject in the midst of the crowd. "I told her you had already made plans for us to go together. Which wasn't exactly true, but I didn't want her arranging a date with me so she could think that I was leading her on. Then she insisted on giving the tickets to me."

"She's such a sweet girl."

"But I told her I wouldn't hear of it and finally persuaded her to let me pay for the tickets." We reached the top of the portico stairs. "Anyway, you and I have been discussing eugenics since college, and I wanted us to hear this lecture together."

"How is Miss Washburn's mother?"

"Not well, I'm sorry to say. I'll tell you about it after the lecture." A look of concern came over Gwen's face, and we fell silent.

The people in front of us moved through the doorway and I presented our tickets.

We stepped inside and I removed my hat. The foyer was packed. A cacophony of voices echoed off the high ceiling as the audience slowly made its way toward the auditorium. One stream of the crowd flowed up a balcony stairway that overlooked the entry hall. There, just above us, I spotted Dr. Adrian as he ascended. He was scanning the crowd below and caught my gaze as I looked up. That cold look came over his gaunt features and he turned back to the gentleman beside him who was speaking emphatically and gesturing with his hands.

A woman just in front of us was saying, "I do hope she isn't going to spend much time talking about moral degeneracy. We heard enough about that in the 1912 scandal."

Through the crowd I recognized Tom Harris and waved to him. He waved back and our paths converged as we moved toward one of the doors.

"I wondered if I might see you here. Tom, this is my old friend Gwen Cook, a nurse at St. Mary's."

"I'm so pleased to meet you, Tom." Gwen extended her hand. "What sort of work do you do?"

"I'm afraid I'm a professional busybody. News reporter."

"How interesting. This event should give you a good story."

"I expect so. Controversy always gets people interested. And with the vote about to go to the legislature, public attention is focused on eugenics right now."

"Surely they'll vote it down, don't you think?" Gwen said. "They have twice before."

"It's a close call. The makeup of the legislature has changed."

A woman behind us interrupted. "Of course they'll vote for it. It's the only right thing for society."

Gwen and I turned. It was Minnie Mitchell, who lived around the corner from me. She wore a stern expression, which matched her uncompromising comment. But her face always seemed to have a harsh look. As soon as she saw me, recognition and surprise passed over her features. But the harshness remained.

"Why, Mrs. Mitchell," I said. "Good evening."

"I didn't recognize you, Dr. Holman."

"Looks like Sunny Grove neighborhood will be well represented this evening," Tom said. "Hello, Mrs. Mitchell."

I introduced Gwen.

"Good evening, Mrs. Mitchell," Gwen said with a smile. She seemed to be studying the faces of the women with Mrs. Mitchell.

"Carl, I think we'd best find seats," Gwen said. "With this big a crowd, we'll be lucky if we don't have to stand in the aisle." She took my arm and maneuvered us toward the auditorium. I nodded toward Tom Harris and said, "I'll watch for your coverage."

Inside the hall we spotted two vacant seats near the back. "Are those two taken?" Gwen called out. We squeezed our way down the row. The din of babbling in the hall demonstrated the crowd's excitement.

After we got settled, Gwen nudged me and nodded toward Minnie Mitchell and the three women with her who were making their way toward seats several rows ahead. She leaned in to whisper,

"That's Elaine Blodgett and Rena Storm that she's with. They're both Loties. I don't know the third woman."

"Loties?"

"I'll explain later."

The audience seemed to be solidly middle class, well-groomed and well-dressed. As they continued to file in, I listened to the gentleman sitting next to me talk to his wife about the "Yellow peril." I wondered whether Joe Locke, my Chinese house servant, considered himself to be a peril to the citizenry of Portland.

It took a long time to get everyone settled, and then the overflow crowd took up positions lining the sides of the auditorium and the back of the aisles. Finally, the house lights dimmed and a man crossed the stage to the podium. He introduced himself as an official of one of the local Masonic organizations and said that they were proud to be sponsoring this lecture. Then "without further ado," he gave a long-winded introduction to Dr. Higgenbotham.

At last, a small thin woman emerged from the wings and took command of the podium. The audience applauded at length.

"Thank you," she said and the applause began to subside. "Thank you all for coming out tonight." The audience became quiet. What she may have lacked in stature, she made up for in energy and presence.

She began with the etymology of the word eugenics and cited its coinage by Charles Darwin's cousin Mr. Francis Galton. "Fit individuals propagate fit offspring," she said and went into some detail about the process of natural selection.

"So what Mr. Darwin has shown us," she concluded, "is that over the eons our ancestors arose out of the primordial mud and slime to crawl upon the land. Eventually, they shed their tails and walked upright on two legs. With the development of superior cranial capacity and a larger brain which enables us to think, and the opposable thumb which enables us to manipulate tools, humans have raised themselves above the other animals on this planet."

I wondered how William Jennings Bryan and the anti-evolutionists would take to this, as well as those devout Christians in the audience. Gwen nudged me with her elbow and leaned in to whisper, "Watch them," nodding toward Minnie Mitchell and her friends. They were whispering among themselves, their hats bobbing and dipping as they turned from one to another.

Next came a digression summarizing the work of Gregor Mendel's research with garden peas, and Dr. Higgenbotham went on to discuss the long history of breeding domestic livestock and Luther Burbank's crossbreeding of plant stocks. She emphasized that Burbank joined the Committee on Eugenics of the American Breeders' Association to encourage the improvement of the human species, and that leaders like Teddy Roosevelt and Woodrow Wilson had also supported the eugenics movement.

This movement had a two-pronged approach. First, encourage white upper class couples to propagate. "Today, with more of our women going to college and entering the professional world, they are having fewer children. Many choose to use the new birth control methods to ensure fewer pregnancies."

A month earlier the wife of a prominent businessman had come to see me. She was in an agitated state, begging me to help her with birth control. She had read a pamphlet by Margaret Sanger that a friend gave her. She said that after bearing three children, she simply could not face another pregnancy. I did what I could, prescribing the foam powders and jellies and giving instructions for their use. But all the while I kept remembering that in 1915, while I was still in medical school, Emma Goldman had been arrested in Portland just for giving a public lecture on birth control.

Dr. Higgenbotham was going on about "race suicide," the Fitter Family programs, and use of European developments in psychology like the Intelligence Quotient Test to help us identify those who are most fit to procreate. She encouraged immigration policies that favored people of Nordic and northern European heritage and discouraged letting in those from the less desirable races.

She went on to describe the second prong of the approach. "We must curb race degeneracy by preventing propagation by those afflicted with poverty, prostitution, feeble-mindedness, insanity, epilepsy, habitual criminality, and sexual deviance, all of which have been proven to pass on to subsequent generations."

Of course, sexual deviance, I thought. While I was in college, the local Portland YMCA was implicated in a high-profile sex scandal involving "unnatural acts." Numerous men, some among Portland's elite, including a physician and an attorney, were indicted for sexual deviance in sodomy trials that were widely reported.

"...but we now have an invaluable tool to fight these menaces to our nation—a simple, surgical operation called sterilization. As a practitioner of the art of medicine, I can attest to the fact that it is efficient, inexpensive, and safe." Dr. Higgenbotham held that, once sterilized, "these unfortunates" could be freed from expensive tax-supported institutions to live productive lives in society.

During the War, I had removed the testicles of a soldier who had been injured in the groin. But I could not square Dr. Higgenbotham's talk of animal husbandry with applying the same techniques to human beings.

"...let us take another example, that of feeble-mindedness. I know many of you are familiar with the case studies of the Jukes and the Kallikaks."

Gwen gently elbowed me again. We had spent hours discussing the Jukes and the Kallikaks back in our undergraduate days when new research on those families had been published.

Dr. Higgenbotham outlined the scholarship on family degeneracy, then continued. "This category has been carefully studied and scientifically classified using mental age testing. Starting with the most unfortunate, we have the idiot, which, of course, we all recognize at once. These are unable to speak or care for themselves and require the care that any one- to two-year-old child would need. Next, there is the imbecile, able to speak and do the activities expected of a three- to seven-year-old. These types necessarily require confinement and care in asylums. But the most dangerous of all is the high grade moron with a mental age of eight to twelve years. These might move through society almost without detection and pass their genetic material on to another generation." She described her personal experience in rural Oregon with a husband and wife of the feeble-minded type with seven feeble-minded children and another on the way. "They were living in poverty and squalor, unable to provide the basic necessities for themselves. Their danger lies in the fact that they cannot tell right from wrong and they are easily recruited into a life of crime and moral degeneracy."

I had met people of this type—like a black New York City shoeshine boy with a beautiful smile and infectious laugh or a young Parisian flower vendor girl with a lovely singing voice—both of a dull but sweet-natured and innocent character. What they had been recruited into was a life of simple, productive work and they were bright spots in the lives of their communities.

"Today, right here in our state, we have before us the chance to pass a law that will improve life for these unfortunates. A new and revised Human Sterilization Bill is poised for passage by the lawmakers of our state." She briefly outlined earlier attempts to pass similar bills in Oregon going back to 1907, including a 1913 bill that was passed by the legislature and signed by the governor, then later repealed in a voter referendum.

"As you may recall, in each of these battles, eugenics legislation garnered greater and greater support. The new bill, considered by legal experts to pass constitutional muster, must be passed. We have, today, this great opportunity to finally enact a law that will improve society, make us all safer, and through surgical sterilization, return many of these defectives to productive lives in the community. I urge each one of you to write letters to your elected officials letting them know that you want them to vote for enactment of this law. We believe the governor is with us on this, so all we need do is get this act through the legislature.

"I entreat your support. With the spirit of reform and the belief in progress guiding us in our many endeavors, we cannot help but create a better race of people and a better world."

Prolonged applause followed. Hearing Dr. Higgenbotham's summary of recent legislation, I realized that the sex scandal of 1912 had undoubtedly influenced the eventual passage of that 1913 law for the sterilization of "moral degenerates" and "sexual perverts."

As we exited through the foyer, I saw attendants selling pamphlets of the lecture to raise funds. I was taken aback when Gwen bought one and foisted it into my hand. She insisted that we needed it to think up counter arguments. Embarrassed, I quickly stuffed it into my coat pocket.

It was dusk as we moved slowly with the crowd out under a half-full moon. I was putting my hat on when Gwen elbowed me and nodded toward Minnie Mitchell and her friends, who stood at one end of the lighted portico talking excitedly. Engaged in their circle of conversation stood Dr. Adrian and his gesticulating friend, nodding and frowning as they talked.

We descended the front steps away from the electric lights into the freshness of the night air. "What was it you were going to explain to me about Mrs. Mitchell's friends?"

"Those two women belong to the Ladies of the Invisible Empire. The Loties."

"The Loties? I've never heard of them."

"They're the ladies auxiliary of the Klan. Elaine Blodgett lives in Astoria and belongs to the same chapter as my mother. And Rena Storm is an official in one of the Portland chapters. She often comes to speak to the Astoria chapter. Mother speaks highly of her."

"Wait. Your mother belongs to the Klan?"

"I'm afraid it's true. I try to change the subject when she brings it up. It's so hard for me to bite my tongue when she starts in on it."

I was about to ask if her father belonged to the Klan too when a booming voice from across the lawn commanded our attention.

"A literal interpretation of the *Book of Genesis* is fundamental. And you can read the truth right here in *The Fundamentals*. For just a nickel. Less than the price of a moving picture ticket." A young man surrounded by a large group of onlookers stood on a soap box under a streetlight. He held a megaphone in one hand and waved a copy of the magazine above his head with the other.

"What you have heard this woman preach tonight is blasphemy," the young man continued. "An insolent challenge to eternal verities. The scriptures were inspired by God and are beyond questioning. Do you want your children being taught this kind of godless atheism by eugenists and Darwinists? Now with the Compulsory Education Act, this is exactly what children will be learning in the public schools. This is an abomination. In that lecture hall tonight you have heard the voice of the Devil enticing you away from the truth."

Gwen took my arm and guided us toward the speaker.

"All around us in modern life we hear the voice of Satan tempting us. In the movie palaces, in the speakeasies, in popular phonograph records. But subtlest of all is this modernist heresy that promotes the view that the scriptures have evolved. You hear this whispering of the Prince of Darkness from the pulpits of the mainline Protestant churches in every city in this nation. They are just putting on Darwinist eyeglasses to look backward on what was established long ago, 'In the beginning God created the heaven and the earth. And God said, Let the earth bring forth the living creature after his kind, cattle, and creeping things, and beasts of the earth after his kind: and it was so.'"

We took a position at the periphery of the onlookers, but a crowd from the lecture hall soon filled in behind us.

"Listen to me, people. 'God said, Let us make man in our own image, after our likeness.' Human beings were created by God. Not descended from apes. We are special, and we have a special relationship with God. This teaching that we arose from a brute ancestry undermines moral principles. I don't have to explain this to you. You see it everywhere. You see it in the envy that is engendered by modern advertising. You see it in the greed of modern industry."

A tenor voice cried out from close behind us. "You can pray to God all you want, but it's John D. you'll have to convince to give you a raise in pay." Here and there a ripple of laughter sounded.

The speaker ignored the comment and went on, trumpeting

through his megaphone. "You see it in the lust that is rampant in movies and publications of our day. You see it in the anger unleashed in the terrible war that has recently taken so many of our young men. Those barbarous Huns used this godless philosophy of survival of the fittest to wage a war of aggression against God's chosen, the Anglo-Saxon peoples."

At his mention of "the barbarous Huns," the elegant vision of the embassy ball in Berlin floated through my mind. And I remembered that manicured Berlin park where Gerald had taken me to the Bach concerts. I remembered the architecture and the art I'd seen there. Could this Christian speaker be referring to the same country I knew? Memories of the many good German citizens that I had met came to mind, most prominently, my two closest German friends, Detlef and Heinz, to whom Gerald had introduced me. Could this churchman possibly be referring to these people I had known?

The same tenor voice called out again. "Lester Sykes, your brother wouldn't have been killed by those Huns if he hadn't volunteered to let himself be used as cannon fodder by the capitalist butchers."

Something in his tone made me wonder if maybe liquor hadn't loosened his tongue. I turned to make out who this apparent socialist was and saw a tall slender fellow sporting a Stevedores Union button on his cap. Standing next to him, smiling broadly at these political jibes, was a shorter, athletic-looking man with bad teeth. I recognized him, an automobile mechanic called Nick with whom I had once shared intimacies. I quickly turned back toward the preacher, hoping Nick hadn't seen me.

"Yes. Bigger guns, more destructive bombs," bellowed the megaphone. "Submarine warfare under the seas, flying gunners in the heavens, poisonous mustard gas creeping across the land. Progress. That's what your great god Science has to offer. We know all about the perfectibility of the human race. We must all wake up and acknowledge that Christian moral principals have been weakened by this Darwinist propaganda. I tell you it's the work of the Devil, and we must fight against it with all that we are worth."

"The devil we need to fight against is the devil of laissez-faire capitalism," the stevedore interjected. "What we need is for the workers to unite in unions and—"

"Hey, bottle it, buddy" came a nearby shout from a tall, burly fellow with a full beard. I turned and saw Nick staring up at the stevedore with a look of admiration and something subtle in the posture of his stance that suggested to me the two were intimate as well. The bulge of a flask in the stevedore's breast pocket confirmed my suspicion about alcohol.

"Yeah, let the preacher have his say," a voice called out. Several others rose in agreement.

"The good Lord taught us to turn the other cheek," the preacher continued, "and I will do the same. It is the meek who shall inherit the earth."

"You sound like one of these Wobblies," the bearded fellow said with rising heat as he moved toward the stevedore.

"You're right. I'm a Wobbly." He drew himself up, standing his ground. "And proud of it."

I leaned in to Gwen and suggested we move along. "Just a minute," she whispered and made a gesture with her hand to silence me.

"I think you've said about enough," the bearded one replied and walked up and gave the Wobbly a shove. A man in a bowler hat stepped forward and said to the stevedore, "Sounds to me like you need to learn some manners."

"God will seek out iniquity and punish the sinners," the megaphone boomed.

The bearded man shoved the stevedore and the stevedore pushed back.

"We must not engender strife among ourselves," the preacher shouted.

The bearded man took a punch at the Wobbly.

"Remember that the lion will lie down with the lamb."

The Wobbly hit back and the bearded man reeled. The man in the bowler grabbed the Wobbly's arm, pulling him around, and kneed him one. Nick gave the man in the bowler a shove. The crowd surged forward to view the fight better. The bearded man recovered his balance and came at Nick. A blow from Nick threw the bearded man backward. He bumped into the man beside Gwen. She lost her footing in the jostling and fell to her knees just as some others collided with us. I reached down and took Gwen's elbow. She quickly pulled herself upright, but her hat fell to the ground and was trampled underfoot. I tried to position my body between Gwen and the combatants, but the crowd surged back the other direction as the stevedore stumbled away from another jab. I took advantage of the opportunity to escort Gwen out of the thick of it. An old man followed us and handed Gwen her battered straw hat.

We continued backing away. The preacher began trying to distract the crowd by rallying them in a hymn, but the pushing and shoving escalated.

He sang the hymn's chorus through his megaphone but no one picked it up. A group of about half a dozen men bustled over from the lecture hall and began trying to restrain the combatants. The scuffling subsided, but raised voices shot back and forth. Then sirens wailed in the distance. Soon things began to quiet down. Finally, Nick and the stevedore were escorted off toward the street. The others in the tussle were led off toward the lecture hall. The preacher had stopped singing his hymn and must have stepped down from his soapbox for he could no longer be seen above the dwindling crowd.

Gwen and I crossed the moonlit lawn toward the sidewalk. Stopping to look back, we saw more men coming from the lecture hall encouraging the crowd to disburse. A police wagon arrived and Nick and his companion disappeared inside it.

"I hope Tom Harris was able to get in on that," I said with a laugh. "Should make for a good story."

"That poor preacher," Gwen said assessing the damage to her hat.

"Misguided fellow."

"Yes. But all the same…There was a sincerity about him."

"Sounded like sheer bullheaded dogmatism to me."

"I know you aren't a believer, Carl."

I didn't want to get into a religious argument, least of all with Gwen, so I changed the subject. "My car is a couple of blocks over. I was planning on driving you home."

She took my arm again and we walked, each of us lost in our thoughts as we passed under a row of trees that shaded us from the moon.

"I am a little uncomfortable," I said, "when I think that our admission tickets are going to support Dr. Higgenbotham's campaign for sterilization. Then you bought that pamphlet."

"Oh piffle. We can use it against them. Besides, the Masons were her sponsors. Maybe some of the take will go to the new hospital."

"Oh, there's yet another controversy."

"I guess any change creates controversy," Gwen said.

"You're right about that. I saw Dr. Adrian there tonight. He was talking with those Lotie women."

"I noticed. It worries me."

We turned the corner where a city street ran alongside the campus.

"You know, what Dr. Higgenbotham didn't stress enough was voluntary birth control," Gwen said. "If Mrs. Sanger were free to spread information and send her sponges and powders through the post, needy women would have the means to limit pregnancies."

"But she argued that it's middle class women who use Margaret Sanger's methods. She even used that old shibboleth, race suicide. Do you think the uneducated would take advantage of those methods?"

"I've had many women who were not so well educated tell me they wished they had some way to keep from having another baby. I suppose it's because I'm a nurse. Some of my patients will confide things to me that they wouldn't tell a doctor. And I know you disagree with me on this, but I've quietly referred a number of women who asked about ending a pregnancy."

"It's not that I object to the operation. I just don't feel right performing it myself. Besides it's illegal and I'm not willing to jeopardize my career."

"I expect you'd feel differently if you had to bear the children yourself."

"Yes, that's something I'll never experience. Even though I've seen my share of pregnancies and births. It just doesn't sit right with me. I can't explain my feelings. Maybe it has to do with taking the Hippocratic oath, which does specifically forbid abortion, and that phrase from the oath, do no harm. It's not a religious thing with me. But having sworn an oath…I guess I feel an obligation to keep my word."

We didn't speak for a time. A breeze rustled the leaves of the trees overhead as we walked.

"I keep remembering a neighbor girl out by the farm," Gwen said. "She wasn't the brightest star in the sky. Came from dirt-poor farming stock. Some said she was born dimwitted. But I'd heard that as a child she was kicked in the head by a horse. So her condition would not have been passed on. But such a loving, sweet, warm-hearted girl. And, my, she was a worker." We stopped at the corner as cars passed. "She was taken away to a home for the feeble-minded and they talked her family and her into a voluntary sterilization. Under those circumstances, being removed from familiar surroundings and forcibly institutionalized, you can hardly call such a decision voluntary."

"And now I find myself a candidate for sterilization," I said.

Gwen glanced at me and gave my arm a squeeze before we crossed the street. We were both preoccupied as I drove Gwen home.

I parked at the curb near the front walkway and turned off the engine. It was a quiet street. The moon threw its light on the white rhododendron blooms in front of Gwen's apartment building. We sat in silence for a while.

Gwen turned and scrutinized me. "Is everything all right, Carl? You seem tired."

"Oh, I don't know," I said. "Sometimes I feel so old. Especially lately."

Gwen laughed. "Carl, 32 is not old." She paused and looked at me. "But you're too old to be without companionship."

"I've been thinking a lot about that."

"How so?"

"Oh…at that wedding reception something made me think of Gerald and I keep seeing his face…"

"Oh, Carl."

I didn't have to remind her how broken up I was after I returned from Berlin. She had been there to comfort me.

"I try to stay busy. I try to just put it out of my mind, but… almost every day something reminds me…" I took off my hat and rubbed my hand over my forehead.

"That beautiful face," I went on. "That face that I loved so much. How could it become smashed to pieces like that? What kind of God would let such a thing happen?"

"Carl, don't," she said gently. "God works in mysterious ways."

"How could that physical presence simply disappear from the face of the earth? Vanish from existence? I've seen enough people die that I should understand. But, you know…I keep feeling like Gerald left me. I keep wondering, where has he gone off to?" Tears welled up and I looked away.

Gwen placed her hand on mine. "Yes." She squeezed my hand. "I know."

Again we were quiet for a while. Finally I took out my handkerchief. "And now I'm afraid to get close to anyone…for fear that…that it will happen again."

"You mustn't…"

"I know." I raised my hands in a gesture of part protest, part resignation. "I have to buck up. Stay open. To possibilities. To change." I put my handkerchief away. "Maybe change is possible." I looked over at her and tried to smile. "You remember how I used to say that tears could heal wounds?"

"Don't be too hard on yourself, Carl," she said.

Just then Charlie came strolling down the dimly lighted walk from the building entrance. She was wearing trousers, which took me by surprise. I'd seen her in slacks at home with Gwen, but I'd never seen her out on the street dressed like that.

"What are you two lovebirds doing out here in the moonlight?" She leaned down to peer into the open car window. "Spooning in this struggle buggy?" She laughed. "I saw you drive up from the front window upstairs."

"Good evening, angel," Gwen said as she opened the car door.

After goodbyes, I watched them walk arm-in-arm into the building, and I started the engine. A vague feeling of agitation regarding Gwen and Charlie arose in my mind as I drove home. By the time I steered up my driveway and anticipated walking into my empty house, I was able to put a name to it. Envy.

THREE

On Thursday, before the dance at the Bisby Grange Hall, I had settled on the idea of sharing a nip of gin as an excuse to talk to Jimmy alone. When I got home from work that day, I grabbed a chair from the breakfast nook and began rummaging around in the top shelves of my kitchen cupboards to find a silver-plated hip flask my grandfather gave me when I graduated from medical school. The flask hadn't seen any use since the Eighteenth Amendment went into effect. I never did drink much even when prohibition became law in Oregon back while I was in medical school. And once drinking became a federal offense in 1920, I stopped carrying liquor on social outings. As I stood there on the chair near the stove, Joe Locke came into the kitchen from the garden carrying a basket of greens and snow peas. In his Chinese accent he demanded to know what I was doing standing on a kitchen chair and why hadn't I asked his assistance.

I took Joe into my employ soon after I returned to Portland and moved into an apartment. At first he came once a week to clean my apartment and attend to my wardrobe and dirty linens, which he took to his family's laundry. When I bought my bungalow, he began coming to the house to cook and clean three days a week. I gave Joe his own key so that he could let himself in if I should be away on an emergency call when he arrived in the mornings. He worked at another household the other three days. I never knew what he did on Sundays.

Joe was intent on becoming American and fitting in. He always arrived in a tailored suit of the highest quality, and he would first carefully exchange his suit coat for a work smock before he began cooking or cleaning or tending the kitchen garden. When attending at meals, he always wore a starched white serving jacket. His grooming was impeccable and his manners superb. He worked hard on his English and he often asked me to correct his pronunciation. When I first knew him, I would ask Joe the Chinese words for common phrases and household objects, but he waved my questions aside, and I soon gave up on it.

Later on, when I asked him to take care of the lawn and flower beds, he became indignant and insisted that he was not a gardener. I said I would hire him for an additional day each week to do the yard work, but he adamantly maintained that he was a house servant. He said he had a cousin who was a gardener and suggested I hire him for those duties. After considerable discussion, I convinced him to help with the vegetable garden since he would be cooking produce from it. But there he drew the line. So, when I could find time, I helped Joe with the vegetable garden, something I had enjoyed since childhood. And I ended up hiring Minnie Mitchell's boy Clark to mow and edge the lawn since he lived just around the corner.

Joe Locke and I had gotten to know each other's habits pretty well after being around each other for almost three years now.

I located the hip flask at last and pulled it out from the back of the cupboard. It was black with tarnish. As soon as I stepped down, Joe whisked the chair away and placed it back in the breakfast nook. He scolded me for not using the small step stool in the pantry.

I stood there admiring the design of the flask, marveling at what good taste Grandpa Travis showed in choosing it for me. Topped with an octagonal cap secured to the neck of the vessel by a small chain, its front was surrounded by a decorative border and engraved in the center with my initials "CTH." My middle name Travis had come from him.

The image of Grandpa Travis proudly dressed up in his suit for my graduation brought a wave of fond memories of him—picking tomatoes in his garden, reciting a popular poem at a Thanksgiving dinner. We had been very close. He presented me at Christmas one year with a board game called Halma, which he taught me to play and it became my childhood favorite. Another year on my birthday he gave me an illustrated book called *The Voyages of Jason and the Argonauts*. He read it to me until I learned how myself and then I read it over and over again.

I handed the flask to Joe Locke and asked him to wash it out and fill it with gin. He said that before he did anything, he would first take some silver polish to it.

The Bisby Grange was out of the way, just as Jimmy said—about thirty miles from town. I got only vague directions when I asked several acquaintances how to get there. At last, I telephoned Gwen and told her I wanted to hear a band that was playing out there.

"That doesn't sound like you, Carl."

I couldn't tell her what was up. "A patient suggested it," I said. It was a white lie—Irene Iverson was after all my patient. "Besides, I thought it would do me good to get out of the house."

She gave me explicit instructions that involved lefts and rights and bridges over country streams as I scribbled down the directions.

I had kept the evening open on my calendar, but I didn't know when the dance would begin. Nine-thirty seemed like a safe bet for the band to be well underway by the time I got there. I didn't want to arrive so early that it looked like I was too interested or too eager. Still I set out early enough to allow plenty of time for getting lost.

It was a balmy evening typical of late May, just after sunset. The weather had been clear but not hot, and the country air was perfumed with newly mown alfalfa. The smell brought back the rural community of my boyhood—the daytime field work putting up hay at Grandpa Travis's place during summer vacations, the nighttime buggy drives with my country doctor father to remote farmsteads or the Indian mission school, and the weekend afternoons on our screened porch playing Halma with the boy from down the street.

I did get lost trying to find the Bisby Grange and was forced to back track a couple of times. Finally I pulled over to the side of the road to study the directions I had jotted down.

It was nearly dark except for an intense blue light in the West and directly before me was a large gibbous moon. I thought of anatomy class, the semilunar valves of the heart. It was the same phase of the moon that hung over that dance at the officers' club when I first met Gerald.

That October evening in 1918 outside of Paris, there was music and dancing with nurses from the base hospital and young ladies from the town. The Yankees were very popular with the French.

After dancing with a nurse, a drunken lieutenant had stumbled and bumped into a pretty mademoiselle, spilling his drink all down the front of her dress. She burst into tears and there was a commotion among the women to help her. The drunk became belligerent and called her a clumsy bitch. Then a friendly captain quickly took charge of the situation. In French he apologized to the women and put his arm around the lieutenant, pulling him away.

"Okay, soldier, I think it's time for us to take a walk," he said. His tone was gentle but firm and he steered the lieutenant toward the exit.

I was somehow drawn to the captain, and I followed him in case he needed assistance. Near the front door the lieutenant turned and tried to free himself.

"I'm not ready to leave yet. I gotta dance with one of them Frenchies." He stumbled again and I stepped in to help the captain steady the fellow. Together we maneuvered him outdoors and the captain arranged with the military police to see that the lieutenant was escorted back to his quarters.

Once we were alone, the captain turned to me. "Thank you, Captain," he said, "you were Johnny-on-the-spot. The backup is much appreciated."

"No, Captain," I said, "you were the one who took the initiative to intervene. I must say, I was impressed."

"Just doing my duty. Why don't you let me buy you a drink." He smiled at me. My gaze met his and lingered. There was a moment of inexplicable familiarity. I nodded.

He indicated a grassy walkway that led back to the club. As we walked, he pointed to the sky. "Look at that funny egg-shaped moon we've got tonight."

"My granddad used to call it a gibbon moon," I said, "but I think what he meant was a gibbous moon."

Then he laughed. It was his laugh that got me.

Remembering Gerald and feeling the loss, I stared up at this humpbacked moon. It could have been the larger half of a playing-card heart, but the ragged edge of the shadow across the face of the moon gave the impression of something that had been torn apart. A broken heart. And beyond sparkled a few scattered stars, like shards of the missing part of that gibbous moon, strewn helpless and isolated across the evening sky.

I started off again and before long drove through the gate of the Grange. The moonlight shone down on the many cars and trucks and the few horses and buggies that were lined up in a mowed field next to the white clapboard building. I parked away from the other cars, at the edge of the field near a stand of cottonwoods. I stepped out and stood for a moment taking in the scene. A small creek whispered beneath the cottonwoods, and the crickets were chirping up a storm, punctuated by the croaking of frogs. I took off my hat and laid it on the front passenger seat, then pulled out my watch and saw by the light of the moon that it was nearly 10 o'clock.

Figures were moving about inside the warmly lighted windows. As I walked toward the building, the murmur of voices drifted out.

I was just beginning to wonder if Jimmy and his friends had cancelled their engagement, when I heard the band strike up. The clarinet bubbled above the rest of the instruments, alternating with the brassy filigree of the cornet, while the piano and other instruments wove in and out carrying the rhythm along. Then the instruments backed off, and I heard a clear tenor voice sing out the lyrics. I was stopped short.

I couldn't make out the words, but the singing had a melodious, crystalline quality. Yet underneath that disarming sweetness was something else—a rough beauty—so strong and dark that the hair on the back of my neck stood up. That's Jimmy's voice, I thought.

After the lyrics came to an end, the horns moved back in to take their alternating breaks and then finished out the tune as it came together, ending crisply. Then there was silence.

A sudden breeze rustled the cottonwood trees and the leaves applauded the performance. The rural setting seemed an unlikely place to be hearing this kind of music. It was new music, different from the sentimental popular songs I was used to, and certainly not what I would have expected at a country barn dance.

Another piece began, and I walked on toward the hall. Here and there among the parked vehicles dim figures talked and laughed. A cigarette coal glowed and then an exhaled cloud of smoke caught the moonlight. One man took a surreptitious swig and passed the paper bag. I mounted the wooden steps and paid my admission to a woman seated at a card table next to the door.

The hall was crowded. Under the open-beam ceiling, young people filled the center of the large room, moving to the sound of this new jazz music. Some older folks tapped their feet to the infectious rhythm and looked on from wooden folding chairs scattered about the perimeter. Others of the older set didn't seem to know what to make of the music and sat without moving, looking on with disapproval, but one old fellow kept asking young girls to dance and at last found a partner. Meanwhile, the youngsters seemed to take right away to the new sound.

The musicians were at the far end of the hall on a low platform. Dressed in tuxedoes, they looked out of place in this rustic setting. I maneuvered through the edge of the crowd, closer to the band. Jimmy played at an upright piano with his back to the audience. Next to him the drummer popped away at his array of percussive instruments. The trombone player swayed back and forth on a chair beside the drummer. Seated in front, a banjo player strummed wildly, next to the trilling clarinet player. And standing, a redheaded cornet player blared out above the crowd into the hall. When he was not blowing his horn, the cornetist was busy leading the band.

The jazz melodies and counter-melodies of the instruments dodged around one another, like the arms of an octopus reeling out and pulling back in. Then the cornet would move center stage and expound on a theme, only to be replaced by the trombone or the clarinet, which would launch off into another flight of improvisation. Occasionally, the other instruments would pull back softly, and Jimmy's piano, though lacking the brash force of the brass and woodwind, would bound aggressively forward, spinning out extended arabesques and gymnastics, taking daring risks, before falling back to pulse out the background rhythm that held the music together and ushered it along. The inexorable forward momentum reminded me of Bach's music and it again brought to mind those outdoor concerts that Gerald took me to that summer in Berlin.

I focused in on Jimmy. His playing was as intense as at the wedding reception, but making jazz, a driving energy propelled him forward, heightened by the other band members and the dancing, milling crowd. I already knew he could play Mozart, but now, listening to the dangerous adventures and rich treasures of his risky jazz improvisations, I began to appreciate what a true Argonaut he was. Again I heard that distant panpipe in Jimmy's piano playing, but now the satyr had grown a lusty tail.

Of course I had heard jazz before. But the music of Jimmy's band stirred a longing in my gut, a floating, nonspecific erotic yearning. It was a hovering, youthful desire that dodged around corners and beckoned down unknown streets. The music was like a well-drilling rig tapping a deep reservoir of emotion that had lain deep inside me, buried for too long. It was not that the music created that longing, but rather it spoke its language and at last gave the feelings a definition, a voice, a song. Now, I felt that perhaps in Jimmy this floating desire had at last found its proper object.

I watched the band pump out the rhythm for a while. Then the cornet player came forward and announced that they wanted to play a song they had worked up recently. He said it was based on a tune from some New Orleans musicians that he heard in Los Angeles. They broke into a dolorous melody and then Jimmy stepped forward and began to sing the lyrics.

"I went down to St. James infirmary

Saw my baby there

Stretched out on a long white table

So sweet, so cold, so fair."

The dripping of water in the metal sink. The sharp odor of disinfectant. The gleam of the white ceramic tiles.

The Grange hall melted from my consciousness.

I was in a quiet realm with nothing but the sound of that dripping faucet in one corner. A few German police officials stood nearby. My eyes hurt as the bright electric lights reflected off the stainless steel examining table.

Then I felt a pain in the middle of my chest that slowly spread downward to the root of my torso, and my stomach seemed to twist and turn over. Gerald's death. The song had unexpectedly brought on a rush of memories. That night in the Berlin morgue when my world was shattered.

A cold sweat broke out on my brow, then a wave of nausea and lightheadedness overcame me. I lurched to the nearest empty chair near an open window. I sat and concentrated on the musical instruments, inhaling slowly. The breeze carried in a waft of fresh air. I took long deep breaths.

Soon the band began a different tune and the spell slowly subsided. The lively tempo and invigorating spirit of the music seemed to restore me. After a time, I felt better, and to distract myself I turned my attention to the dance floor. Young couples glided past me, an old couple seated nearby laughed out loud, some children scurried around the back of the hall playing. Outside of my own mind, nothing had changed.

The band played a few more tunes then took a break. This is my opportunity, I thought. I was already excited to see Jimmy and now that I had my chance to approach him, an airy nervousness rose from the pit of my stomach. To talk to Jimmy is why you drove all the way out here, I told myself. I stepped forward. Jimmy stood next to the platform, talking heatedly to the busy redheaded cornet player. When the band leader withdrew, I walked up beside Jimmy.

"Hey, ace piano player. You fellas sound great." I agonized through an anxious moment when I wasn't sure he would recognize me. "I met you at the Iverson wedding," I added. "Carl Holman." I extended my hand. A cloud disappeared from Jimmy's face as his expression lit up with a sunny smile of recognition. He shook my hand.

"Oh, yes. Doctor Holman, isn't it? It took me a minute. Boy, did you have as much trouble finding this place as we did? We were driving around for hours till I'd like to panic."

"I got directions from an old friend of mine," I said, "but still it took some work finding it."

Jimmy's forehead glistened with perspiration, and he took out a crisp, ironed handkerchief. "It's warm in here. I've got to step outside for a minute before we start up again." He wiped his brow. "Come on. How about a cigarette?"

Double doors on the side of the hall had been opened to let in the night air. Some of the dancers had gone out onto the field where the light from the Grange spilled out. As I followed Jimmy through the crowd out into the dark, he took out a pack of cigarettes and offered me one.

"Thanks. I don't smoke," I said holding up the palm of my hand. Jimmy lit his cigarette. "You fellas must rehearse a lot."

"Five days a week." He shook out the match and threw it down, stubbing it into the dirt with the toe of his patent leather shoe. "Diggs' father owns a warehouse—Diggs is the horn player," he gestured toward the hall. "We get together over there at night."

"How long have you been playing the piano?"

"Oh, heck, since I was a kid. My mother started teaching me when I was 5. I had a string of piano teachers after that. I don't think this music is what my mother had in mind when she first taught me to play though." He laughed.

"Did you grow up in Portland?"

"About eighty miles east. My dad has an orchard near Watney Junction."

"You don't say. I grew up in a little town outside of Greenville near the Indian reservation." Greenville was some ninety miles south of Watney Junction. "I bet you used to go swimming at Canyon Creek in the summers."

"Yeah. My uncle used to take me and my cousins out there. One place had a big old cottonwood right on the bank and there was a rope you could swing out over the water and let go. That was some fun."

"I'll bet," I said. "Our family used to go to Canyon Creek for picnics with friends. We'd set up by this huge rock right by a deep part of the creek. Us kids used to dive off the rock there. My mother was always having a fit about us getting hurt, but no one ever did."

The redheaded band leader approached us. "Hey, Jimmy," he said going through his pockets and shuffling through pieces of paper, busy as a bee. "What do you say we start our next round with one regular set and finish with you singing? Then me and the others will try those horn pieces we've been working on."

"Heck, Diggs, that will make about half an hour I won't get to play."

"Let's just try it out, okay? We haven't done those pieces in front of a crowd before. This would be a good place to try them out."

"Okay. You're the boss," Jimmy said. Diggs headed back toward the hall.

"I better get back," Jimmy turned to me. "Nice talking with you…Dr. Holman."

"Please. Call me Carl." I moved a bit closer and lowered my voice. "Say, Jimmy, if you aren't going to be playing for a while, later on, we could share a drink from my flask," I patted my breast pocket and raised my eyebrows.

He hesitated a moment as some mechanism worked round in his mind. "Sure." He smiled at me. "Why not? I'll slip back out here." Jimmy stepped on his cigarette butt. "Catch you later," he said and went off into the hall.

I wasn't ready to go back in yet so I wandered toward the creek thinking about Jimmy. The night air was intoxicating, fresh and cool. The moon had risen higher, and more icy blue splinters of stars were spread out like playing cards scattered across the night sky. It was a gamble, I thought, but perhaps I might have a chance with Jimmy.

Moonbeams shimmered on the surface of the brook and the crickets and frogs kept up their own brand of jazz, punctuated by an occasional hoot of laughter from the distant crowd. Then the band struck up again and I wandered slowly back. The side doors had been closed so I headed toward the front entrance.

A group of men were filing into the hall under the electric light of the entry porch. A small billy club, like a scaled-down police nightstick, was slung through the belt of one fellow's trousers. I stepped in line at the bottom of the stairs that led up to the porch, waiting for the men to move forward. In front of me, a man in shirtsleeves stood two steps above, his backside at eye level, and I could see his hip pocket bulging with a small heavy blackjack, the handle of which stuck out right before my face. A man in bib overalls next to him was similarly armed.

"Hello, Walter," said the woman at the card table. "I didn't see Evelyn at the meeting Tuesday night. I hope she hasn't been ill?"

"No, Mildred, it's her sister hasn't been well, so she went up to help out."

"I'm glad you and your boys made it over here tonight to keep an eye on things." She handed him his change.

The men slowly entered and I followed a few steps behind. Just inside the hall the man named Walter turned and said, "Hey, Norm, why don't you and Mitch see if the others outside need help. We'll be able to handle this group." Two of the men went back outside and the others dispersed throughout the hall in pairs.

I sat and listened to a few tunes and began to think I ought to be participating in the dancing. It wasn't so much that I wanted to dance. Rather, it was an awkward feeling of obligation. Maybe it was being back in the rural setting of my youth. The purpose of a dance was for boys and girls to get together. So I felt it was my place as a male to ask one of the young women to dance with me. As if to give myself an excuse to conform to convention, I told myself, Come along, it won't kill me, besides it will make me feel more a part of the music.

I wandered to the edge of the dance floor. Standing nearby, a young woman in a pink dress was giving me the eye. Maybe it was because I was one of the few men wearing a suit. She had a pleasant, innocent look about her. The music was making me tap my foot. I gave in. Why not dance? So I made my way to her side and asked. We hadn't moved halfway around the periphery of the dance floor when an anxious young fellow wearing cowboy boots cut in on us.

"Hey, that's my girl you're dancing with, buddy," he said. A couple of the billy-club boys approached us. The young woman gave the cowboy a sheepish smile, and I wondered in passing if she had not calculated that accepting my invitation to dance would rekindle his interest in her.

I held up my hands as I let go of the young lady. "Don't worry about it," I said to the young fellow. "It's only a dance."

He took her hand and they danced away. The billy-club boys passed on through the crowd. That, I told myself with considerable relief, fulfills my obligation to participate in this ritual. I made my way to the side of the hall, up near the front where I could watch Jimmy and the band. I was content to sit back and listen. I felt a widening gulf between myself and these established boy-girl proceedings.

After a while Jimmy came forward and sang another song in that silvery tenor voice. His singing spoke of something that the song lyrics did not, something that the lyrics could not even approach. Maybe it was his sense of rhythm and delivery, I don't know—but for me it was simply magical. After the verse, the band chimed in with an improvised passage, and then Jimmy's distinctive voice came in again with the lyrics of the chorus:

"It's right here for you
If you don't get it
It ain't no fault of mine."

By the time he finished the next verse and the second repetition of the chorus came round, two of the billy-club boys were approaching the bandstand. The fellow named Walter was holding up his hands and shouting over the sound of the band.

"Hold on there. Just a goddamned minute. You can't sing them nigger songs here. Hold up there. That's downright indecent."

The fellow with Walter had taken out his billy club and was holding the handle in one hand as he slapped the business end of it against the other palm.

Jimmy stopped singing and backed away from the front of the platform. Some of the dancers in the front of the hall stopped dancing and turned to watch. Diggs turned to the band and called, "Keep on playing. Never mind the lyrics. Finish the tune. Jimmy, take up the piano." Jimmy went to the piano and began playing. Diggs quickly turned to Walter and the billy club fellow and hopped down from the platform. He began talking rapidly to them, his hands gesturing, his mouth working a mile a minute, joking, apologizing, and cajoling. He placed a hand on Walter's shoulder as he talked and guided the two men off to the side of the room where they continued their discussion for a time. Finally, the three started to laugh and nod together, and after a bit Diggs walked away with a smile on his face.

Diggs made his way back and crossed the bandstand to the piano where he leaned down, placing a hand on Jimmy's shoulder, and said something in his ear. Jimmy turned, glanced up, and shot Diggs a look, then went on playing. Diggs walked slowly back to the center of the stage, moving in time with the music, and resumed playing his horn. Soon after, the musicians brought the number to a close.

Immediately, Diggs turned and said something to the band, then counted a few beats and launched into another tune. Jimmy got up from the piano and left the bandstand. I followed him directly, winding my way through the crowd trying to catch up, but he had a head start. As I emerged into the cool night he was lighting a cigarette, half turned away from the building. The match flame lit up his profile.

"Swell music," I said, approaching.

"Thanks," Jimmy said. I could hear a sullen edge in his voice.

"And the crowd likes it."

"Yeah," Jimmy said. "Except for those two numbskulls."

I reached up to his back, gently placing my hand between Jimmy's shoulders, and with a gesture of my other hand directed him away from the building.

He gave me a look.

"I think they've got some of their buddies out here," I said quietly. "Let's walk." We wandered away from the building and I reluctantly removed my hand from Jimmy's back. Besides the presence of the billy-club boys, I wanted to put a discreet distance between us and the crowd.

"Those bastards," Jimmy said under his breath. I could feel his agitation. We walked a good distance away from the building into the shadow of the cottonwoods. The sound of crickets surrounded us. Shaded from the moonlight, I pulled out the newly polished flask from my inside breast pocket. Removing the cap, I offered it to Jimmy.

"Premium gin. It will do you good after that. Doctor's prescription."

Jimmy looked up. "Maybe just a taste." He took a swig from the flask and shuddered. "Whew." He handed it back. I took a sip and the clean, sharp taste of the gin burned my mouth.

We were walking near the burbling creek now, serenaded by the intermittent crooning of the frogs. Jimmy crushed out his cigarette and picked up some stones. He tossed one into the water. Then he hurled another with greater force. "Who do those bastards think they are, anyway?"

"Probably the local church morals committee," I joked.

Jimmy unleashed a series of violent pitches, striking the trunk of one of the trees. "Those dirty...god...damn...bastards." His voice got louder with each word and each throw. His aim was true and each stone connected solidly with the tree trunk.

I walked up next to him and placed my hand carefully on his shoulder. His breath heaved with exertion and anger. In the corner of his eye a tear glisten with moonlight.

"It's okay, Jimmy," I said softly. "You have every reason to be angry. They had no right to stop your singing."

He didn't move except to turn his face away. He inhaled a long sniff, tilted his head back, and let out a sigh. I took my hand from his shoulder and offered him the flask. He took a long drink and handed it back to me.

"I'm sorry," he said. "I lost control." He picked up more pebbles and tossed them gently down the stream. "It's just that the music should be strong enough to cut them off." A soft plunking sound arose where each of his pebbles entered the water. "I need to learn to sing so well that it stops them dead in their tracks."

"I doubt if they know anything about music," I said.

"They sure as hell don't know anything about the Blues."

We were quiet for a time. Jimmy tossed the last of his pebbles and leaned down to pick up more.

"Where do you fellas get your songs, anyway?" I was hoping to get his mind onto another topic.

"I have a friend who buys these race records from a Negro maid. That song I was singing when those dimwits stopped me is one of Mamie Smith's recordings."

We walked along the creek in silence and Jimmy continued to pitch his stones.

"You've got quite an arm," I said.

"Oh, I used to play baseball when I was a kid," he replied as he tossed his last one. "I was better as a batter though, than I was as a pitcher." I passed the flask back to him. Jimmy took another drink and then held the silver container up so that the decorative border caught a glint of moonlight through the trees.

"Classy," he said and handed it back.

"It was a gift from my granddad when I graduated from medical school."

Jimmy looked at me. "Oh yeah?" He seemed to be at a loss for words for a moment and looked away. After a bit he said, "Boy, these frogs are sure singing to beat the band. I'd like to see those bastards stop them from singing."

I chuckled. "Did you ever try to catch frogs when you were a kid?"

"Oh, I guess so." He looked at me again. "Did you?"

"My grandparents had a place with a pond where I used to catch tadpoles. I'd keep them in a jar of water and watch them grow. I guess that was one of the things that first got me interested in science. I couldn't believe how something that was all head and tail could develop into an animal with four legs and no tail at all."

"So is that how you got interested in becoming a doctor?"

"Partly. I guess it runs in the family. My father was a doctor, and when I was a kid, I used to go with him to see patients sometimes."

"Must be tough work."

"It can be. The hours are long sometimes. And I never know when I'm going to get a call in the middle of the night."

He took out a cigarette and lit it.

"Pretty little stream," he said. "I bet it would be good for fishing."

His remark caught my attention. All at once, I decided to take a chance. "Do you fish?"

"I used to." He puffed on his cigarette.

"Hey, you want to go fishing sometime?"

"Gee, that might be fun. We used to fish a lot. I haven't done it for a long time. I guess I still have some tackle stored away at my place."

"Where are you living?"

"I've got a room in a boarding house downtown—near the library."

"Let's see. Are you free next Saturday?"

"We've got another music date that night and I'll be waiting tables in the afternoon."

"You wait tables, too? Where's that?"

"At Hansen's, downtown on 6th Avenue. It helps pay the rent. I'm hoping I can quit once we get more music jobs lined up."

"How about next Sunday? Are you free then?"

"Sunday?...Yeah. That's okay. But not before 1 though. I play the church organ Sunday morning."

"Boy, you have a busy schedule."

"I usually try to take Monday and Tuesday off. But I enjoy playing the organ at the church. That was the first job I got when I moved to Portland last year. I used to play at church back home before I went away to college."

"I see. At the wedding reception you said you picked up jazz at college. Were you studying music there?"

"Yeah."

"What was that like?"

"Oh, boy." He sighed. "A lot of hard work. But good. I learned a lot."

I took another drink and held the flask out to Jimmy. He shook his head and laughed. "I've gotta stay sober enough to play. I'd better head back."

I capped the flask and put it away, then took out a business card.

"Here. Give me a call at my office sometime this next week and we'll plan a fishing trip."

"Sure." He took the card.

The warmth of the gin was spreading through my body. We turned back toward the hall. One more question lingered that I needed to ask Jimmy before we parted company.

"Between your music and your restaurant job and all, you must not have much time for girls."

"I don't. I haven't met that many people since I moved here, besides the fellas in the band. But, there's my fiancée, Mary. She's a painter. My muse. She's the friend I mentioned who buys the race records. We met in college. Lives with her aunt and uncle in Portland. It's their Negro maid who picks up the records."

I was crestfallen to hear the word *fiancée*. "So you're engaged to be married?" I tried to make the question sound like a neutral request for information.

"We haven't told our parents or bought rings or anything yet. But we've talked about it and she's planning ahead. I figured we should wait till I'm better established."

We were approaching the side door of the Grange hall, again. The music and light spilling out from inside.

"I should go in," he said.

"Okay, Jimmy. I'm glad we got a chance to talk." I extended my hand and he shook it. "Give me a call next week."

"You bet." He started to turn, then paused. "And thanks for the medicine, Doc. I feel a lot better." Jimmy smiled at me, then walked off into the music.

I stood and listened for a while in the cool night air, looking up at the stars. Waves of relaxation from the gin spread through me as I turned our conversation over in my mind. Before long I heard the piano keys rejoin the band. Listening to him play, it occurred to me that Jimmy was like an arrow, all speed and forward motion, racing toward its target, but at the same time rigid and inflexible like an arrow and not cognizant of anything outside of its goal. And with Jimmy, the goal was jazz.

Yet an inkling persisted, weighing on my mind, an unresolved feeling about him that I could not put my finger on. I guessed it would have to wait until I knew Jimmy better.

I decided it was time to go home and headed around behind the Grange toward my car, mulling over the evening. Rounding the corner of the building, in the shadow cast by the moon, I ran smack into a group of the billy-club boys. They were smoking and laughing and my sudden appearance caught them off guard.

"What do we have here," one of them said, approaching me.

"Evening, fellas," I said.

"Lose your way, buddy?" Another one stepped forward.

"Oh, I just came out the side entrance," I said. "My Ford is parked over yonder."

"I believe I smell the curse of alcohol," the man nearest me said, and I was quickly surrounded by four figures in the darkness. Two stood behind me and held my arms while another patted me down and took the silver flask out of my breast pocket.

"Well, now, what's this? Hey, look, Mitch."

"So I did smell the devil," Mitch replied.

"Why, it's half-empty," said the man holding the flask. He uncapped it and sniffed. "The devil's brew, no doubt about it." He began to pour the remaining liquor out onto the ground.

"This just might save your soul, buddy." The last of the alcohol dribbled out.

"Don't you know liquor is an illegal substance?" Mitch said. I didn't know how to answer. He grabbed my lapels and shook me. "God help us, you smell like a saloon. You know there is a law against possession of alcohol?"

"Yes," I said. "Yes, I know. I guess I broke the law."

Mitch let go of my lapels. "You're not from around here, are you?" He patted down my suit coat and reached in the pocket where he felt my business cards. "Bring him over here in the moonlight, boys."

By the light of the moon I could see that Mitch was tall and stout. He held up the business cards and read. "Carl Travis Holman, M. D." He sounded impressed. "From Portland. A city fella. And a sawbones." He regarded me for a moment. "Let him go, Norm. I guess he's all right. Now, look, Doc. Out of respect for your profession, we're gonna let you off easy. I suspect you need to carry around a little alcohol for medical reasons. But remember, you're not supposed to drink that stuff." They all laughed. "It's polluting. A man of medicine should know better. What do you say?"

"You're right," I said. "It was a lapse in judgment on my part."

"Yes, it was. Wasn't it? Well, you sound like an intelligent fella to me. We're gonna send you on your way. Go and sin no more. And remember your Hippocritic oath." He slapped me on the back and directed me toward the parked cars.

I turned and looked at him. "Thanks." I felt awkward and reluctant, but I had a humble appeal and I knew no other way around it. "Can I ask you a favor? May I have the flask back? It was a gift from my granddad…when I graduated from medical school."

Mitch looked at me for a moment.

I added, "It's sentimental, you understand. My granddad died a couple of years ago."

"You heard him," Mitch said. "Give the doctor back his flask."

One of them handed over the silver container with its cap dangling by the chain.

"Now you drive careful on your way home, Doc."

"You bet I will," I said and turned toward my car. As I walked away, I could hear their laughter behind me.

When I got to my car, I realized my shirt was drenched with sweat. It was not from exertion. I took off my coat before I drove away.

I was pondering all that had happened as I drove home along the moonlit country roads. Turning a corner onto a bench of land that overlooked the valley below, the head lamps of a number of cars off to the side of the road came into view. I slowed to make out what was happening. A band of white-robed figures in pointed hoods stood in the lights of the cars. I remembered Tom Harris's remarks about the Ku Klux Klan, but I had never seen any of them in the flesh.

As my vehicle approached, two of the masked figures carrying flaming torches walked out into the road and flagged me to a stop. As they peered inside my car to make an inspection, I made my own inspection of the scene beyond.

In a field, five automobiles surrounded a sixth, all pointing their headlamps inward. Beside the central vehicle three of the masked figures were holding a young man bent over the front of the car. His pants were pulled down around his knees, his buttocks showing white in the headlights. A fourth robed figure was administering a spanking using a wooden paddle. Off to the side, two hooded figures flanked the young woman in the pink dress. They held her arms behind her back, forcing her to watch the punishment. A dozen Klansmen looked on from a semi-circle surrounding the spectacle.

When the inspectors concluded that I was a man driving alone and not carrying crates of booze, they waved me on.

So, I thought, that was the story on the "local church morals committee" as I had dubbed them. Apparently, the Klan was monitoring the dance at the Grange to make sure everything remained within the bounds of propriety. And, here, at what was no doubt a popular spooning location overlooking the valley, they had caught a young couple in the act. The Knights of the Invisible Empire planned to make sure it would never happen again. At least never again with this couple, I thought, and probably never again in this location, once word got around.

I decided I'd better be careful to mind my P's and Q's in these rural areas.

FOUR

I wasn't at all certain Jimmy would telephone me. Not wanting him to think I was overly interested, I had avoided asking how I could get in touch with him. By being too forward, I might scare him off. He could disappear altogether, and then only chance would determine our next meeting. Unless Jimmy decided to avoid me.

Trying to be optimistic, I phoned Gwen, who was a fishing enthusiast. She told me to call up a farmer named Arvid Phillips and ask permission to fish in the stretch of Falls Creek that ran through the east end of his farm. "Remember that time we drove to Alder Lake? Out toward Mount Hood?" she said. "It's out that way, but not so far. Arvid is an old friend of my father's. He used to live near us. Tell him you're a friend of mine."

"Oh, is Rebecca Phillips his wife?" I said. "I've treated her in our clinic."

"Good, then tell him that too. I've been fishing at his place a couple of times with Dad. You shouldn't have any trouble catching something there. Say, Carl, I never knew you were interested in fishing."

"A friend of mine persuaded me to take it up," I said.

When I telephoned Mr. Phillips, I mentioned Gwen. He said he'd known her since she was an arm child. His wife might remember that she saw me for her bunions, I told him, and sparked his memory. He said he'd be glad to have me fish on his property.

On Thursday afternoon, Jimmy finally phoned. When the receptionist announced his name, I closed the door to my office before I took the call.

"Hey, Doc. This is Jimmy Harper. Your patients keeping you busy?"

"They sure are. And how is your band doing?"

"We're all tuned up. Busier than ever. That's why I phoned. About fishing on Sunday? We just lined up an afternoon tea dance for that day. It's a gold-plated opportunity we can't pass up."

My hopes crumbled. Maybe he'd reconsidered the whole situation and was backing away.

"Can we make it another day," he said, "like the following Sunday? Assuming we don't get another booking. I'm sorry about the change."

My outlook brightened. "The following Sunday..." I glanced at my desk calendar. A Sunday dinner with the family of a hospital administrator was penciled in on that date, but I figured I could manage to wiggle out of it. "Sure. Let's plan on that. Why don't you give me a call Thursday or Friday before, just to firm things up."

He agreed.

"Say, Jimmy, I think you should know about something that I saw on my way home from that dance at the Bisby Grange." I told him about the paddling incident I'd witnessed with the Klan.

"Holy smokes. We heard that the Klan was active out there, and Howard guessed that's who those men with the billy clubs were."

"Did you have any other problems after I left?"

"The Klan fellas wouldn't let me sing any more songs, but they let me play the piano. There wasn't any more trouble. But it doesn't matter now. We aren't going to be playing any more of those rural dances. Diggs has gotten some of the country club set interested. That's where the tea dance is on Sunday, out at the Milton Heights Country Club. And we'll be playing a couple of college dances on Friday and Saturday night."

"It sounds like things are taking off for you fellas. You're not overextending yourself?" I would have asked if he was getting enough rest, but I checked myself before I got to sounding even more maternal.

"Oh, not at all, Doc. I'm happy we're getting more opportunities to play."

"Jimmy, you can call me Carl."

"Okay, Carl. Sorry."

"Jimmy, while I'm thinking about it, let me give you my home telephone number if something else comes up for your band. Do you have a pencil?" I gave him the number. "And if a Chinaman should answer, don't think you have the wrong number. He's my housekeeper."

There was a pause. I assumed Jimmy was writing down the telephone number. After a moment he said, "Thanks, Doc—I mean, thanks, Carl."

"And, Jimmy, just in case I should get an emergency medical call, can you give me a telephone number where I could let you know?"

He gave me the number for his boarding house. I felt a sense of exhilaration, as if he had opened a door into his life for me. Then he added hastily, "Look, I've gotta dash. I'll call you next week and we'll plan that fishing trip. I can't remember the last time I was fishing."

My hopes rose. "Okay, Jimmy. Give me a call." Maybe he wasn't trying to put me off, after all.

Jimmy phoned the next week to arrange the fishing trip. He gave me the address of his boarding house and we planned for me to pick him up on Sunday at 2. But he stressed that he had to meet up with the band at 7.

The sky was cloudy when I drove up to Jimmy's address. He was reading a newspaper on the front stoop of a large Victorian house. I barely recognized him in workmen's clothes and an old felt hat, his fishing gear leaning against a pillar beside him. I hopped out and Jimmy folded the paper and came down to the sidewalk. I extended my hand. That slightly crooked smile spread across his face as I felt his firm handshake.

"How ya doin'? I'm not used to seeing you without a tuxedo."

He laughed. "Formal wear for fishing. Now there's an idea."

I stowed his gear in the back seat.

"Hey, this Ford looks brand new," he said climbing into the passenger seat.

"I try to take good care of it." I started the engine and passed him my map with directions to the Phillips place. "This is supposed to be a good spot. I guess we'll see."

Once we were alone in the car, an uneasiness settled over us. He was the young bohemian musician and I was the established professional man, several years his senior. We had so little in common and we were not comfortable together, not yet. Maybe this was too soon to be on such an elaborate outing. As we headed out Thornhill Boulevard, I felt I needed to try to make some conversation to put Jimmy at ease.

"Where did you play last?" I asked over the sound of the engine and the wind.

"A dinner dance at the Willow Creek Country Club last night."

"My, my. You are coming up in the world."

"Yeah. Diggs is pretty well connected. He's managed to get us bookings every week for a month."

I had trouble thinking up anything to say beyond that. Stories from my medical practice were all that came to mind, and I didn't want to bore him. At last Jimmy said, "I heard a good one the other night," and he proceeded to tell me a story about a man who lost his coat.

The story itself wasn't all that funny, but something about Jimmy's way of telling it and the timing of his delivery were so perfect, that the longer he went on, the funnier it got. I kept wondering if it was something he had polished up to slip in between songs for the bandstand audience. Maybe it was just my growing affection for Jimmy, but by the time he got to the part about the pockets, I was laughing so hard I thought I would have to pull over. We both felt a bit more relaxed after that.

The city quickly gave way to the countryside. The day was warm and the clouds were breaking up. The sky began to show patches of blue. Neither of us felt compelled to talk over the noise of the engine, and we silently took in the scenery. Every once in a while as we came around a bend, Mt. Hood would rear its blue-white summit like a diamond standing aloof from everyday life. But still it was connected to us as a source of the watershed that helped feed the river through Portland and the sole source of Falls Creek, our fishing destination.

"The native Indians must have had a name for Mt. Hood," I said to Jimmy, "but I don't know what it is." He told me he'd heard it and pronounced the name for me, but the sound was so foreign to my ear that I wasn't able to keep it in my mind.

When we got farther out into the country, we had to watch the map more closely. The game of finding our way became a kind of scavenger hunt. First, we had to find Meyer's Creek Bridge, just beyond a red barn. Jimmy navigated and we kept our eyes peeled for road signs. "Zorn Road should take off to the left up here," he said. "There. Part of the sign is missing, but I can make out the Z." Before long we found Arvid Phillips' place. I parked in his drive and asked if Jimmy wanted to come to the house with me but he said he would wait in the car. I walked up to the house to have Farmer Phillips direct us to the creek and to pay my respects to him and his wife.

A few minutes later Jimmy and I were driving up a rise along a dirt road toward a wooded area. The mountain loomed to our left. When we came to the barbed-wire gate that Farmer Phillips had mentioned, Jimmy jumped out and opened it while I drove through and he closed it behind. A bit farther on, we came to a fallen-down shed and beyond that was the creek. I parked just past the shed in the shade of some alder trees. We stepped out to look around.

"What do you think, Jimmy?"

"Nice spot. Looks like good fishing."

The alders stood about a hundred feet from the stream across a sloping grassy area. Large boulders lined the water, which stretched out in a wide shallow expanse over the rocky stream bed.

We were getting our gear out of the back seat when Jimmy asked, "What's all this?" indicating a picnic hamper.

"Oh, I thought we'd want a little snack later on."

Jimmy cocked his head and gave me a curious smile.

We walked over to the stream and sat near the bank arranging our rods and tackle. Jimmy moved efficiently and purposefully with what I was coming to understand was his characteristic intense concentration.

I laid out my fishing pole, tied a hook on the end of the line, pinched a lead sinker onto the line, and took out a small can of worms I'd dug from my garden that morning. I tied a red and white bobber several feet up from the hook and carefully laced the hook through one of the worms. Then I walked over to the stream and found a deep pool near the boulders. Sitting down on a large flat rock, I plunked my line in the water.

Jimmy meanwhile was fiddling with his line and rod and pulling things out of his pockets. I sat and watched him, waiting for him to join me. He glanced up and noticed me waiting. When he saw my red and white bobber, he broke into laughter. Then noticing that I was a bit taken aback, he stifled his laugh, with difficulty, and asked, "Where did you learn to fish, Carl?"

"I went fishing a couple of times with my cousins in Texas— when I was a kid."

That provoked another involuntary chuckle that Jimmy tried to control. I waited while he regained his composure. "I'm sorry, Carl, I don't mean to laugh. I'm just surprised. I didn't give it any thought, I just assumed you were a fly fisherman. But I see you're not."

"Oh, you mean those little artificial insects?"

"That's right. Here, these." Jimmy came over and knelt down beside me and reverently opened up a leather folder. Inside were rows of hooks with colorful feathers and other materials tied onto them. "This one is a woolly spinner. And this one is a royal coachman. And this is one of my favorites. It's especially good for rainbow trout in the right situation." He could tell from my expression that this was all Greek to me. "You haven't done a lot of fishing, have you?"

"When I was 14, we visited family in Texas and my cousins took me to catch catfish with them a few times in a muddy lake. I'm afraid that's about the whole of my fishing career."

"What you've got there might catch you a catfish in a Texas mud hole, but I'm afraid you won't get too many trout. Here, let me show you." He began taking a fly out of his folder. "When I was a kid, I went to stay on my uncle's ranch every summer. We would herd the cattle, castrate and brand the calves, that sort of thing. It was a lot of work. But afterward, as a reward, Uncle Wally would take us fishing. He was a fanatic about trout fishing. It was like a religion to him. He and my cousin taught me the art of fly fishing. And that's what it is—an art. Like playing the piano. I can show you enough to get started—if you're interested."

"Gee, and I had visions of a relaxing afternoon on the creek," I said. "I guess I'd better take notes."

"That's okay. We don't have to knock ourselves out."

So Jimmy spent the next hour patiently giving me a brief introduction to the art and religion of fly fishing. He told me that trout had excellent eyesight and they could see you standing on the bank or in the stream, so you had to outsmart them. He described how they thought, where and how they spent their days, and what they fed on. This led to a discussion of how to select the best fly for a particular situation. Then Jimmy demonstrated how to hold the rod and how to cast, and he insisted we take turns using his fishing rod so I could practice. He placed special emphasis on the importance of casting the line.

After a while we waded out into the stream so he could show me how to actually catch a fish. The water was colder than I expected. Jimmy gracefully whipped the line out over his head and expertly placed the fly exactly where he wanted it to land in the stream. All during this elaborate performance, Jimmy was singing quietly under his breath, unconscious, I was sure, that he was vocalizing.

"It's right here for you

If you don't get it
It ain't no fault of mine."

I happened to glance down into the water where his feet were firmly planted in the stream bed with the current lapping against his calves. There, swimming against the current in the clear water, dozens of small fingerlings dodged around his feet, as if drawn to him by the magic of his voice. His voice was magic to my ears anyway.

A strike yanked Jimmy's line taut. He pulled back on the rod and then lowered it and let the line run out until I was sure he would lose his catch. He slowly reeled it in and let it out, playing the fish with intense concentration. At last, Jimmy brought in the trout and held it up in his small hand net, as it flipped frantically, flashing silver in the sun. The fish was a good twelve inches long. Jimmy called to me to bring him the creel from the bank, and I waded over slowly through the cold water, steadying myself against the current.

"You know, playing jazz is a little like fly fishing," Jimmy said, lowering the trout into the wicker basket. He closed the cover and submerged it in the stream. "You want to catch the attention of the audience, and then let your line of music out as far as it will go without breaking, then you want to reel it back in, before the audience senses that you've gone too far." He laughed and handed me the fishing rod as he took charge of the creel.

We went on taking turns using Jimmy's rod. By the time he'd caught his third fish, including two he threw back because they were too small, I still hadn't caught a thing. I found myself standing near the side of the stream with the line hung up in a bush behind me, and Jimmy helping untangle it. In the process, the line knocked my hat off and it landed on its crown in the water. Before I could reach it, the current swept it away, and like an open boat, it floated off down the stream.

"Maybe you'll find it in town later on," Jimmy said, "floating down the river under a bridge."

At that point I said, "How about breaking for a snack?"

"Swell idea," Jimmy said as he freed the line.

I reeled it in and handed the rod to Jimmy, then waded over onto the bank and tried to shake the water out of my shoes. Jimmy started for the spot where he'd left his creel full of catch, wedged between rocks near the edge of the creek.

"I'll clean these fish and be along in a minute," he called to me.

I slogged and squished back to the car in my cold wet shoes. From the back seat, I pulled out the picnic hamper and a blanket. Choosing a level spot near the creek under the dappled shade of a cottonwood tree, I spread out the blanket and began unpacking the hamper's contents.

When he finished taking care of the fish, Jimmy came up from the creek, holding the fishing rod in one hand. He stopped and stared. "Holy smoke, Dr. Holman."

The blanket was spread with china plates full of finger sandwiches and pastries, cheeses and fruits, strawberries dusted with powdered sugar, silver flatware with white table napkins, and a bottle of champagne with two wineglasses.

For a moment I felt a rising doubt about all my fastidious planning for the picnic. Maybe I was only making myself appear foolish in Jimmy's eyes. But he had been gracious enough about my Texas fishing habits.

A smile replaced the astonishment as he took in the spread, and he looked at me and chuckled. I felt somewhat relieved, and I hoped he was not just being polite.

"Don't just stand there," I said. "Why don't you take off those wet shoes and socks and sit down." I'd left my shoes to dry in the sun nearby. Jimmy laid down his rod and reel and knelt down on the edge of the blanket.

"Look at all this." He studied each plate. Then he looked me in the eye and said, "You've sure gone to a lot of trouble."

"Oh, I didn't do so much. My housekeeper and the Chandler Hotel caterers did most of the work. I contributed the wine. Of course, the Hotel wouldn't have alcohol now, would they?"

He removed his old felt hat, tossing it to one side, and continued to regard me for a moment with a curious expression. Then he turned sideways and sat with his feet off the edge of the blanket and began struggling with his wet shoelaces, occasionally casting a sidelong glance at the food and then at me.

I opened the champagne and filled each wineglass half full. Jimmy set his soggy footwear off to the side.

I picked up one glass and handed the other to Jimmy. "Let me propose a toast," I said.

He took the glass.

"To a long friendship."

We looked at each other and raised our glasses until they touched with a tiny clink. At the last moment Jimmy glanced away, and we drank. The liquid seemed to evaporate into bubbles as soon as it touched my tongue, the bubbles tingling all the way down my throat.

"Mm, that's tasty," Jimmy said. "What kind is it?" He reached for the bottle. "Oh, boy. I've never had French champagne," he said, studying the label.

"Try one of these," I indicated some little pastries. Jimmy bit into one and chewed for a moment. A smile broke over his face.

"I remember these from the wedding reception," he said.

"'Food for the gods,'" I quoted him. "I figured a picnic would not be complete without food for the gods. Especially a fishing picnic."

Jimmy laughed and gave me another amused glance. Then he turned back to the label of the wine bottle.

"Where did you find French champagne? That must be hard to come by these days."

"I bought it in France. After the War."

Jimmy whistled with surprise and then looked up at me squarely. "What was that like? The War?"

"I didn't see much actual fighting. I arrived in France a few months before the armistice. I'd just finished medical school and I spent a little time doing triage at a dressing station at the front—

sorting out the bodies to see which ones we might be able to save. I thought I'd seen a lot of bad cases in medical school, but that was pretty gruesome." I glanced at Jimmy who was listening intently. "After that, I was moved to a field hospital. Then I spent most of my time in an American army hospital outside of Paris. After the Armistice, I joined the occupation force in Germany—working in a base hospital in Koblenz."

The image of Gerald's shattered face floated up.

"But let's not talk about that over lunch," I added quickly. "Have some food."

We filled our plates.

"There were lots of good things that came out of my time in the service though. In Germany I got to know some of the people—I made some good friends. I still correspond with them. It was an extremely interesting time." I paused for a moment remembering Detlef and Heinz cooking dinner for Gerald and me. "I'd say it changed my life."

I couldn't tell Jimmy all my experiences in Germany just yet. But other memories rushed up.

Jimmy asked, "How's that?" His voice called me back from my reverie. The memories must have left an odd expression on my face because Jimmy was studying me with a quizzical look. "How did it change you?" he asked.

I considered for a moment, trying to decide how much I could tell him. "I'd say it made me a bigger person. It's just that people are different in other countries. They have different customs, you know. I believe Europeans are more open to different ways of thinking." I watched Jimmy's face to see if he understood. He was biting into another salmon pastry and I couldn't tell what impression my remarks were making on him.

"I thought people were the same everywhere," he said. "That's what the poets say."

"I suppose the human heart is the same everywhere. It's just all that external stuff. Society."

"So what's different over there?"

"Here's one example. The German military—some of them—believe that it is healthier to be out in the sunshine without clothing—that it builds stronger bodies. So there are some commanders that train their men outdoors in the nude."

"You're kidding."

"No. That's the truth. Of course, in ancient times, the Greeks used to practice their sports without clothing."

Jimmy was quiet for a few moments as he chewed on a sandwich and watched the stream. "I always dreamed of going to Europe to study music."

I watched his face, and a little breeze ruffled his hair.

"When I was a kid, my mother used to bring me into Portland sometimes to play for Mr. Gustav. He was this old German man who taught piano. He'd known a bunch of those composers you read about in books. He met Richard Wagner once. After I'd have a lesson with Mr. Gustav, I'd dream about playing piano in Europe. But later on when I started hearing jazz, I decided that there was nothing like that in Europe, and that America was the only place to be. Nowadays, I dream about going to Chicago and New Orleans."

"Then you ought to do that, Jimmy."

"Yeah. Diggs and the fellas in the band, we've been talking about that. We're working on plans. We need more experience playing first. But we'll get there, I know it. I can feel it."

"Tell me about your music background. You said your mother first taught you to play?"

"Yup. She taught me to sing first. As a child. She wasn't a piano teacher, but she plays pretty well. She didn't force the piano on me. I just took to it. The whole thing. I was fascinated by the way different combinations of notes made you feel. Not just major and minor, happy or sad, but all these in-between feelings. Subtleties that you can't even talk about. I don't know. It's hard to put into words. Then I went away to college and studied music there. That was pretty intense. It exposed me to a lot of new music, new ideas."

"That's when you started playing jazz?"

"I started by picking out tunes on the piano at college. Some of the students were interested in jazz and we would listen to new stuff on the phonograph and then improvise on our own—outside of class, of course. The faculty didn't approve of it. That's how I met Howard—he's the clarinetist in our band. He went to the same college with me. Then when I came to Portland, after I graduated, Howard introduced me to Diggs, and Diggs knew some other musicians. The first time we all got together was at Diggs' house one afternoon. They have a big swanky place up in the hills. But his mother didn't like all the noise, so we started using a room in one of his dad's warehouses—he's in the shipping business. We all pitched in and rented a piano to leave down there. We have a great time. And now we're getting more bookings all the time. I plan to quit my job waiting tables next week. If we get much busier, I may have to quit playing the organ at the church too."

"You do keep busy."

"Yeah." He reached for a piece of cheese.

"It's good you can let the waiter job go. Maybe we can celebrate when you quit," I suggested. "When's your last day?"

"This coming Friday."

"Can I buy you dinner Friday night?" I asked.

Jimmy hesitated.

"Anywhere you want to go," I said. "You name the place."

"I've got a date that night." A sheepish smile came over him.

"Oh. You must be seeing your girl." I tried not to let my disappointment show.

"Yeah," he said.

"Tell me about her."

"She's from Chicago. We met in college. Now she's living with her aunt and uncle and her cousin here in Portland. She works as a typist in her uncle's insurance firm. But she sings, too. She has a beautiful voice. Sometimes I accompany her on the piano. She won't sing in public though. She's shy about it. She also paints pictures. She's terrifically talented. Back in college, she painted a portrait of me—at the piano. It's wild. Lots of subtle colors. It's done in this modern style. She calls it cubist. You wouldn't be able to tell it was me. She was trying to paint a picture of my music. She's a first-rate girl."

"She sounds multi-talented."

"Maybe you can meet her sometime," Jimmy said.

I looked down at the picnic food and let the comment pass.

Then after a moment I asked, "Have you talked to her parents yet—set a date and all?" I had to know how serious he was about this girl although I suspected that he wasn't sure himself.

"Huh?" Jimmy seemed surprised by the question. "Oh, that. Well, no." He picked up a strawberry, bit into it, and chewed for a moment. "I guess Mary wants to go ahead and tell them. We've talked about it." He paused and swallowed. "But I think I ought to have some money saved up and get a little more established in my career." Jimmy didn't seem comfortable with this line of conversation. He finished off his wine, then stretched and lay back, gazing up at the blue sky. I was glad to let the subject drop.

Nearly all the clouds had dissipated, leaving only a few fluffy white puffs scattered about. I sat listening to the whir of the grasshoppers and the gurgle of the stream, glancing over at Jimmy now and then. The sun had become hot, but it was still cool in the shade. We had finished off most of the champagne and eaten a good deal of the food while we talked. I was feeling relaxed.

"This is the life," Jimmy said, lacing his hands behind his head. We were quiet for a time. The trees rustled in the breeze.

"Hey, Doc." Jimmy looked over at me with a sly smile and said, "Let's go skinny dipping." He sat up and started to unbutton his shirt.

"But Jimmy, what if Mr. Phillips comes round? We are supposed to be fishing."

He stood and pulled off his shirt, standing there in his undershirt as he began unfastening his trousers. "That's okay. He won't care. We'll just tell him it got too hot to fish."

"But—" I was more surprised than shocked.

"We used to do it all the time—with my cousins when we were kids. Come on. We'll be like those German soldiers, training in the nude." He slipped out of his pants and walked toward the creak in his underwear, carrying his pants and shirt. "Come on, Carl," he insisted over his shoulder. "Last one in is a rotten egg."

This was more than I could have hoped for, but it was all so sudden. Did Jimmy know what he was doing? I had no way of judging his level of awareness, and I didn't know how much significance to attach to his actions. His attitude was much too casual and innocent for me to believe that he was acting with any overt intention.

I jumped up and walked quickly over to the creek. Jimmy had peeled off the rest of his clothes and left them in a pile on the large flat rock where we had organized our tackle. His body was slim, just saved from being skinny by his slight muscular development. His skin was pale, his chest hairless. I couldn't help noticing that he was circumcised.

As I fumbled to remove my clothes, Jimmy walked carefully into the stony creek bed toward the pool. Then with a sudden splash, he plunged into the deeper water. His head emerged almost immediately with a shout. "Christ, it's cold!"

I stood naked at the side of the stream, inching my way into the icy water, grimacing with each step. Jimmy approached and began splashing me and laughing.

"I'll get you for that, Jimmy Harper." By now I was so wet it didn't matter, and I lunged into the pool toward Jimmy, but he evaded me. I was in up to my neck, and when the impact of the cold water hit me, I began hooting. Jimmy laughed and continued to splash water at me. I submerged my head and opened my eyes under water just long enough to catch a glimpse of Jimmy's body beneath the surface of the clear water. For a moment everything was quiet and the mottled, wavering light played on Jimmy's white skin and on the boulders of the creek bed. I quickly emerged and shook the water from my head. The cold produced an aching sensation that slowly became a numbness.

"Hoo-ee!" I yelled. "This is too refreshing. I can't stay in this water, Jimmy."

He submerged himself and swam a couple of strokes, then re-emerged. "Hey, you can swim against the current," he said and began doing the breast stroke upstream. His body stayed in place with relation to the shoreline.

I slowly picked my way over the stones to the bank and stood on the large flat rock near our clothing. I stripped off the water with my hands and sat on the warm stone surface watching Jimmy swim. Before long he made his way to the edge of the stream. I thought he kept looking over at the dark hair on my chest, but with the strong shadows cast over his eyes by the bright sunshine, I wasn't sure. Walking carefully over the rocks, he came up and sat just an arm's length away. Little spasms of shiver rippled over his body and his breath came fast from the exertion.

"Let me grab that blanket for you," I said, starting to rise.

"Naw, I'm all right," he said glancing at me. He began rubbing his arms and legs. Then he shook his head and raked his fingers through his hair. Laying back he stretched out flat, cupping his hands behind his head and closing his eyes. He let out a sigh and shivered again. "Ain't this the life?" he said again.

"Yes, indeed," I said.

Jimmy seemed to have no idea how provocative his behavior was for me. As he lay there, I wanted to reach out my hand and feel the pectoral muscles of his chest and touch that mysterious place where the thigh and the hip join the torso, which the ancient Greek sculptors learned to depict so well. But this wasn't the right time or place. I didn't know Jimmy well enough to be sure how he would react, and I couldn't take a chance on scaring him off. Right then, I was happy just to be sitting next to him.

Bird song punctuated the quiet.

"Listen to that," Jimmy said raising his head. "Meadowlarks." His rectus abdominis muscles tightened as he raised himself up on his elbows and listened a moment. "When I was a kid, I always thought they were singing 'A. J. Whitaker.'" He sang it out to match the lilting birdsong.

"A. J. Whitaker." The larks called back to him. Jimmy laughed and lay back on the rock.

"Ever meet anyone with that name?" I asked.

Jimmy laughed. "No. I never have," he said turning his head to look at me. "But if I ever do, I'll tell him that the meadowlarks are asking for him." We laughed together. Then he closed his eyes again and lay quietly for a time.

I glanced over at him, and I felt as if my heart would burst. How could this fellow be so charming without even seeming to try?

"Have you ever heard of King Oliver's Creole Jazz Band?" Jimmy asked without opening his eyes.

"No. Who are they? A local group?"

Jimmy laughed. "No, they're from New Orleans. I keep hearing a tune in my head from one of their records." Then he sang, "Da-doot Doot Doot. Doodle oody oody."

"You love music, don't you? It's good to have something you're passionate about."

Jimmy raised his head, squinting against the sun. "Is that how you feel about being a doctor?" He raised up on his elbows and looked at me.

"I do. I guess it's a lot like music in that it's a pretty all-involving career."

"But you must have a girl too. I take it you aren't married. You don't wear a wedding ring, and you didn't have a girl with you at the wedding reception—or at that Grange dance."

I was happy to think he had been observant enough to notice.

"I'm not married."

"Playing the field, huh? You must have a whole black book full of girlfriends."

The thought made me laugh out loud.

"Oh, I go out occasionally with my friend Gwen—a nurse. But I guess I just like spending time by myself."

"What do you do when you're by yourself?"

I was flattered to have him show so much interest.

"Oh, I read books. I try to keep up with medical journals. I work in my garden. There is something therapeutic about digging in the earth and watching things grow. I don't know. I guess I lead a fairly quiet life."

"You don't get lonely?"

I looked right at Jimmy and said, "Sometimes I do, Jimmy." He held my gaze for a moment, then looked out at the stream. We were silent for a time. Then he sat up.

"Well, there's one thing I can tell you for sure. You're not a fisherman." He laughed. "But I bet you're a pretty good doctor."

He sat up cross-legged like a picture I once saw in a magazine of an Indian yogi sitting on a rock. Then he picked up some pebbles and began tossing them in the water.

The intimate turn in our conversation emboldened me. "Jimmy, are you sure marriage is the right thing for you, right now?" I had been wanting to get back to the subject, and this seemed the right time. I had to know how he felt.

"Am I sure?" He paused. "Of course," he said turning to glance at me, but he didn't sound convinced. He went back to tossing pebbles. "Besides, my family keeps asking me when I'm going to get married."

"You know what? My parents keep asking me the same question. I just keep telling them I'm not ready. There's no good rushing into these things."

"Do you have something against marriage?" he said.

"I've never thought of it that way. I guess it's just that I see a lot of unhappy marriages in my medical practice. Pregnant women who hate their husbands. Husbands who get drunk and beat their wives and their children. So I think people should be pretty careful about making that decision."

Jimmy looked over at me for a moment. He seemed to be considering my words.

"You see, Jimmy, it's just that music is not a stable career. You talk about waiting until you get better established. But unless you get a permanent position teaching music or something of that sort, you may never get established, as you put it."

Jimmy appeared to consider this for a moment. "But," he said at last, "I've got to try to make it as a performer. I have to at least give it a go."

"Yes. I know you do. I understand that. Maybe you need to pursue that dream before you think about marrying. Just remember that there are all different kinds of success. And if performing doesn't work out, it's not the end of the world."

He tossed another pebble.

"I thought the world had come to an end once," I said. "But as it turned out, that wasn't exactly true."

He glanced at me for a moment with curiosity, then looked back toward the stream.

We were both quiet for a long time.

The sun was hot and we were mostly dry now. I could tell by the angle of the shadows that the afternoon was passing. Jimmy continued tossing pebbles out into the creek, like he had after that incident at the Bisby Grange. Maybe he needed to sit alone and think. I hoped my comments hadn't made him angry. Besides, I was feeling too exposed and I continued to worry that someone might happen by.

"Maybe we'd better get dressed," I said. "You don't want to get sunburned." I felt like reaching out to touch his bare shoulder but restrained myself and stood up. I began slowly pulling on my clothes while Jimmy continued to throw pebbles. When I finished dressing, he was still sitting there cross-legged on the rock beside his clothes. I squatted down beside him.

"I hope you aren't cross with me for anything I said about marriage."

"No," he said. "Naw, I'm just thinking." He gazed out at the creek, his brow knitted.

I reached over and placed my hand on his shoulder and gave it a squeeze. "There's plenty to think about in this old world." I took my hand away and stood. "We probably ought to start thinking about heading back in a while," I said. "If you have to meet your band, I don't want to make you late."

Jimmy glanced over his shoulder at me and said, "Yeah, I guess you're right."

I walked back to the picnic hamper and started gathering up the dish ware and the remains of the feast. Jimmy sat tossing pebbles for a time, then began dressing slowly. Finally, he went to the stream to retrieve the creel full of fish.

"Hey, Doc, you take these fish home with you," he said approaching the car. "I don't have any use for them at the boarding house."

"I'll tell you what," I said. "Let's give them to Farmer Phillips."

Driving home, I was feeling good that the outing had gone well, but Jimmy seemed so pensive that I began to worry. When I dropped him at the boarding house, I asked once again if I could take him out to dinner to celebrate the end of his waiter's job. He reminded me he was seeing his girl on Friday night. I realized I had put that detail completely out of my mind. Jimmy added that he was playing with his band on Saturday night.

"How about lunch on Saturday?" I suggested.

He paused and considered for a moment. Then, much to my relief, he agreed.

I told him I'd drop by around noon to pick him up.

FIVE

It rained that following Saturday. My plan was to take Jimmy to a nice restaurant. But he insisted we go to a small diner that he liked, not far from his boarding house, so we walked, sharing my umbrella. I was pleased to have Jimmy close to my side, protecting him from the rain. We ordered sandwiches and sodas, and when I asked about his band, Jimmy told me about playing for the opening of a dance marathon on Thursday.

"This one sheba was wearing a dress that showed her knees, and she and this sheik were doing some new steps they called the Camel Walk. It's the berries, I tell you. We heard they picked it up in Southside Chicago."

"I wish I'd been there to hear you play."

"The marathon came up out of the blue, and I didn't even find out about it myself till the last minute."

When I asked where he'd be playing next, he specified a few engagements that he said had been nailed down, according to Diggs.

As I jotted down the dates and locations on a napkin, Jimmy told me that Larry, the banjo player, had come to the marathon in a nifty new suit. "It was just like ones I've seen in the movies," he said. "What do you think? Should I buy a suit in that style? I could get it on the installment plan at Waldstein's."

"I can't advise you about styles—that's something you know more about than I would, especially for the youth and music set, but you want to be careful not to overextend yourself with installment buying. I think a lot of people get in trouble with that these days."

Jimmy asked about my work and I shared with him some humorous encounters I'd had with patients recently. Then he told me a funny story about his Uncle Wally's gall bladder operation.

Hoping to prolong our afternoon together, I asked him about taking in a movie after lunch. He glanced up at the café clock and thought for a moment. Then he said, "Sure. Why not? You know, the Osiris is playing a couple of Chaplin films that I've been wanting to see. Do like him?"

"Sure, I like Charlie," I said.

"Me, too. I think he's the greatest. A real artist."

As we walked to the movie theater, I told Jimmy a story I'd heard during the War from an American neuropsychiatrist serving in France. "A young soldier who had gone mute from shell shock went to see a Charlie Chaplin film and afterward he was able to speak again."

"You don't say." Jimmy shook his head. Then he laughed and added, "Like I said, Charlie is the greatest."

The Osiris was one of several lavish new movie palaces in Portland. Its architecture was meant to evoke ancient Egypt, and I suspected the name had been chosen to create an air of exotic orientalism. But I wondered how many Americans knew the story of Osiris, the god of the underworld and the dead, his body dismembered and scattered by his brother Set. The theater walls were decorated with a dizzying array of hieroglyphs and Egyptian motifs and a lot of gold paint. I asked Jimmy if he didn't agree it was a bit gaudy.

"Oh, no," he said. "Egyptian style is the bee's knees. This is my favorite theater in town." Entering the auditorium he whispered, "Let's sit over to the side there, where we can watch the organist play."

Jimmy fidgeted with his hands and kept craning to make a show of watching the organist. I still felt self-conscious in his company, especially sitting so close beside him in the theater seats. So when the lights went down after a couple of popular tunes from the organ, the movie was a welcome distraction. The feature was preceded by a one-reeler called *The Woman*. It began with a series of mishaps, after which Charlie attempted to get himself out of a tight situation by disguising himself as a woman. Two men with whom Charlie had gotten in trouble began making passes at the unknown woman. She coyly enticed them both to kiss her simultaneously, one on the left cheek, the other on the right. At the last moment, she ducked out of the way and the two men ended by kissing each other on the mouth. The scene made Jimmy laugh out loud. Next came the main feature, *The Kid*, in which Charlie adopts a foundling. We both found it funny and touching by turns. As we were walking out, Jimmy said how much he liked that one, and I felt glad that we now had one more thing in common.

The rain had stopped, and as we headed back toward his place, we strolled along a busy street looking in the shops. Jimmy paused at a jewelry store window where he seemed to pay particular attention to the engagement and wedding ring sets.

A couple of doors down, I saw the Halma game.

One rarely sees Halma sets anymore. Sometime around the late 1920s, the game board was reconfigured into a star and given the snappy new name "Chinese Checkers."

This set was displayed in the window of a purveyor of fine stationery, which also sold typewriters, expensive fountain pens, and books of the newfangled crossword puzzles. Next to the Halma game an elegant boxed set of mah-jongg was laid open on an embroidered Chinese cloth.

The Halma board was an eighteen-inch square slab of dark walnut. The checkerboard pattern covering the playing surface was defined by alternating squares of white ash inlaid in the walnut. Surrounding this was a decorative border like a small parquet floor. The four different groups of playing pieces stood in the four corners of the game board, each looking like a phalanx of chess pawns ready to charge forth. My mind was flooded with memories of childhood summer afternoons.

"Hey, Jimmy, look at that Halma set. Isn't that a beauty? I haven't played that in years."

Jimmy told me he'd never seen the game before. I stared at the set for a moment. "A neighbor boy and I used to play for hours. My folks' house had a screened porch under a big old elm. It was one of the coolest places to be in the heat of summer. Johnny and I would lie on the floor and play one game after another. He was a champ at it too. It was tough to beat him. Say, let's go in. You're not in any hurry, are you?"

"Naw," he replied.

In the store Jimmy studied the fountain pens in the glass case while I said hello to the young lady behind the counter. I told her I was interested in purchasing a game and she seemed relieved when I pointed toward the front window and said it was the Halma set I wanted to know about.

"I was afraid you might want a mah-jongg set," she said. "We can't keep them in stock, they are so popular."

Jimmy looked up from the pens and said, "I heard from that fella at the dance the other night that the Chicago stockyards are shipping cattle bones to China so the Chinese can turn out more mah-jongg sets."

"I can believe it," the store clerk said. "We've had them back-ordered for more than a month now."

"No, I'm only interested in the Halma set," I told her.

"Isn't that beautiful?" she said. "An old British gentleman here in Portland makes them by hand. I thought that since we couldn't keep the mah-jongg sets in stock, we might be able to sell some of those Halma games. We've actually sold two of them. But his work is so meticulous and slow. It's been hard to keep those in stock too."

The set was more expensive than I anticipated, but I had already decided I wanted to buy it. Walking out of the store I asked Jimmy if he wanted to learn to play Halma sometime.

"You'd pick it up in no time. The rules are simple." I began to think maybe I was being too insistent.

But he replied casually. "Boy, I haven't played a board game since I was a kid." He laughed.

"Hey, why don't you come over this afternoon," I blurted out before giving it any thought. "That way you can see my place and we'll play a game or two." It occurred to me that my enthusiasm for a mere board game must appear rather juvenile.

Jimmy hesitated.

Before I could consider, I found myself saying, "You don't have plans, do you? I know you don't have to wait tables this afternoon."

"Hallelujah," Jimmy replied. "Sure, I can come over for a little while. I don't have to meet the band till 7."

In the back of my mind, I felt relief that Joe Locke was never at my place on the weekends. Jimmy and I would have the place to ourselves. But then, as we were getting into my Ford, I began to feel a sense of nervous anticipation. As we drove toward my bungalow, which was across the river and a ways from downtown, I began rambling on, explaining how Sunny Grove neighborhood had been developed barely ten years earlier, how the curving streets and sidewalks had been laid out by a renowned architectural team, and other information I had read in promotional brochures. I must have sounded like a real estate salesman as I chattered on.

But as we drove into Sunny Grove, I saw it with new eyes, as I imagined how it might appear to Jimmy viewing it for the first time. Many of the lots were vacant, and numerous others had skeletal wood frames still under construction. The existing homes were set back from the sidewalks with room for generous front lawns, but a number of them had yet to be landscaped and displayed only an expanse of bare dirt.

"I bought my bungalow from the original owner," I continued, unable to stop myself. "He and his wife just had her third child, so they wanted a bigger place. I thought the house would be a good investment." Maybe all my banter put us both more at ease. Jimmy took in all this information with apparent interest.

I parked at the top of the sloping concrete driveway and got the Halma set and my umbrella out of the back seat. Jimmy seemed a bit surprised as he got out of the car.

"A brand-new neighborhood," he exclaimed looking around at

my house, the lawn sloping down to the sidewalk, the small trees planted along the street. "I guess I never thought much about where you lived."

"Come on. I'll show you around." I led him toward the garage at the back of the house. "I want you to see my garden." A robin flew up from the vegetable rows as we approached. Everything was still wet from the rain.

"I've got tomatoes over there. Those are potatoes." Feeling a bit professorial, I realized I was pointing with the tip of my umbrella, and I tucked it under the arm holding the Halma set. "This is lettuce," I gestured with my hand, "and a few herbs. My houseboy helps me take care of it. I'm hoping to put in more flowers later on." I smiled proudly and looked over at Jimmy, who was standing there shaking his head as if in amazement. What kind of impression must I be making? I asked myself. Maybe I'm displaying too much enthusiasm.

I looked away to survey the sky where some blue patches were beginning to show through the clouds. "Looks like it might clear up." I glanced back toward Jimmy, who was looking up and down the garden rows. Was it just politeness? He looked skyward a moment and nodded. Then he glanced my way, and we looked at each other awkwardly.

"Nice garden," he said and looked back at the tomato plants. "My mother always keeps a vegetable patch."

"So did my granddad. He loved having fresh tomatoes."

The robin's song rippled from the rooftop of the Beasleys' house behind mine.

"Well," I said, turning, "shall we go in?"

He followed me back down the drive to where a wide porch stretched all the way across the front of the house.

"Part of the reason I bought the house was this swell front porch," I said, climbing the low steps to the end of the porch. We crossed to the front entrance.

"I liked that you can enter from the drive on the side or from the front walkway across the lawn. Someday those little ash trees on the parking strip will be big shade trees," I said. "And the woman who used to live here planted these little rhododendrons in front of the porch. They made a mass of pink blooms a few weeks back." I wanted to tell Jimmy about my plans to plant a lilac at the far end of the porch and to hang a porch swing next to it, but I felt I had already said too much.

"Here, hold this a minute." I handed the Halma box to Jimmy and fumbled to unlock the front door. My thoughts were racing as to what I should do next as I led the way into the dim living room. We're just here for a friendly game of Halma, I told myself, and took a deep breath.

When I left the house earlier, I was in such a state at the prospect of having lunch with Jimmy that I hadn't thought to open the curtains in the living room and dining room. I never expected I would be having him as a guest. But now there seemed something furtive about the dim room, with the sun growing brighter outside so I drew back the curtains and at the speed of light the room changed.

"Have a seat," I said as I put my umbrella in the stand and hung up my hat. Jimmy scanned the room and took a seat on the sofa laying the game box next to him. I was feeling a bit warm and I slipped off my suit coat and hung it on the back of a chair.

"Here, let's have a look at that." I held out my hand and Jimmy passed the Halma game to me. I knelt on the carpet and began unpacking the game.

"Do you want anything?" I asked. "Coffee? I believe I've got some rum." I glanced up at Jimmy. He sat on the sofa leaning forward with his hands on his knees looking around the room.

"Yeah," he said, "maybe just a taste of rum. This is a fine place you've got here, Doc. That's a terrific fireplace." He looked across the room at the decorative tiles on the facing around the firebox.

"Glad you like it. Why don't you make yourself comfortable? Take off your jacket and come over and help me with this." Jimmy laid his suit coat on the back of the sofa and sat on the carpet opposite me, the playing board between us. I set the cardboard box aside. Its contents were scattered on the carpet. There were four paper bags full of playing pieces and a booklet of instructions.

"Open one of these bags and set the playing pieces out in that corner of the board. Like it shows in this picture." I handed him the instruction book and tore open one of the packages. "Should be nineteen pieces each. These other corners are only used if you are playing with four people. Then each player only gets thirteen pieces. Here, like this." I set out a few of the playing pieces. You finish setting up while I go fix some drinks."

In the kitchen I nearly overturned one of the tumblers in my haste to prepare the cocktails. When I returned to the living room, the two sets of pieces stood ready for play, and Jimmy was squatting beside of the hearth reading the titles on the built-in bookcase.

"Boy, you must read a lot," he said without looking up. "*Myths of the Ancient World?* And this looks like a whole set of Shakespeare."

"Yes, I've been interested in those old Greek myths since I was a kid. And when I bought that Shakespeare set, I had big ambitions, but *Hamlet* is as far as I got. I like that the plays are each bound separately—so you don't have to hold a heavy volume of the complete works when you're only reading one play. Say, that reminds me." Setting down the drinks by the game board, I pulled out a large art book that Gerald had given me in Berlin. Flipping through the pages, I located the reproduction of Thomas Eakins' *Swimming Hole* and handed the book to Jimmy. "This one reminded me of our fishing excursion." I watched his face. Jimmy laughed, catching my reference, then studied the painting of the naked young men on a rock next to deep water.

"That's beautiful," he said.

I glanced over the picture of the bathers for a moment and said, "Yeah. He's a great painter. Look at the next page. That's his portrait of Walt Whitman." Jimmy took in the face for a moment and handed the book back to me. I guessed that Whitman held no special meaning for Jimmy. "There's a medical painting, too. *The Gross Clinic.*" I flipped to a bookmark. Jimmy looked at the painting of the surgical operation for a moment, then grimaced.

"Maybe that one is a little gruesome if you aren't interested in medicine." I returned the book to the shelf wondering if maybe I was being too self-indulgent.

"Shall we play?" I said, motioning toward the Halma set.

We sat down on the floor at opposite corners of the board. I picked up my drink. "May the best man win." I raised my glass to Jimmy and took a sip. He followed suit.

"The object of the game is to get from here to there." I indicated the two corners where the playing pieces were clustered. "You want to get all your playing pieces over here to the opposite corner. I'll take these dark players, and you use the light ones there."

I showed Jimmy how one playing piece could be moved one square in any direction and how they could jump over adjacent pieces to extend their progress toward home. He quickly got the hang of it, and we were soon engrossed in the race to get our players across to their home fields. Before long, it was clear Jimmy's pieces were about to reach home, while I had stragglers inching across the board. Finally Jimmy moved his last piece into place and looked up at me with a smile.

"You catch on fast, jazzman. Here's to the winner." I raised my glass.

"Must be beginner's luck," he said and took a drink.

"Shall we play another?" I asked. "I need a chance to redeem myself."

"Sure," Jimmy replied.

As we turned the board around to start again, Jimmy pointed out a seam at the outer edge of the parquet border. I felt a thumbnail groove on the lower edge and discovered a small drawer.

"I'll be darned. It looks like he's put hidden drawers along the sides to store the playing pieces," I said.

Jimmy leaned in closer to look. I caught the scent of his shaving lotion mixed with his sweat and body heat. The wooden drawer fit tightly, not having been used, and in trying to open it fully, I jerked the board and sent playing pieces rolling off across the carpet and the hearth tiles.

"Oops." I reached to move my drink out of harm's way. Crawling on my hands and knees in front of the fireplace, I began pushing the playing pieces off the hearth toward the playing board on the carpet. Jimmy joined in. A number of pieces had disappeared beneath the sofa, and he stretched out on his side, sweeping the playing pieces from under it with one arm. I moved along on hands and knees, whisking the players out from the other end of the sofa. Our hands touched briefly and I looked over at Jimmy. His face struck me as particularly handsome with his expression so intense. I glanced down at his body laid out on the carpet, his suspenders stretched tight across his chest, and I remembered his body lying on the rock after swimming in the creek. A wave of desire swept over me. Maybe this was the right time and place.

"Jimmy…there is another secret drawer."

He looked up at me. "What?"

I looked him in the eye and said, "I have a secret drawer here in my heart…and the object of the game is to get from here," I tapped my fingers against my chest, "to there." I reached out and touched his sternum. Jimmy raised up on his elbow and stared at me. He cocked his head ever so slightly as several gears seemed to turn about in his head. "How do you mean?"

"I guess what I mean is…I want to kiss you." I moved forward slowly and kissed him lightly on the lips. He didn't move. I pulled back slightly and looked at him.

"I…" He didn't say anything more but glanced down at the carpet. Then he gave a short exhaled breath that was almost a laugh, and the corners of his mouth twitched slightly, almost a smile. He looked back up at me somewhat bewildered.

I leaned forward and kissed him again, longer and more firmly. When he did not pull away, I kissed him again and slowly maneuvered him onto his back on the carpet. As I continued kissing him, I felt his hands on my back, and then one hand moved slowly up to the back of my neck. I moved closer so that my body lay next to him, and we continued to kiss. My hand found its way onto the side of his chest to caress his pectoral muscle while I pressed my torso closer to his. He responded to my kisses, parting his lips and letting our tongues touch. After a time, I was certain that Jimmy could feel my erection against his hip.

A quiver rippled through his body and he made a little sound in his throat. He quickly turned his head away and rolled over on his side with his back to me.

"Jimmy?" I said reaching out and placing my hand on his shoulder. "Jimmy, are you okay?"

He raised up on his elbow and pulled his knees up. "It's all right. I'm fine...I'm just...." He jumped up to stand and my hand fell to the carpet. Keeping his back turned, he grabbed his coat from the sofa and held it in front of him. He walked quickly to the door and half-turned toward me with the jacket draped over one arm and the coat collar clutched tightly in his other hand. "I've gotta go." He didn't look at me. "I'm sorry." He reached for the doorknob.

I jumped up. "Jimmy, don't go."

He opened the door.

I went quickly to him and put my hand on edge of the door to keep him from walking out. "Jimmy, let's talk. Please."

He forced the door open and pushed his way past the screen door and out onto the porch. The sun was out full now and the wet street was blinding. I reached for his arm.

"Jimmy, we're still friends. At least tell me we're still friends." As I caught his arm, he turned slightly, still holding his suit coat in front of him.

He glanced up at me and said, "We're still friends." Then he pulled away looking down at the porch. "I've just got to think things over." He turned and walked away.

"Let me give you a lift," I called.

"I need to walk," he said over his shoulder, descending the steps to the front yard.

"Jimmy...wait. Please..."

He kept walking and I called after him. "Please telephone me."

Without looking back, he walked away in the brilliant sunshine. I stood in the doorway until he disappeared down the street. Then with a heavy sigh, I went in and closed the door. The room was filled with a deafening silence. I didn't know if I would ever see Jimmy again.

"Damn," I whispered as I slammed the side of my fist against the doorframe. I stood there for a long time looking out at the street through the small beveled windows in the front door.

After what seemed an eternity, I turned and picked up the rest of the pieces from the Halma set and hid them away in their secret drawers.

It wasn't until late Monday night that I heard from Jimmy. The phone rang around midnight, waking me from a sound sleep. At first I thought it was the hospital or one of my patients. When I recognized Jimmy's voice, I felt like the sun had just burst through the clouds on a rainy day. But as he spoke, I realized Jimmy was drunk. And he wasn't just tipsy. Jimmy was stewed. Music and voices in the background made me guess he was calling from a speakeasy. Even if he was intoxicated, I was still glad to hear from him. The significance of him choosing to call me when alcohol loosened his inhibitions was immediately apparent. I meant something to him.

But it didn't take long to understand that there was no possibility of a conversation with him. His speech was slurred and his thoughts incoherent. Finally, I reluctantly told him to go home and get some sleep and call me in the morning. When he insisted he had to see to me right away, I told him it was late and he should call me at my office tomorrow. His voice trailed off. I waited and finally I heard him say, "Okay."

"We'll talk tomorrow," I said, then added as firmly as I could without sounding angry, "Goodnight, now." I heard a click on his end.

When I hung up, I thought that was that and went back to bed.

About an hour later the doorbell rang and then there was a knocking at the door. As I pulled on my bathrobe and made my way down the hall, the knocking became insistent and a voice began calling. "Dr. Holman. Dr. Holman." It was Jimmy. I felt a momentary thrill to hear him there on my porch.

He must have taken a taxi, but it was gone by the time I got to the front door. I switched on the porch light. Jimmy was halfway turned toward the street, as if deciding whether to leave. I unlocked the bolt and opened the door wide. He swayed unsteadily as he turned toward me. His hair fell down across his brow and his neck tie was askew.

"Jimmy, quiet down," I said. "You'll wake the neighbors. Come on in here."

He teetered at the doorway a moment, his head downcast. Then he stepped unsteadily inside. I closed the door and as I turned around, Jimmy grabbed me in a bear hug, burying his face in my shoulder. "Doc, you're the only person I can talk to."

He clung to me for a time, and I could smell the alcohol on his breath. He was holding my arms pinned against my sides in his awkward embrace, but I worked free enough to hug him back.

"I feel like some kinda freak," he said. "Like I'm no longer a member of the human race."

"It's okay, Jimmy. It's okay."

"Doc...I wish I was dead. It'd be better that way." The image of Gerald's body in the Berlin morgue flashed through my mind. I had considered suicide myself after Gerald died. But not because of self-hatred.

"No, Jimmy. It's going to be all right."

"I should ask Howard to borrow his gun and go off in the woods someplace."

"No, don't talk like that."

"Or just jump off a bridge."

"Jimmy, stop." I squeezed him in my arms and gave him a little shake. "Don't even think that way."

"You're the only one who'll understand," he mumbled. "I like you, Doc. You're a real swell person. And now everything's gone crazy."

"It's okay, Jimmy. Everything is going to be all right."

We stood there holding each other for a long while until I gently pulled away. Putting my hands on his shoulders I looked him in the eye and said, "Listen to me."

He looked up at me but his eyes weren't focusing too well.

"We can talk. We can talk any time you want. But you're in no shape to talk tonight."

"You're right," he muttered.

"Look, have you eaten anything?"

"I dunno. Don't remember."

"Come on, I'll fix you something." I sat him down in the breakfast nook and brought him a glass of milk and a package of saltine crackers. "Here's your medicine. Now be a good patient and follow the doctor's orders. Eat up."

We sat in silence while he nibbled at the crackers. His white shirt was rumpled and it looked like he had spilled liquor down the front. But I was happy to see him again even though this drunken visit in the middle of the night put us both in an impossible position.

"I'm going to get dressed and then I'll drive you home."

"No. I don't want to go home. I want to stay here…with you."

His naked body on the rock beside the creek. The smell of the alcohol on his breath. A vision of Joe Locke finding us in bed together in the morning.

"You can't stay here, Jimmy. You need to go home and sleep this off." I put my hand on his shoulder and leaned down to look him in the eye. "I'll talk with you tomorrow. All right?"

He looked at the floor and shrugged.

I left him there and went down the hall to dress. *What do you do with a drunken sailor?* All the time I was putting on my clothes, the song lyric kept going through my mind. *Throw him in the hold until he's sober…* And if you don't have a hold? I thought. Hold him in your arms? As much as I desired it, this was no way to start.

When I got back to the kitchen, Jimmy wasn't there. I panicked, remembering him wishing he was dead. I had seen enough suicide attempts to know what was possible. Would I have to track him down out on the streets and bring him back here?

But I found him in the living room pitched over on the sofa. When I tried to rouse him, he didn't respond, and when I tried to lift him, his body had the dead weight of a corpse. Let sleeping dogs lie, I thought. It was just as well this way. Now I wouldn't have to worry about him making some foolish suicide attempt. Dead drunk was better than dead.

In spite of the handicap of too much alcohol, he had accomplished the Odyssean task of navigating his way to me through a hostile and drunken sea in order to blurt out the impossible words that he liked me and needed my help. Having achieved that, he had given in to the blackness. So I gave in and let him sleep it off where he had fallen.

It wasn't that I didn't want Jimmy here. I just didn't want him here in that condition. And in the morning, he wouldn't want to be here in that condition either.

I got a pillow and blanket for him, took off his shoes, and tried to make him as comfortable as possible. Then I squatted down and stroked his forehead, watching his face for a moment. He was out cold.

Jimmy was still asleep on the sofa when I got up at 6. I had resolved to get him out of the house before Joe Locke showed up at 7:30. After I showered and shaved and dressed, I went to the kitchen and made coffee and toast. Then I went to rouse my sick patient. It took several attempts and a cold, damp towel to get Jimmy upright on the sofa. At first he didn't know where he was. Then when he figured that out, he didn't know how he'd gotten there. He sat with his face in the wet cloth, groaned softly, then after a moment he said, "I'm sorry, Carl."

I placed my hand on his shoulder and told him it was okay. "You don't have to talk about it now. We'll talk later. For now, as your personal physician, my prognosis is that you are going to survive. Can you stand up?"

"I don't know," he said.

I stood and helped him up. He groaned and wobbled but was able to hold himself upright. With an arm around his shoulder, I guided him to the bathroom while I explained the situation. "I want to get you out of here before the houseboy shows up. I'm going to drop you off at your place on my way to the clinic. Now wash your face and pull yourself together." I handed him a dry towel. "We've got to get moving. Understand?"

"Okay, Doc. Thanks." I left him to his business.

After insisting on a bite of breakfast, I finally got Jimmy into the Ford, and I backed into the street. My next door neighbor Maude Williams was collecting the morning paper. She couldn't have missed seeing that I had a passenger with me, for even at that early hour the June sky was light with morning sun. I caught her eye as I passed, but from her expression, there was no telling what she was thinking. She probably didn't give it a second thought, but in my state of mind, I was sensitive about what the neighbors might think. All I could do was give a friendly smile and wave.

When I dropped Jimmy at his place, I asked him when we could get together to talk. He thought for a moment with one hand steadying himself on the open car door. "Oh, God, what is this? Tuesday?" He clapped his other hand on his forehead and closed his eyes. "Let me think. I'm not sure…Let me telephone you later on." He looked over at me and gave a helpless, indefinite gesture with his hand. "But soon. Let's talk soon. Maybe tomorrow afternoon. I'm just not thinking clearly right now. I'll phone you."

"Jimmy…promise me you won't hurt yourself."

"What do you mean?"

"Well…you were saying some pretty crazy things last night."

He gave me a puzzled look.

"Oh, never mind. Just be sure and phone me."

Jimmy closed the car door but kept hold of the handle, looking down at the sidewalk. Then he looked up at me through the open window.

"Honestly, Carl, I'm sorry. Thanks…Thanks for being so swell about all this."

"You can make it up to me by taking care of yourself. Now get some sleep. And remember to call me."

SEVEN

I continued to worry about Jimmy's mental state throughout the day. But later that afternoon he phoned my office. At the sound of his voice the room brightened. He sounded like his old self, direct though chastened. I set aside my worries.

"Good to hear your voice, Jimmy. How are you feeling?"

He assured me he was fine and suggested that we meet the next afternoon, his voice businesslike but subdued. The next afternoon seemed an eon away. I checked my desk calendar.

"I've got a meeting at 4 tomorrow. Is there any chance we could meet this evening?"

Jimmy had a rehearsal.

"My meeting tomorrow will probably run about an hour. How about 5:30?"

"That's okay."

"Where shall we meet?" I asked.

"I thought Pioneer Park would be convenient for both of us."

The wet leaves. The overly strong scent of violet perfume. Pioneer Park at night.

I hesitated, unable to answer. "We could meet by the fountain," he said.

It was a logical choice. The park was several blocks from my clinic and fairly close to Jimmy's boarding house.

"I'll be there." I wanted to say something more, something

intimate, but being at the office I felt constrained. "5:30 then."

We said goodbye and I hung up. Immediately I regretted that I'd been unable to think of some way to reassure him, to let him know how much I cared for him. But I was caught off guard by the mention of Pioneer Park.

The fountain at Pioneer Park was an ornate monstrosity with a muscular Poseidon high in the center surrounded by lithe sea nymphs and mermen pouring water from seashells and grotesque fish spouting arcs from their mouths. This hydraulic superstructure spilled down into a low, wide basin some thirty feet across where little boys often sent small boats off on odysseys into the roiling waters near the center. It was a gift to the city of Portland from a wealthy timber baron who instructed an American sculptor to design something based on fountains that the donor had seen on travels in Europe. The resulting creation was installed near a corner of the park by the intersection of two busy streets. Concentric walkways with park benches surrounded the fountain, and curving flower beds ornamented the site.

The fountain offended my sensibilities on a number of levels. It depicted too many figures and gave an impression of too much busy detail. The bodies were not so skillfully rendered, and it was an American imitation of a French imitation, which I felt turned the dignity of Homer's ancient Greek gods into a frivolous fairy tale. How could Americans possibly know what Poseidon, that awe-inspiring force of nature, meant to the hearts of the ancients?

As an added insult, the genitals of all the figures were carefully covered or hidden in the composition. Even the breasts of the female nymphs were veiled by what appeared to be wet seaweed, showing not a trace of nipple, obviously inspired by a prudish American Puritanism that ran so contrary to the Greeks' open appreciation of the human form. In contrast, the chests of the male figures were fully detailed with disk-like areolae and nipples set on well-developed pectoral muscles.

I was well familiar with the fountain because it was not far from my office, and I occasionally took a walk on my lunch break and ended up passing by. I had once seen a crudely drawn penis and the word "suck" in pencil on the side of the basin. It had brought to mind a magazine article that mentioned ancient Roman graffiti on the Egyptian pyramids. The markings on the fountain were quickly removed, probably by city officials, because they were gone when I passed by the next day.

Pioneer Park was one of the oldest parks in the city and covered several city blocks. It was populated by large old trees, some dating back to before the pioneers. Aside from the fountain, it had a popular formal rose garden, a duck pond, and many secluded walkways with park benches. The park also had the reputation, among those who knew such things, as a place where men could meet each other, especially after dark.

My ruminations about Pioneer Park were interrupted by the telephone. Vivian, our receptionist, announced my next appointment, a new patient named Gilmore.

He was an otherwise healthy male in his late 20s complaining of what he called "piles." Upon examination, I found that he was not suffering from hemorrhoids but rather from significant condylomata of the anus. I had occasionally seen these warty growths on the genitals of females and males, and as anal growths in both sexes. That these lesions were associated with sexual activity was well known to me from the medical literature. Experience had taught me that it was not wise to question men directly about the cause. Instead, I offhandedly inquired if Mr. Gilmore was married. He told me he was a bachelor. I had no idea of the statistics, but I wondered how many men in our society never married. I asked if he had experienced any recent trauma to the area, hoping to solicit any comments he might be open to making. He simply shook his head, and I proceeded to treat the lesions.

One thing I value about medicine is that it looks truth full in the face, be it life, sickness, or death. It forces us to deal with the private parts, the hidden organs, the blood and urine and semen, the raw physical evidence of the individual human being. Secrets do not keep long with the probing of medicine.

Soon after I first took up medical practice in Portland, I concluded that men in my community were having sex together. Men like Gilmore would come into my office complaining of hemorrhoids or vague bowel ailments. I let them maintain that fiction and treated the problem. The way they had acquired the malady was obvious to me. What I didn't know then was how such men found each other.

Gilmore made a follow-up appointment with Vivian, and I returned to my office where I studied my calendar. Wednesday, 5:30, JH at PP.

Pioneer Park. I felt a slight quickening in my blood, a hunger, a nervous anticipation—and a disquieting resistance. What was it? Shame?

Until I decided it was too dangerous for me professionally, I had, in states of desperate loneliness, gone there myself. Never underestimate the power of loneliness.

Yes, I had a sexual history—like everyone. We all have things in our past that we wouldn't tell our mothers. Of course, the truth is that our mothers do, too. The human heart is riddled with secret drawers, some of which we keep locked up tight, others we don't even know are there.

Love stories can get messy, especially when you get to the sexual part. And sex is always messy. Not only are there all the bodily secretions, but there are all the messy emotions as well. And, messiest of all, these emotions become harnessed by the heartstrings to fate and destiny, and the course of one's whole life hangs in the balance.

Love stories get especially messy when the love is forbidden. The story of Romeo and Juliet would have been a simple one if their families had not made their love dangerous. But love will flourish, even when it is forbidden.

Sometimes it is necessary to take forbidden things out and examine them, as on an operating table. Now, looking back all these years, I believe we must speak openly, put all our cards on the table, all our actions, even our sexual activities, out in the open for history to see. For just as the ancient Greek tragedies place the murder offstage and the imagination amplifies the horror, it is the thing that is unspoken that takes hold of the mind and leads one to suspect some heinous transgression, when in reality, the unsaid thing is simply an act of physical desire at worst, or at best, an act of love.

Like water, love and desire go where they will. When they cannot find an open pathway through which to flow along in the sunshine and fresh air of the upper surfaces, these feelings seep into secret underground caverns. But instead of groping girls at petting parties, or getting young women pregnant in the back seat of a struggle buggy, instead of spending nights at unhealthy cat houses, I went to this park at night searching for release, yearning for companionship, and hoping I wouldn't get caught by vice agents.

I recalled Dr. Higgenbotham's lecture when I'd realized that the case involving our local YMCA had influenced the eventual passage of eugenics laws for the sterilization of those who might be "a menace to society." I knew the highly public nature of the YMCA scandal, the indictment of prominent men, the hints of sexual deviance, the sodomy trials. That widespread airing of the topic of homosexual sex, bringing it out into the open, made it possible for it to be named and spoken about, and hence, after the scandal, the sodomy laws were broadened to include oral-genital contact. So I was not innocent of the risks involved in seeking male companionship.

The first time I went to Pioneer Park at night was almost by accident. It was in mid-October the first year I settled in Portland. I had simply been walking around downtown, wandering aimlessly after a couple of drinks. It had rained earlier in the evening, and then the rain had stopped. The temperature was mild and I was enjoying the fresh night air. I happened to notice a couple of young men talking furtively on the street. When they walked off toward the park, I followed them at a discreet distance. They strolled past the ornate fountain and into a wooded pathway. A few other men wandered along singly or loitered on park benches. I had heard of this kind of activity when I was in New York City in the military, waiting to be shipped over to Europe. I had even been approached rather openly on the street a couple of times when I was in uniform. However, I had shied away from participating in that sort of thing. It struck me as unseemly and dangerous to be out searching for sex in public streets and parks, so instead I chose to spend my time trying to meet men like myself in certain Greenwich Village cafes and drinking establishments. I never imagined that such blatant open-air soliciting went on in my straight-laced, sleepy little Western town. And now I had stumbled upon it in my casual wanderings.

I walked around in the park for a time, observing the surreptitious promenade under the dim electric lights that dotted this part of the park. Finally, I sat down on one of the benches. No one was in the vicinity just then, and I waited for a time, feeling ill at ease. After a bit, a young boy walked out from behind some fir trees across the way and came toward the bench where I sat. He looked to be about 13 or 14 and wore frayed, dirty workman's clothes, which were too large for his small frame. His dark, curly hair hadn't seen a barber in a spell, but he was a good-looking kid. He eyed me intently as he approached and then took a seat near me on the bench.

"Hey, you got a cigarette, mister?" he asked.

"Aren't you a little young to be smoking?"

"Hell, I'm old enough."

"Where do you live, kiddo? Isn't it time you were home in bed?"

"I ain't got no place. My folks are dead."

"Come on. Give me the real story."

"That's the god's truth. I'm on my own."

"Don't you have some family around?" I was concerned for the kid in spite of his tough exterior.

"Naw, I like it this way. There ain't no one I gotta answer to."

"You must have a place to live."

"I been sleepin' here in the park," he said.

My incredulity must have shown on my face.

"Honest," he insisted.

It was just a feeling, and I didn't know why, but I thought the kid was untrustworthy.

"Hey, look," he said, "you seem like a nice man. Can you help me out with some spare change?" He looked up at me. "I ain't eaten since this morning."

"What's your name, kid?"

"Billy. Billy Butler. What's yours?"

I hesitated a moment then decided there was no risk in telling him my first name. "I'm Carl. Listen to me, Billy. You know there are places that will take you in."

"Yeah, yeah. I know all about it. You can forget about trying to sell me on that crap."

"Billy, you've got to eat. Winter's coming on. How are you going to get by? At your age?"

"Hell, I'm old enough. I'm old enough to know a thing or two. Maybe I can do you a favor." He moved a little closer to me. "I mean, I can make you feel good." Then he reached out and put his hand on my thigh and slowly moved it up toward my crotch.

"I can show you a good time," he said and he watched my face carefully. "You can cornhole me. Or do it between my legs. I'm better than any girl. Let me show you." His fingers found a sensitive spot and began to explore.

I pushed his hand away. "Hey, take it easy, kid. You're too young for this kind of stuff."

"No, I ain't. Come on. Let me show you." He reached for the inside of my thigh again. His other hand began fluttering around feeling my coat pockets. I pulled his hand away from my pockets, holding him by the wrist.

"Stop it," I said firmly.

"Please, mister, give me a try," he pleaded, reaching up my thigh with his other hand. I began to fear this might be some kind of trap, and I took him by the other wrist as well and stood up, holding him at arm's length.

"Just a dollar," he said. "I'll satisfy you for just a dollar."

"No. Now be quiet. I'm not interested in sex with you."

He was quiet for a moment, looking up at me, and I thought I caught a hint of fear in his eyes.

"Tell me the truth, Billy."

"Okay. Okay. I'll tell you the truth. Just let go of me first." I released his wrists and he backed off a few steps, out of reach, and shoved his hands in his pockets.

"I run away from home. Out in Idaho." He gave me a sullen look and then stared down at the ground. "I hopped a freight down here with a friend to go to work in the apple harvest upriver. While I was workin' there, I got hooked up with this jocker who talked me into coming to Portland with him. Said he wanted to be my friend and make me his very own punk, but when we got to town, he started selling me to trade. He wanted me to suck cocks for a quarter, but I wasn't having any of that. I'll do the other, but none of that fairy business. So I ran away from him. Now I'm just trying to get back to Idaho." He looked up at me again. "Can't you just give me some change to help me get back home?"

This story of Billy's made more sense than anything else he had told me, but still I wasn't inclined to trust him. Yet I didn't feel I could simply tell him to get lost and go on my way. And I wasn't about to take him to my house and give him a place to spend the night. I fumbled in my pockets and took out a business card and a dollar bill and held them out to him. I knew it might be taking a chance, but that was all I could think of at the moment.

"Here, Billy. This ought to buy you a room someplace for tonight and something to eat." He threw me another sullen glance. "My office address is on this card. It's right downtown here. If you come round to see me tomorrow, I'll take you to the train station and buy you a ticket back to Idaho."

Billy stepped up and grabbed the money and the card and stuffed them in his pocket. Then he quickly backed away from me saying, "Hell, I ain't goin' back to Idaho." He gave a scornful laugh as he continued to back down the pathway. "I ain't never goin' back there." Then he turned and ran off.

I didn't hear from Billy, much to my relief. The business card I gave him did turn up again a couple of weeks later, however. An itinerant laborer about my age came into my office smelling of campfire smoke and wearing a few days of beard. From his accent and the name he gave, I gathered that he was Greek. With him was a blond boy about 15. The older man presented my business card, worn and folded and smudged with dirt. "Billy Butler says you would help us out," he said and nudged the youth forward. The kid had injured his arm falling off a moving freight train. He was tough, barely grimacing while I examined the arm and found one of the bones in the forearm was broken.

"Is this your son?" I asked the man.

"Naw, he's a punk I met at a timber camp up in Washington. Early snow put an end to the logging for the year, so we hopped a freight down here. That's when he fell, jumpin' off the train."

I wondered how many unmarried men were working in the logging industry of our region, and it struck me as ironic that the timber baron who had erected the Greco-Roman fountain in Pioneer Park had created a social milieu that brought thousands of bachelors together in remote forest camps.

"How long ago did this happen?"

"Yesterday."

I gave the kid something for the pain and set the bone, then splinted his arm.

When I was done, the older man said, "We ain't able to pay you nothing, Doc. We got no jack. Been living in a hobo jungle outside of town."

"Don't worry about it," I told him. "Keep the splint on for a month and loosen the wrappings if it swells." I instructed them to come back in a week, so I could check to see how the bone was healing. But of course neither one ever returned.

I sat back down on the park bench to collect my thoughts. I wasn't a jocker looking for punks or a wolf looking for lambs. Unlike the adult male citizens of ancient Athens, I was not inclined toward boys and women. But even still, Billy Butler's proposition and his manual groping had inflamed my mind.

At the same time, the whole encounter was so unsettling that I decided maybe it was time for me to head home. I wasn't sure what game Billy was playing, but I felt more certain than ever that I was right not to trust him. Could he be working with the vice department?

I stood up to leave and had just started walking away from the park bench when a uniformed sailor came toward me along the dim pathway. You never can tell about military men. Some of them will kick you in the teeth if you proposition them, some will gladly let you suck them off, but they won't let you kiss them. Still others will get downright romantic with you. This sailor sized me up as he approached, then he paused, fumbling in his pocket and came right up to me. Again I felt that spark of erotic curiosity that had first drawn me to the park that night.

"Hey, buddy, got a light?" he said and took out a pack of cigarettes. He was weaving slightly as he stood there and I knew he had been drinking.

I always carried matches with me even though I didn't smoke, mainly to be prepared for any emergency that might present itself to me as a physician. But after dealing with Billy, and now confronted with a drunk, I decided to skirt this encounter as gracefully as possible.

"I'm sorry, I don't smoke," I said.

But he didn't give up easily. He stood there beside me and took out some matches to light his cigarette. He seemed unaware that he had just asked me for a light.

By the flame of the match, the sailor appeared about my age, and though he was no great beauty, his face had a manly attractiveness. Maybe it was only the uniform, but he reminded me a little of Gerald. Even still, I could tell he'd had one too many, and I knew from past experience that was not a recipe for a satisfying sexual encounter.

"Say, you know a place called the Green Daisy?" he asked. "I been lookin' for it all night. Supposed to be a good place to get a drink."

"Why, yes, I've heard of it, but I can't tell you where it's located. I've never been there."

"You never been there?" He laughed. Apparently, he didn't believe me. "Aw, come on, toots, you can be aboveboard with me." He moved in close and put an arm around my shoulder. I could smell the liquor.

"Wouldn't you like to have one of the smoothest wolves in the Navy give you a good browning?" he asked.

"I beg your pardon?" I said. It was an innocent reply. Although his speech was slurred, I understood perfectly well what he was suggesting and I wasn't offended. He had simply caught me off guard.

"I'm sorry, sweetheart," he said, "I took you for a pogue. You wouldn't be in the mood to suck off the ol' trouser snake now, would you, dearie?"

The encounter had gone on long enough. "Excuse me, but I think you've got the wrong idea."

He immediately backed off, removing his arm from my shoulder. "Hey, buddy, I'm sorry. I thought you were a fairy. Hope you'll 'scuse me. You upper class types always strike me a bit sissified."

I knew I was attracted to men, but I also knew I wasn't a fairy. During the War I had met a number of soldiers and sailors who preferred the effeminate fairy types because they knew they could treat a fairy like a whore but wouldn't have to pay money for it. They were also under the mistaken impression that they could get a venereal disease from a female prostitute but not from having a fairy perform fellatio.

"You ain't miffed with me, are you?" he said.

What can you do with a drunken sailor? But even if he had not been drunk, I had already decided this fellow was not my type. With all his brash aggressiveness, I sensed he was the kind who was completely inept with girls so he turned to fairies.

"Don't worry about it, pal," I said.

He paused as if he were trying to decide to stay or go.

"Hey, look, I got a room down here at the YMCA and there's a li'l bottle in my duffel bag. Ya wanna have a drink with me?"

He now appeared lonely and vulnerable. At that moment I felt a wave of empathy for him. His loneliness was right there on the surface and it was a loneliness I shared. But I knew he was not the right person for me. I also knew the reputation of the YMCA and I wasn't about to take the professional risk of being seen there. "Thanks, but I've got to be getting home," I said. "It's late."

"Yeah," he said, "I guess it's time to turn in." He began to raise his hand in a gesture that looked as if maybe he were about to salute, but he caught himself at the last moment. Then he turned and walked off down the path.

I waited a bit, then followed him a distance to be sure he was leaving the park. He headed off toward the city lights. The sailor had resurrected Gerald's specter and with my loneliness and yearning rekindled, I ambled around the park for a spell. I eyed the few men who passed by and they gave me the once-over without stopping to initiate an encounter. Finally, I took a seat on one of the benches again. I was determined to learn how to play this game, and I decided I had better take advantage of the next opportunity that came along.

After a while, a hatless young man with an effeminate manner approached—it was something in the way he walked. As he passed beneath a nearby lamppost, I could see that he was blond, probably in his 20s, and quite a handsome fellow—a little too handsome. And he was a bit on the heavy side for my taste. He kept his gaze on me as he came near, and I looked him in the face. He took a seat at the other end of the park bench and fidgeted for a while, running his fingers through his hair, then smoothing it down to make sure it was in place. Finally, he turned to me and said, "I beg your pardon. Have you got the time?" His voice had a distinctive quality, not exactly high-pitched, but there was a lilt to it.

If I had been more experienced and on my toes, I would have replied that I had all the time in the world. Instead, I quietly reached into my vest pocket. As he watched me take out my pocket watch, I had the peculiar sensation that I was participating in a sexual act. I told him the hour. He took out a pack of cigarettes and asked if I had a light. This time I took the overture in stride. I pulled out some matches and moved in closer to light his cigarette. The pungent scent of a cheap, violet perfume assaulted my nostrils. As I struck a match and held it for him, the light of the flame revealed that he was wearing lipstick and his eyebrows were tweezed. His hair was bleached blond with the roots showing a bit of dark brown. And he wore a red necktie. No one but a fairy would adopt such grooming and attire, I thought. On the wrist of the hand that held his cigarette, he wore one of the newly fashionable wristwatches, which used to look so effeminate to me because their unexpected appearance always reminded me of a lady's bracelet. Consequently, I had always preferred a pocket watch.

He offered me a cigarette. Even though I don't smoke, I had decided that I was going to go through with this thing, so I took one and lit it for myself. He told me his name was Jerry but said I could call him Germaine if I liked. He asked my name. When I hesitated, he quickly said, "Oh, sweetie, you don't have to tell me your real name."

The timbre of his voice and a gesture he made with his cigarette gave free rein to his feminine side. It was his maleness that attracted me, yet this blatant display of femininity in a male body caused a repugnance to arise that put me off balance.

The medical literature used the term "inversion." It specifically referred to a female nature trapped in a male body. Jerry may have typified this category, but I felt completely masculine within my own body, while I felt desire for other masculine men. I always thought the term "invert" did not square with men like me.

"My name is Curt," I said at last.

"Hello, Curt. Pleasure to make your acquaintance. That wasn't so hard, was it? A good first step." He waited a moment to see if I would take up the conversation but I said nothing. After we sat in silence for a moment longer, he said, "I guess you probably didn't come to the park for stimulating repartee, did you? Do you want to take a walk with me?"

My throat had gone dry with sexual anticipation and I croaked out the word, "Sure."

He stood and it took me a moment to collect my thoughts. "Oh, don't worry. You can trust me," he said.

"No, it's not that…" I stood up.

Jerry gestured down the way with a jerk of his head and began walking. I followed him off the path into the trees. The glow of his cigarette veered through some bushes to the trunk of a large tree. Its bare branches were silhouetted against the glow from the city reflected in the heavy clouds of the night sky.

We put out our cigarettes in the thick mat of wet leaves and Jerry turned to me. He moved in close and brought his face up to kiss me. Something made me turn my face away from him. Maybe it was the thought of his lipstick or the scent of his perfume. I don't know.

When I was in the military, I had known men who would have sex with you but would never kiss. As long as they didn't kiss and were not on the receiving end of a male sex organ, they thought sex with another man was okay. I guess that way they felt their manhood couldn't be called into question. I always disliked that, and I never considered myself to be like them, but there I was, treating Jerry that same way. I can't explain my reaction to him, and I won't try to justify it.

"Oh, you're one of those," Jerry said quietly, but the bitchy undertone was clear. "If you don't kiss, then you're not a fairy, right? Okay, just call me Jerry the Fairy. Let's make the most of it. Take out your dick. I can service trade as well as anyone. But I'm always hoping for something more than that."

"Trade." It was the same term that Billy Butler had used. I don't hear it much in recent years, but at that time it was understood by those in the know as slang for "normal" men who took the active role in sex with fairies. I had never been called "trade" before, and I wasn't sure I liked it. But I didn't take up with women so I didn't consider myself normal. Maybe I could "pass," but I knew I was different.

While I unbuttoned my overcoat and opened my fly, he said, "You're not a flatfoot, are you? No, I wouldn't expect you to tell me if you were. Not till you pull out your badge and make the arrest. We might as well try to have some fun in the meantime." This patter fascinated and amused me, while I was repelled at the same time. Before I knew it, he was on his knees with his mouth on my penis. I watched as he performed fellatio on me and masturbated himself at the same time.

I felt I was being sexually stingy, yet my feelings about Jerry were so mixed that I didn't know what to do. I wanted to apologize to him in some way, but I couldn't find the words to express the confusion I was feeling. Maybe there were no words. Still, I had my needs and my desires, so I just let him do what he pleased. It struck me as odd that what I was doing was considered the active role in the encounter, when Jerry was the one doing all the work. But at the moment, he seemed to be getting what he wanted out of the transaction. Still, later on, I felt somehow guilty and ashamed.

Had the situation been different, the whole sexual encounter could have turned out otherwise. I could just as well have been the one performing fellatio. I had no qualms about that. However, Jerry was making certain assumptions and I was feeling reticent in such a public place, so the course of our interaction seemed a predetermined comedy of errors. Under better circumstances we might have been more open with each other and perhaps become friends. But I was caught up in the demands of a whole society that could not accept people like Jerry the Fairy.

It was all over quickly. Afterwards, when we had closed our flies and buttoned our coats, he offered me another cigarette. I declined. As we walked back toward the fountain, he said there was an all-night diner a few blocks from the park. "I don't suppose you'd want to join me for a cup of coffee."

"No, I've got to get going," I said.

"I thought so," Jerry said. "Back home to the wife and kids, eh? Well, it's been fun. Maybe I'll see you around here again." He made a little wave with the hand that held his cigarette, then turned and crossed the street.

I returned to the park a week later and hooked up with a trim, athletic fellow with bad teeth and a nice smile. Unlike Jerry, he came across as a regular fellow. We didn't kiss, and the only act we did together was mutual masturbation in the bushes. Afterward he asked if I wanted to go for a drink. I didn't want to be seen out in public with anyone who might be of questionable reputation, so I told him that I had to be going home soon, but that we could sit on a park bench and talk for a bit. He told me his name was Nick and that he worked as an automobile mechanic at a garage. That explained the grime under his nails. I told him my name was Curt and that I had returned from the War recently. He had to be home early, too. He had a wife and two kids. He said that he loved his wife and enjoyed sex with her, but that he liked men, too. So he would tell his wife he was going out drinking with some of the boys and then come to the park. His story was so straightforward and casual, lacking any hint of guile, that I trusted him completely.

I ran into Nick a couple more times in the park. At our last encounter there, he invited me to come to a party on the next weekend. I found Nick attractive and he seemed like a nice sort, so I agreed to go, since he said that the party was at a private residence. We would meet at the fountain in the park at 8 the following Saturday evening. When Nick arrived that night, he had cleaned his fingernails for the occasion.

The party was given by an effeminate man in his late 40s named Dixon Calder. He ran a couple of speakeasies that the authorities kept shutting down. His apartment was decorated with Chinese screens and furnished with low tables and cushions on oriental carpets. Incense perfumed the air, and candles lit the rooms, which were filled with an assortment of vases with extravagant bouquets of cut flowers. I could easily imagine orgy scenes in such a setting, and that contributed to the uneasiness I was feeling, aside from my nervousness that I might run into someone there who knew me. It turned out to be a small gathering. Aside from the host, there were only three other gentlemen there when Nick and I arrived. They appeared to be sedate, ordinary fellows, probably in their 30s or 40s. They drank cocktails and chatted.

After a while, Jerry the Fairy arrived with two effeminate friends, all of them wearing make-up and flamboyant clothing. Jerry had a lavender scarf around his neck and another fairy wore a lady's cloche. They were full of chatter and campy jokes, using mannerisms that made me uncomfortable. Soon after he arrived, Jerry glanced over at me and there was a moment of recognition on his face, then a smile with a tinge of disdain. I excused myself and left before Jerry had a chance to talk to me. I had hoped to spend some time with Nick that night, but we never saw each other again. He was just trade, but we might have developed a friendship. However, I suspect I would have dropped him sooner than later, even though I felt a strong attraction for him. I couldn't see continuing on with a man who had a wife and children. I spotted Nick around town a few times after that and always tried to avoid him, just like that night after the eugenics lecture.

I ran into Jerry once more a few weeks later. I had gone to lunch with Dr. Bleeker at his club down the street from the clinic. On our way back, I stopped into a small haberdashery to pick up some new handkerchiefs and Bleeker accompanied me. When I looked up from the glass display case, there stood Jerry behind the counter. His hair looked newly bleached—no dark roots showing—but the shade was a bit too light to appear natural. I froze as we recognized each other.

"How may I help you?" he asked. He made it sound like a perfectly natural question for a store clerk, but we were both aware of the innuendoes and I thought I detected a slight smirk as he asked the question. Bleeker stood nearby looking over the ties and I hoped he was not paying any attention to the exchange.

After my moment of panic subsided, I blurted out, "Just browsing." Then without meeting his gaze, I said, "Thank you" and turned away. Bleeker had crossed the room and seemed engrossed in examining the belts. To get his attention I cleared my throat, but he must not have heard me. He took down a belt and ran it around his waist to check the fit.

I went to his side and said, "They don't seem to have my brand. We'd better get back."

"I think I'll purchase this one. How do you think it looks, Dr. Holman?"

I was perturbed that he had used my name and I kept my back to the counter where Jerry stood.

"Good-looking piece of leather," I said.

He walked up to Jerry and held out the belt. "I'll pay with a check," Bleeker said. While they completed the transaction, I busied myself inspecting the shirts in the other corner of the room.

When Bleeker was finished, I walked out of the store as quickly as I could without seeming to rush.

I didn't want to be associated with Dixon Calder's circle of fairies and queers. I'd heard of such social groups, but I thought such associations were too dangerous professionally. I longed for like companions, yet there was no safe place to meet men like myself—men who preferred men but ones that were not effeminate. Even if there were such a place, the threat of blackmail always lurked or the fear of having my business associates find out.

The dangers of sex in the park may have held an added element of excitement for some, but that wasn't my cup of tea, any more than gushing pansies were. I wanted something besides a quickie in the bushes. Like Jerry, I always hoped for more than that. I wanted someone with whom to spend leisurely mornings in bed on weekends, someone to come home to after work, someone to share my life.

After that party at Calder's apartment, I resigned myself to loneliness. Still I hoped that someone would come along—a discreet meeting with the right person. Now Jimmy had come along, but I wasn't sure what he was feeling. He probably wasn't sure either. But after his drunken visit in the middle of the night, I was hopeful.

EIGHT

The next afternoon I arrived late at the fountain, sweating from exertion, having nearly run the few blocks from my office. My clinic meeting had detained me past 5:30, and I was afraid that Jimmy might not wait for me. On top of that, I was suffering the nervous excitement of having agonized through the last twenty-four hours waiting to see Jimmy again.

A substantial number of people were scattered in the garden around the fountain, and my eyes searched frantically for Jimmy's familiar figure among those strolling along the flower beds or lounging on benches, enjoying the sunny June afternoon. Finally, with joyous relief, I spotted him sitting off by himself, arms folded across his chest, staring at the wet statuary. He looked sharp and well-groomed, as usual, in contrast to his appearance at our midnight meeting. I stood catching my breath for a few moments, admiring him from a distance. When my breathing slowed somewhat, I walked around the basin toward Jimmy Harper.

He must have been lost in thought for he didn't see me until I neared the bench where he sat. He stood up quickly and said hello.

"It's good to see you, Jimmy." I extended my hand, although what I wanted to do was put my arm around his shoulder and reassure him.

He shook my hand firmly and looked me in the eye. His face was serious and clouded with concern. I could smell alcohol on his breath, though he didn't seem drunk. I figured he'd had a drink to bolster his courage.

"I'm sorry to be late," I said. "Something always comes up at the last minute when I'm trying to get out of the clinic on time. Have I kept you waiting long?"

"No, only a few minutes," he said. "Let's walk a bit."

He led us away from the fountain into the park. As we walked slowly under the tall, old sycamore trees, I asked if he was familiar with the park.

"Oh, sure," he said. "Mary and I…" he paused, "we used to come here on Sundays."

We passed down a path under large maples.

"Ever been here at night?" I asked.

"Why, no," he replied. "Why would I come here at night?"

"Just curious," I said and let the subject drop. He obviously attached no significance to the question. He gestured to a bench set off by itself in the shade of a spreading oak that overlooked the duck pond. We sat down. I was careful to leave an acceptable distance between us on the park bench. I didn't want Jimmy to feel that I was moving in on him, and at the same time I didn't want to appear standoffish. Across the pond an occasional stroller passed by on the footpath, but there in the dappled shade we were quite alone.

Jimmy apologized again for his drunken visit at my house, and I said that he must have had a good reason for getting drunk.

"Yes, there was a good reason why I got drunk," Jimmy began. "I may as well just tell you everything." He looked out at the pond. I supposed it was easier for him to talk if he didn't look at me directly. Hoping not to inhibit him, I kept my eyes on the water as well.

"When you kissed me on Saturday," Jimmy began, "I started to say that I'd been kissed by a man before. Not a man, really, a boy at college—another student." He paused and took a deep breath. "I guess he was infatuated with me, but I didn't like him. He was kind of a milksop and the other fellas made fun of him. I didn't want to be associated with him. But he was overly forward and kept approaching me to make conversation. One night, I was alone in one of the practice rooms at the end of the music building. I was gathering up my music to go home when he knocked at the door and came in with some sheet music. He started asking me about piano technique in the piece he was working on. He sat down on the bench next to me and played some passages, and I showed him how I would play parts of the piece. Then before I knew what was happening he had his hand on my leg and his arm around me and he was kissing me. I was so surprised I didn't know what to do and he kept kissing me and feeling between my legs. I started to get aroused and it was so confusing that I just sat there. And then he… he started talking sex talk, saying he wanted to suck me off, and… and he undid his trousers…he was hard. And he had a terrible body odor about him. I was so shocked I just got up and left—without saying a word."

He shifted his weight and pulled at his shirt cuffs.

"I never spoke to him again. I avoided him when I could and snubbed him whenever he came around. I felt bad about it all, but I never liked the kid to begin with, and after what he did that night, I hated the sight of him."

Jimmy reached down and picked up a twig and began fidgeting with it.

"So when you kissed me, I wanted to tell you about all that, but I couldn't—not right then. And then…." Jimmy sighed.

"You know what happened next….I came in my trousers while you were kissing me. I didn't even…I wasn't even hard. I didn't understand what was happening. And it all happened so quick. I just…I just don't know what's wrong with me. I thought I was normal and now—"

"There's nothing wrong with you, Jimmy," I said.

He held up his hand to stop me, still looking down at the ground. After a pause he continued. "So…so I made a date with Mary for Sunday evening. When I talked to her on the telephone, she said she had a surprise for me. Well, the band played an afternoon tea dance that day, way the heck out at the Randall's Ferry Country Club. We planned to meet back here in town for drinks at our regular speakeasy afterwards. Howard agreed to let me borrow his car to take Mary out that night, and I was going to get the car from him there at the bar. I arranged for Mary to meet me there. I thought we could have a drink with the band so she could get to know them better. She said she could get a ride down to the bar with her cousin and some other girls.

"I got away from the tea dance late because I was riding with Howard, and he kept flirting with a girl after the dance. Diggs and the others arrived at the speakeasy first. When Howard and I got there, we parked in the back lot and came in the back way like always. I didn't see Mary so I figured she and her friends hadn't arrived yet."

A flock of tiny birds fluttered past and settled in a nearby bush, then just as quickly, flew away.

"So I walked up to the bar, and Diggs comes up to me and says, 'Hey Jimmy, have I got a story for you.' He said when he walked in that afternoon he spied this attractive young thing at the bar in a pretty yellow dress. He said, 'Boy oh boy, what a looker. So I put the moves on her.' Then she told him that she was waiting for me. It was Mary he was flirting with.

"Diggs got a big laugh out of that. He told me that she said she'd wait for me outside, and then she and her friends ran off. He said I should let him know if I decided not to keep her. 'I'll take her any ol' time.' He said it right to my face."

Jimmy paused and shook his head. "I told him he had a talent for butting into the wrong situation. I asked him, didn't he recognize her? I've introduced him to her a bunch of times." Jimmy continued to shake his head slowly from side to side. "I swear, anything in a skirt. They all look the same to Diggs. He just shrugged and said he didn't mean to mess things up for me. So I went out front and found Mary and the girls sitting in their car talking. I hardly recognized her, myself. Her big surprise was that she had bobbed her hair. It's real short now. My God, she looked like a little boy. She used to have this beautiful long blonde hair. That threw me for a loop right off the bat. But I tried to be complimentary about it. Told her it looked swell. But I don't think she believed me.

"After all that, I didn't want us to stick around. I borrowed Howard's car, like I planned, and Mary and I went to dinner. I took her to the Chandler Hotel and during dinner I…I proposed to her. With a ring and everything—I even put it on her finger. It was just an opal. I couldn't even afford the smallest diamond they had. And it still cost me a good chunk of my savings for the down payment."

Jimmy paused and let go another sigh. "I bought the ring on Saturday afternoon after I left your house." He glanced toward me and looked away, then paused to gather his thoughts.

"After dinner, we went on a long drive up in the hills just after sunset and found this secluded meadow where I parked the car. We spread out a blanket there in the grass."

Jimmy paused again. Then after a moment he continued.

"I guess I may as well tell you that I've never done it with a girl before. So I talked Mary into letting me have sex with her… there in the meadow…and I…" He heaved another sigh. "I couldn't. I couldn't do it. I didn't get hard."

Jimmy broke the twig in half and twisted the two pieces between his fingers. I waited for him to continue. He was quiet for a few moments, looking at the ground. Then he took in a long breath and, looking out at the pond, began again.

"Afterwards I told her I was sorry. She kept saying, 'It's all right, it's all right.' But I had to explain to her, you know? I told her about us—that I'd had a…a sexual experience with another man. In her face I could see this terrible poison spreading through her, and I knew I'd lost her. She started crying and got up and ran off into the meadow. She must have turned her ankle or something and she fell. I went after her and helped her back to the car and got her calmed down. She said she had to go home. We didn't say anything more. We drove home in an awful silence and when I got to her place, she took off the ring and left it on the seat of the car. Then she jumped out and slammed the car door and limped into the house. I couldn't move. I didn't even get out and see her to the door. We never even said good night."

Jimmy stopped. Then he said, "I don't know, Doc. I just don't know." He sighed again and paused for a moment.

"Jimmy, I—"

He cut me off. "That's not the worst of it." He continued to stare off at the pond. "Monday night Diggs brought some new music to rehearsal. It's this terrible sweet music—the kind of stuff I hate. At speakeasies, people like the hot jazz. But that country-club crowd likes their music more civilized. And that's the audience Diggs wants to go after—because they pay better. So Diggs and I got into an argument. I told him his music stank and he...he called me a nigger lover. I couldn't believe my ears. Then he..." Jimmy paused as his voice started to quaver. "He threatened to...get a new piano player." A quiet sob racked his body and he began to cry. "I just..." Another sob choked off his words. Jimmy was quiet for a minute while he struggled to regain control.

"I feel like everything in my life has...has gone to hell all of a sudden." Another sob silenced him for a moment.

He began again, talking through his tears. "I thought everything was going the way it was supposed to. I thought I was normal and that Mary and I would get married and have kids. And I'd play jazz with the band." He paused to snuffle. "Now I don't know about anything."

He stopped and tears ran down his face. Then he blurted out, "I don't want to end up a lonely old fairy." His voice gave way to another sob, and he covered his face with his hands. After a time, he took out a handkerchief and wiped his eyes and blew his nose. "You're the only person I can talk to about any of this."

I knew this would take a long time, but I wasn't in any hurry. I waited for Jimmy to say more but he didn't. I looked over at him. His face was troubled, but he had regained his composure. It must have been some relief to him to have gotten it all off his chest.

He was leaning forward with his elbows on his knees, his shoulders tensed. I wanted to reach out and touch him, to somehow reassure him. But I didn't want to crowd him—his mind was already crowded enough. Leaving a comfortable distance between us, I turned slightly toward Jimmy and laid my arm on the back of the bench.

"First," I began, "I want you to know that I've had the same kind of experience you had with Mary—I couldn't get an erection—more than once. That happens to most men at one time or another. Believe me, a number of my patients ask me about this, and I've read some of the medical literature. It's not uncommon. There is nothing wrong with you, Jimmy. You understand?" I looked over at him and waited to make sure he did understand, but he only sat there looking at the ground shaking his head. "You're okay, Jimmy, believe me."

He was silent.

"Now the other thing." I paused. "Look, Jimmy, you're not effeminate. You're not a fairy. Personally, I'm put off by effeminate men. But I find you attractive. Does that make me effeminate? I find you attractive because you're a man, Jimmy. If I were interested in someone feminine, I'd go after a woman. Why, I've read that two men having sex together makes them both more masculine because there isn't the mediating effect of a woman.

"There's no reason that two men can't love each other and have sex and be happy together. Never mind what it says in the Bible. Never mind the sodomy laws. Why, even the famous Dr. Freud is adamant that inversion is not a sickness and should not be subject to the law. And you can't listen to what society says either. You've got to listen to your own heart. Your own feelings."

"But my parents..." Jimmy said. "Everybody expects me to get married."

"Look, Jimmy, times are different now. The War has changed everything. We don't have to do things the way our parents did.

"Let me tell you a story. I had a number of experiences with women when I was in college and medical school but that was never satisfying for me. I always felt like something was missing. Then during my time in the military, I had a few sexual experiences with other men and I discovered that was what I wanted. The more I thought about it, the more I realized that is what I wanted from the time I was a boy. I started to remember a lot of things I felt growing up. As a kid, I had always dreamed of having a special male friend I could share my thoughts and feelings with, someone I would travel with and see the world."

He continued to fidget with his handkerchief.

"Then during the War, when I first went to the front near Meuse-Argonne, I saw a lot of things that changed my way of thinking about the way the world was and the way it ought to be. I saw soldiers torn apart by bombs. I did my best to sew them back together. But that was only the material part, the blood and slime of the battlefield. The psychological part was worse. Doing triage was like playing God. I hated making those decisions about who got treated and who didn't. But we couldn't help all of those young men. There weren't enough doctors and nurses or supplies and drugs. There wasn't enough time." I paused to look at Jimmy, but he continued to stare at the ground.

"One of the worst cases was a young soldier who had his abdomen ripped open by a land mine, and when they brought him in, his intestines were hanging out. I triaged him to the lost causes. To this day I remember the expression on his face as he looked down and saw that he was holding his own intestines in his hands and he looked up at me and said, 'Can't you do something for me, Doc?' There was no use trying. Peritonitis would soon set in if it hadn't already. There was nothing I could do. I couldn't even give him morphine because we had run out." Now I could sense Jimmy listening intently.

"I never found out what happened to him. An extra ambulance arrived at the last moment and since he was still moving, he was evacuated to a nearby town with a couple of the other severely wounded soldiers. I never saw him again. But that memory still haunts me. I always hoped that maybe, by some miracle, he made it through."

A crow in a nearby tree let out a series of croaks. I paused until it was silent.

"That was just one soldier, though—and my inability to make a difference. Beyond that small moment, there was the vast catastrophe of the war. It's hard to convey the immensity of the war machine that developed—on both sides. Not just the huge artillery cannons and the thousands of machine guns, but the endless columns of troops marching into war and the countless supply trucks and rail lines bringing in more and more rations and munitions. A massive industrialized web that entangled everything."

A child across the pond threw a stick into the water and a couple of ducks paddled away from the shore.

"And then there was the devastated landscape. Homes and churches destroyed, whole towns reduced to rubble. Millions killed and maimed. Families torn apart—children separated from their parents, wives from their husbands. Millions of innocent people displaced and scattered. The unimaginable extent of human suffering caused by the War. And for what? I began to hate the whole normal civilized world that had made such a futile, senseless…disaster. I began to question everything. I was determined to live my own life in a different way." I paused. "Then I met up with an American soldier named Gerald."

The dappled sunlight played on the side of Jimmy's face.

"He was an officer on the administrative staff of a base hospital outside Paris. We worked closely. As Gerald and I became friends, we discovered we both felt the same about the War and about the society that caused it. After we'd known each other a while, we discovered that we had a lot more in common." I paused and glanced at Jimmy. "We ended up having sex and we…well, we fell in love—there's no other way to put it."

Jimmy half-turned his head toward me, but he was still staring at the ground. "We were always discreet, of course. But we spent all our free time together. With Gerald, my childhood dream of a male companion came true." With the memories, an inadvertent smile came over me.

"After the armistice, I was transferred to an allied occupation hospital at Koblenz on the Rhine in Germany. Gerald pulled some strings and got himself stationed at the same hospital as an administrator. It probably helped that he spoke German fluently. He met a couple of German men at a beer hall and he introduced me. Heinrich and Detlef lived in Berlin and were visiting Koblenz on business. Heinrich spoke pretty good English and I knew a little German, so he and I could talk, and the four of us all became good friends. It didn't take long to realize that they loved each other, too.

"Heinrich and Detlef had been together since before the War. They were about the happiest couple I had ever known. I mean, when I compare them to my parents—they certainly got along better than my folks did."

Jimmy turned to glance at me with a thoughtful expression, then looked back at the ground.

"Gerald and I would arrange to get leave together and take the train to Berlin to visit Heinrich and Detlef. They took us out to some of the cabarets there, and those places were like nothing I'd ever experienced, even in New York City. You might see anything there: men dancing with men, women dancing together, high society couples, fairies, masculine-looking women, prostitutes. The people were so much more open in these places. And the entertainment. You could see transvestite musical revues with satirical lyrics and parodies of popular songs. Heinrich had to explain the lyrics to us because they were so full of German slang. You even heard American-style jazz there." I glanced over at Jimmy and his head half-turned as if I'd caught his interest.

"Heinrich and Detlef were involved with a group of people in Berlin who were trying to get Paragraph 175 repealed. That's the German version of the sodomy laws here in the States. There were magazines and pamphlets being published—it was a whole political movement. So Gerald and I were reading all that literature—and books, too, not just pamphlets. That's when I first read Thomas Mann and Andre Gide and Oscar Wilde, and some social scientists who were writing about sex. Even Walt Whitman—I had never read his poetry until then—when I saw what respect these German fellows had for his writing." I stretched my legs out in front of me but a bit more in Jimmy's direction.

"Of course, there was also enormous opposition to that life—to that kind of love—in Germany, just like here. Especially from religious groups. The churches there are outraged that the law might be changed—as you'd expect. I still get letters from Heinrich and Detlef, and Paragraph 175 still hasn't been repealed. But, Berlin was a revelation to me. I saw that there was a possibility of living a life with another man—without guilt or shame. For the first time, I realized that it might be possible for men like Gerald and me to be happy together. That was a good time for me." I found myself smiling at the thought. I looked over at Jimmy.

He continued to stare at the ground, but I could tell he was listening.

"But it didn't last long. One weekend while I was on duty in Koblenz, Gerald took the train to Berlin. I was going to meet him there on Monday. Heinrich and Detlef took him out to a cabaret the night he arrived, but he was tired from his trip and left early to return to his hotel. Heinrich and Detlef stayed at the cabaret with friends." I paused and looked out at the duck pond.

"As near as the German police could determine, Gerald was attacked by thugs in the street. They may have been fanatics who had it in for the clientele of the cabaret. His body was found in an alleyway near the place. Or maybe it was because he was American. There was a great deal of anti-American sentiment in Germany then. It's hard to say. He died at a hospital the next day. His attackers had stolen his uniform and all of his identification papers, so it took the German authorities a while to find a witness who could tell them the victim was an American soldier. Eventually, because I was an American military doctor and happened to be in Berlin, I was called down to the morgue to examine the body. The face was so disfigured that I had no idea who it was. I had to examine the rest of the body to make a positive identification. At first, I thought I recognized the shape of the hands, then I saw a scar on the left shoulder. Finally, I recognized a small mole on his foreskin."

Jimmy looked over at me with concern. A light breeze stirred and a dead leaf skittered past.

"In that moment of recognition, my heart shattered into a thousand pieces. Like shrapnel from a land mine. I couldn't work for days. I talked with one of the other military doctors and told him I was suffering from shell shock—of course, I couldn't tell him what had happened. He gave me a medical leave. I stayed with Heinrich and Detlef for a couple of weeks. They took good care of me and that helped. But it took me a long time to realize that Gerald was never coming back."

A curious squirrel approached and then scampered away.

"When I came back to Oregon after I left the Army, that all seemed like a dream—like a fairy tale—'long ago and far away.' My father put me in contact with Dr. Gowan, and I started working at the clinic. It seemed like the harder I worked and the more hours I put in, the more I could…just not think…about Gerald. Or anything. I reconnected with my old friend Gwen, and I was able to talk to her about what happened over there—with Gerald. She is a nurse with a great understanding for healing and she was enormously comforting to me." I pulled my arm from the back of the bench and leaned forward.

"That was three years ago. Since then I've had a few casual encounters with men here—but no one like Gerald." I looked over at Jimmy. "Then I met you."

I couldn't say any more for fear of making Jimmy feel some sense of obligation. I looked away. Maybe I'd already said too much.

Jimmy turned back to watch the duck pond. We didn't speak for a while.

Then he turned to me and took my hand and held it between his palms. My heart leapt. Jimmy looked down at my hand as he stroked the hair on the back of it. Then he gave it a squeeze and glanced up at me.

"If I had a piano right now," he said, "I'd play a Bach piece for you. It's the saddest, most beautiful music in the world."

"But I'm not sad when I'm with you, Jimmy."

He held my hand for a moment longer, both of us looking into each other's faces. Then he squeezed my hand again and looked away. An awkward feeling arose.

"Maybe we should walk some," he said. He withdrew his hands and stood.

I followed suit and we walked slowly up a rise and around the duck pond. A light breeze moved through the oak trees that surrounded us, shading the walkway.

"Aren't these wonderful old trees?" I said.

Jimmy seemed lost in thought. "I'm sorry, what was that?" he said, looking up at me.

"These trees. I was just reminded of a neighbor kid, when I was growing up. He used to say that trees were the hands of God. I didn't believe the God part, but I still always think about it when I see trees like this." I looked at Jimmy. "What were you thinking about?"

"Oh…that my problems seem pretty puny after your story."

"No, Jimmy. Your concerns are important. Each one of us is the most important person in his own life." I paused. "But I believe that war and death help us put other things in perspective."

We passed on out of the trees into a wide, open area where the formal rose garden was laid out in a rectangle crisscrossed by diagonal paths. The roses were in bloom, each labeled with the name of the variety.

"Pick out your favorite rose," I challenged Jimmy. We passed back and forth examining the many colors and shapes and sizes of blooms. Jimmy's choice was a two-toned yellow and red rose named "Fandango."

"Jazzy," I said and sniffed a bud. "But it doesn't have much of a smell."

I chose a white climbing variety named "Snow White" that had large full flowers and a sweet, spicy fragrance. It bloomed in profusion on an arched trellis that spanned the walkway. Jimmy walked over and smelled one of the blooms. "Yes," he said, "I guess a rose without a scent is like a bird without a song."

I laughed.

We walked slowly back toward the fountain. Jimmy seemed deep in thought. We passed back under the open shade of the sycamores and Jimmy stopped and checked his watch.

"Carl, I've got to head back and get ready for rehearsal tonight. But let's get together again soon and talk some more. You've given me a lot to think about. I guess what I need right now is time to try to sort things out."

"You seem less troubled."

"I guess so. Thanks. Thanks for talking with me." He paused and thought for a moment. "Are you free Sunday afternoon? Maybe we could take in a movie or something."

"I'd like that, Jimmy."

He was obviously feeling more comfortable now, and I was thrilled that he initiated the invitation.

"Why don't you come by my place?" he said. "Maybe 1:30."

"Sounds great."

"We can talk some more. I'll show you around. You haven't seen my room." This sounded so much like an invitation to intimacy that I was warmed with delight, and I searched Jimmy's face for some hint of a sexual innuendo. But he seemed completely innocent in his offer.

He stood there for a moment as if he were reluctant to go. I waited, wishing to prolong our visit. "Well…" he said, squinting against the sun.

"I'll see you to the corner," I said.

We walked past the fountain toward the auto traffic in the street. Jimmy turned to me and paused. I wanted to embrace him and I got the feeling he did too, but it seemed inappropriate and he extended his hand. As I shook it, he said, "You're a real pal, Doc."

"I hope to be, Jimmy." He must have felt as awkward as I did, not wanting the handshake to end, but we smiled at each other and let our hands part, and then he turned and crossed the street.

NINE

Jimmy was reading a newspaper on the front steps of the boarding house when I drove up on Sunday afternoon. He looked sharp in his suit and tie, sitting there in the sunshine. As I walked toward him, I could see he'd gotten a haircut.

When he saw me, he quickly folded the newspaper and leapt up. His energetic, carefree manner had returned. A warm smile lit up his face as he approached and shook my hand.

"Hi, Carl. Swell day, huh?"

"It certainly is."

"Come on in and see the place." He led the way up to the front door. "Don't mind Mrs. Burroughs, my landlady. She's a little crazy. But so are the other inmates." He paused and laughed. "Me included." He glanced at me and then looked away.

Jimmy ushered me into the entry hall. There was a steamy smell of food and old wood. We passed the polished banister of a wide staircase, and I followed him through an archway into a large living room. He walked over to an upright piano against one wall and without sitting down at the keyboard rippled off a few phrases of a ragtime tune. An old man sitting in an armchair across the room lowered a newspaper revealing a face adorned with an extraordinarily long, white mustache that nearly hid his mouth. "Hey Jimmy, play Anna Marie," he called out.

"Mr. Dalrymple, you know I'm not familiar with that one. Besides I can't play right now, I'm on my way out." Jimmy sat down at the piano and said, "I want to show you something." He reached under the keyboard and engaged a mechanism then began pumping a foot pedal. All by itself the piano played a lively ragtime tune. "It's a player," he said with a smile. "But listen. It's a piano roll made by Scott Joplin."

I stood listening closely and after a bit Jimmy stopped and rewound the piano roll. "Isn't that something? Imagine, from his hands to this piano. A bit old-fashioned, to be sure, but he sure knew how to compose. I've got some Jelly Roll Morton piano rolls too. He's terrific. I'll have to play them for you someday when we have more time. Sorry to disturb you, Mr. Dalrymple."

Jimmy led me back to the entry hall. Pointing through a double doorway to a long dining table, he said, "Mrs. Burroughs serves our dinners in there."

As we went up the carpeted stairway, we were greeted from above by a stout little woman with an untidy mass of graying hair knotted on top of her head. She came down toward us carrying a feather duster in one hand and a broom and dustpan in the other. We met on the landing, and Jimmy introduced me to Mrs. Burroughs.

"Oh, Jimmy, poor Mr. Crugnale isn't well again. He's going to spend a few days with his sister. So you won't have to worry about disturbing him till he gets back." She leaned in toward me and in a lowered voice said, "Dr. Holman, be glad Mr. Crugnale isn't one of your patients. I think he's a hypochondriac, do you know. Pleased to meet you, Doctor." She passed on down the stairs. Jimmy showed me up to his room, which was halfway down a dim hallway with dark wainscoting and a worn carpet.

The door opened into a large room flooded with sunlight. A three-windowed bay overlooked a small side yard.

"This is my humble abode," Jimmy said. "Let me take your hat." He closed the door and hung my hat on a hook.

"What a swell room," I said.

Either Jimmy was excessively neat or he had spent considerable time cleaning up before I arrived. The bed was neatly made and next to it, on top of the chest of drawers, a comb and brush lay squarely placed on a clean white dresser scarf. A bouquet of flowers sat on a writing table near the windows. Had he gone to special effort just for me? In one corner of the room stood an upright piano, its lid closed over the keyboard, and a bookcase against one wall held music books and sheet music all carefully arranged. A wooden Victrola cabinet stood nearby, tidily closed up.

"Have a seat," Jimmy indicated the single overstuffed armchair. "I have something for you." I sat down while Jimmy went to the closet and began rummaging around. I wondered if he felt as awkward as I did. I cast about for some bit of conversation to put us more at ease.

"Is this your piano?" I asked, glancing around. On a small table next to the armchair lay a book titled *Music and Spirituality*.

"Yes," he called in reply. "My father gave it to me when I graduated from college. The movers had a devil of a time getting it up here."

He emerged from the closet with a large flat paper bag.

"I thought you would appreciate this," he said handing it to me and pulling over the straight-backed chair from the writing table.

"This is for me?" I said as Jimmy sat down. I opened the bag and pulled out a marbled cardboard folder. Opening it, I was dazzled by the bright opalescent colors of an art print of three young men in a rowboat surrounded by swimmers in the glittering, clear waters of a rocky shore. Several of the figures were nude and the painter had expertly depicted the sunlight flashing golden off their bodies with vivid greens and blues reflecting up from the water. One boy standing in the boat was shirtless and wore white pants, while another, seated at the oars, wore a brilliant red shirt. At the bottom of the print was inscribed: "Henry Scott Tuke—Ruby, Gold and Malachite—1901."

"Why, Jimmy, this is beautiful." I looked at him and smiled. "What a lovely gift."

His grey eyes gleamed. "I just happened to run across it at a bookshop that had a bin of prints for sale. After you showed me that Thomas Eakins picture, I knew this one had your name on it."

"Thank you, Jimmy. Thanks a lot." I studied the print for a moment and held it up at arm's length in the light from the window.

"Such striking colors. Why, next to this, Eakins' palette looks like mud. This picture fairly sparkles."

I was truly touched. That Jimmy had been thinking about me at all meant a lot. But still, I wondered what it signified from Jimmy's point of view. Was it just a casual gift that he ran across accidentally, or could it be an overture?

I looked up from the bathers to Jimmy's face and he smiled back at me with a disarming openness that was hard for me to decipher. I was afraid to read too much into it.

"I'll have to get it framed," I said.

Just then the marbled folder and the paper bag began to slip from my lap and, as I reached to grab them with one hand, I lost my hold on the picture. All of the paper fluttered to the floor. Jimmy and I both bent down to gather up the pieces, and our hands brushed in the retrieval.

"I guess I'd better put this away before it gets bent," I said and put the picture back in the folder and fumbled putting the folder back in the paper bag. There was an awkward silence.

"How's the band doing?" I asked.

"Oh, boy, things are sure heating up. We start playing at a speakeasy this next Wednesday and that goes through Friday. This is the first time we've played anywhere more than one night. The band is real excited about it. This could lead to a lot more work. Then Diggs thinks he's lined up another country club dance for Saturday. And we're getting more pay from that club than we ever made for a single night. Besides all that, I think we're getting to be pretty darn good. We're learning a bunch of new pieces. Say, you want to hear something? We just got some new recordings."

"Sure."

Jimmy jumped up and went to the Victrola cabinet where he began excitedly sorting through record albums. "Howard got these new race records from a Negro musician he just met. Some fellow up from Los Angeles. This sound is something."

We listened to the recording, while Jimmy went to the piano and followed along on a sheet of music paper that he occasionally notated in pencil as the tune played. When the music came to an end, he said, "I've been writing this one out so we can work it up with the band."

He put another record on and cranked the machine. "This is Mamie Smith and her Jazz Hounds. It's that song I was singing when those thugs at the Grange stopped me."

We listened to her band play while Mamie warbled. Recalling Jimmy's distinctive singing voice, I had to admit I preferred his version to this one. When the record ended, I said as much.

"Yes, ain't she a bit sweet," Jimmy said. "I like her band better than her voice. But she's got pep. Let me play you another. This is a New Orleans band led by King Oliver."

We listened to a few of King Oliver's recordings and I was no longer in Portland, Oregon. I had been transported to exotic Southern ports, where tawdry honky-tonks teemed with a raw, jungle sound that dragged a whole history along behind it. The music writhed and pulsated like a heart on an operating table, refusing to stop beating, pounding with joy and rambunctious freedom.

This wild music contrasted sharply with the staid boarding house. The neatness of Jimmy's room seemed a thin eggshell, mutely encompassing a whole world of sounds that I imagined lived unheard in his mind until he could turn on the Victrola or sit down at the piano. The silent music books, so fastidiously arranged, the tidy stacks of sheet music, the albums full of black lacquer records, all sat unassumingly on their shelves, noiselessly encoding great torrents of emotional sound yearning to be unleashed into vibrating air. Jimmy's was a world waiting to unfold.

After the last record came to an end, Jimmy turned off the Victrola. He stood at the machine with his back to me for a moment. There was a silence as if he was hesitating to say something.

"Carl..." he said finally, without moving, "let's not go to the movies." Then he turned and walked over and sat in the chair next to me. He leaned forward with his elbows on his knees and looked down at his hands as he fidgeted with them. He pushed aside something in his mind and looked up at me and said, "I want to play

Halma with you."

The air crackled. A faint smile crept across his lips and there was a question in his eyes. Then he leaned forward and kissed me softly on my mouth. I smelled a familiar barbershop shaving lotion that reminded me of new rain. As he sat back, I reached out and placed my hand on his and smiled. "There's nothing I'd like better," I said.

There was a moment in which we looked at each other and almost imperceptibly inclined forward, anticipating the fulfillment of a more passionate kiss.

A loud knock at the door broke the spell and Jimmy lurched to his feet.

"Jimmy, it's me, Mrs. Burroughs."

He went quickly to the door and paused with his hand on the door knob as he took a deep breath. I picked up the art print package and stood up from the armchair. Jimmy opened the door wide, as if to show the landlady that he had nothing to hide. "Yes, Mrs. Burroughs?"

"I just wanted to know if I should set an extra place at the supper table for your guest. We'd be pleased to have you, Dr. Holman."

"Oh, thank you, Mrs. Burroughs," Jimmy said, "but we're just headed out to the pictures. I'll catch dinner out."

"All right, Jimmy. Nice to meet you, Doctor."

"Pleased to meet you, Mrs. Burroughs," I said with a nod.

Jimmy closed the door as she moved off down the hall. He turned to look at me and we both laughed.

Still holding the art print in one hand, I walked toward him and he took a step forward. I placed my free hand on the side of his smooth neck and smiled into his eyes for a moment before our lips met again as if tasting the first course of a feast. The softness.

After lingering there for a pleasant eternity, we broke away.

"Let's drive over to my place," I said.

Jimmy smiled and without saying a word, he turned, handed me my hat, and ushered me into the hallway.

The hand that had been resting on his neck as we kissed now longed to touch more of his skin.

Our skin is a peculiar organ, the largest of the body. The illustrations in the medical books show it up close at the cellular level. In cross-section you can see the layers of cells making up the epidermis, the outermost portion of the skin.

Just above a basement membrane of fibrous material, lies the *stratum germinativum*, where the basal cells reside—the only living cells of the epidermis. These generative cells at the bottom layer continue to divide, regenerating themselves to create daughter cells that build up from this base. As these cells are pushed upward toward the surface, they flatten out and develop into fish-scale-like squamous cells, becoming tough and durable. Slowly these cells mature, creating a protective barrier, a boundary between the body's inside and its outside, between the self and the non-self. The boundary between my hand and Jimmy Harper's neck.

Below this epidermal layer that covers the entire outside of the body lie the living cells of the flesh and blood that we call our own. Here, in the subcutaneous tissue reside the blood capillaries and the scattered neurons that send out nerve fibrils up near the epidermis like frontier scouts. These tactile receptors, most numerous on the fingertips and the palms, in the tip of the tongue and the lips, the nipples and the most sensitive parts of the genitalia, all connect back to the brain and give us the myriad sensations of touch. And what entity, I always wondered, perceives these impressions of an outside world that we seem to be separate from?

Meanwhile, the skin cells themselves, at the outermost surface, are dead. Like the outer bark of a tree, these cells have ceased to be a living part of the body, and in time they become part of the rest of the universe, as they flake off into dust motes floating in sunbeams, finally collecting on floors in the corners of our rooms.

And so this outer layer of dead cells gives to the dry human epidermis its velvet quality. Like the mounded buckskin of grass-covered hills. Like the feel of kid gloves brushing against each other.

Like the vibration of a rosined horse-hair bow passing over the catgut strings of a cello. Like nothing so much in this whole world as itself alone, the skin.

It was Jimmy's skin I couldn't help imagining as we drove to my house. Once there, we did get out the Halma set. I purposely left the curtains closed this time. Jimmy set up the playing pieces on the living room floor while I poured gin cocktails for us. But it was just a pretext. Before long we began kissing and touching each other and then slowly unfastening clothes and helping each other out of them, there on the living room carpet. At last I suggested we might be more comfortable in the bedroom.

And so, there was, then, the falling into bed, falling into each other's arms, into each other's skin.

Jimmy and I shared the pleasure of those sensations, touching that velvety sheath of epidermis. We delighted in the way the pliable, soft skin rides over the bony areas and adheres to the muscled parts of the body, in the sensations of warmth from the flesh attached by sinews and ligaments to the sturdy armature of skeleton. Jimmy's hands were no less curious than mine, journeying over the folds and ridges of the contoured skin, a deltoid, a pectoralis, a vastus lateralis. But he shyly avoided my glance, maybe out of embarrassment, because the intimacy of the eye seems even greater than that of the hand.

Soon we were tangled up in each other's skin, comforting in all its lovely softness, as if the boundary had dissolved. We were drawn to stimulate those parts where the nerve cells are most numerous. And then saliva dampened a surface here, an area there, and beads of sweat began to form, and blood began to pound faster through our veins, filling the secret caverns of the erectile tissue.

There was no penetration of orifices that first time. We each used a hand to stroke the other's organ until we became excited. Jimmy was over-anxious and twice I tried to hold him back. But it was already too late. Jimmy gave a little moan, and I could feel a quiet rumbling deep beneath the surface, like the heated water of a geyser, gurgling up from the depths, and then spewing forth. I let myself go and came off with him.

After the excitement subsided, Jimmy clung to me tightly for a long time.

Later I got a towel to dry us off, and then we lay quietly in each other's arms, occasionally moving a hand to stroke or caress. I turned on my side and smoothed back the locks of hair that had fallen down into Jimmy's face, and I looked into his eyes as he stared at a corner of the ceiling. In the dim light of the bedroom his pupils were dilated. A breeze through the window screen shifted the bedroom curtain and a burst of sunshine lit up the room. As his pupils contracted against the light, Jimmy's irises expanded and I could see in them the striations of varying shades of slate and pale grey, like the polished cross-section of some semiprecious stone.

Was there some worry in his look? Or was that something in my mind that I was projecting outward? Had this act of touching broken down a boundary and brought us closer together? Or would some societal hold on Jimmy's mind give rise to guilt and shame that he would use to deny the pleasure of these moments, that he would use as a barrier to provide an excuse to say it was all a mistake? There was no way to know what he was thinking. He probably didn't know. But these doubts were more than I could abide.

"How are you feeling?" I asked.

"Boy, I don't know." He glanced at me and looked away. "It's like hearing a new kind of music." He paused a moment. "I guess now I know how these flapper girls feel when they throw away their corsets." We laughed. The breeze stirred the curtains again and somewhere in the distance a bird twittered.

"Tell me this, Jimmy. When you suggested skinny dipping—when we were fishing—did you ever think we would end up in bed together?"

"Hmm." Jimmy thought for a time. "I don't know. I didn't think about it. Not…not in the melody, anyway. You know how I mean?

Maybe it was back with the cellos and basses somewhere. Maybe I wanted something that I didn't know I wanted."

"A secret drawer?" I said.

Jimmy glanced at me with a smile of recognition. "I guess so." He paused. "I remembered something else after we talked in the park." He seemed to compose his thoughts for a moment.

"What's that?"

"I remembered, when I was about 14, I did something with my cousin Phil, who was a couple years older than me. Remember how I said I used to go down to their ranch and help out with the cattle? One spring we were rounding up a bunch of two-year-old bulls and herded them into a corral. They were all crowded together as they went through the gate and some of them would jump up and mount another one. You could see their cocks sticking out and everything. I asked Phil what they were doing and he said they were practicing. Later up in the hay loft, just the two of us, Phil started talking about girls. Then he pulled out a tin of Vaseline and he suggested we try practicing like the bulls. He said it's just pretend sex. We didn't cornhole each other—he said you shouldn't do that, you shouldn't go inside, you know, or it would turn you into a woman. So we took turns rubbing our cocks between each other's thighs. I liked it, but I thought it was just kids' stuff—you know, like practice for being with girls later on. He wouldn't let me kiss him or anything like that. I asked him another time, later on, if he wanted to do it again and he made fun of me. He called me a sissy. Heck, it was his idea in the first place. That confused me and hurt my feelings. So I guess I kind of buried it. But, maybe…maybe I felt some attraction for him— back then. Even though I didn't know it." Jimmy looked at me. "I guess I'm attracted to you now."

I put my arms around him and rolled him back and forth. "Well, honey-boy, I'm attracted to you. I was from the first time I saw you playing the piano. And there ain't nothing sissy about you." We lay quietly for a time. "Did the other kids call you sissy when you were growing up?" I asked. "You've never struck me that way."

"Yeah, I got teased a lot because I played the piano. But my older brothers were both good at baseball and they were popular at school. So some of that reflected on me, I guess. When I was little, my brothers and I used to play baseball out by the orchard, and they taught me to bat. We had a Louisville Slugger that my dad gave us for Christmas one year and I got pretty good at hitting the ball. I wasn't great at pitching or catching, but I seemed to have a knack for hitting a baseball, so I got by in school." He looked over at me. "Did you get called a sissy when you were a kid?"

"Sure did. I was always a real bookworm as a youngster, and I was never interested in sports. Also being the son of the town doctor, I guess the other kids thought I was different."

"Tell me this," he said. "When you asked me to go fishing, did you think we would end up in bed together?"

"I was sure hoping. I thought it would be a manly way to get acquainted with you—without scaring you off. But I was angling for you, not for fish."

Later on when the daylight faded, we got up and I cooked us omelets. We ate in the breakfast nook wearing only our underwear. Then we actually did play a game of Halma before we went back to bed.

Jimmy spent the night with me and I dropped him at his boarding house early Monday morning on my way to work. I was careful to get us going early enough so we'd be gone before Joe Locke arrived.

After Jimmy reluctantly got out of the car and closed the door, he lingered, his hands on the edge of the open car window. I didn't want to leave him, but I had to get to work.

"There is a song that Mamie Smith sings," Jimmy said, and then leaning in closer he sang quietly to me through the window.

"Remember what the singin' rooster asked the hen,

'When you comin' round to harmonize again?'"

He looked at me with a question in his smile.

"Didn't you say you weren't working on Mondays and Tuesdays?" I asked.

"That's right," he said.

"Why don't I swing by and pick you up after work this evening?"

"Okay. It's a date."

We smiled at each other for a few moments—too long. If I look at him another moment, I thought, I'm going to have to get out and kiss him right here on the street. With immense effort, I turned my eyes forward to the windshield. "I hate to leave, buddy boy," I glanced back at him, "but I've got to get to work."

"Yeah, I know," Jimmy said, and he slowly backed away from the car. "Bye." He gave a little wave as I pulled away.

Leaving Jimmy standing there on the sidewalk made me ache in the center of my body. I wanted to turn back and take him in my arms. All the same, I drove off to work a bit distracted and with a smile spread across my face.

TEN

The clock-like arrow set in the marble wall above the elevator seemed to be stuck on the brass numeral 4. I took out my watch. 6:23. The lobby was empty as usual for that time of morning. I normally tried to get to the clinic before 7, but today I was especially early, wanting to get Jimmy out of my place and back to his boarding house before we might run into anyone. He had looked so handsome that morning when I brought him a cup of coffee and he pulled himself out of the bed, his eyes bleary with sleep and his hair falling across his forehead.

I slipped the timepiece back into my vest pocket and tried to focus my attention on going back to work after this momentous weekend. My gaze fell on the business directory in the glass case between the two elevators. There we were under "Fifth Floor." Suite 503. The Gowan Clinic: Robert Gowan, M. D.; Harold Bleeker, M. D.; Carl Holman, M. D.

The first time I entered this lobby was in late 1920. I had just returned from Europe, and my father suggested I look up Gowan with whom he'd studied medicine. At that time, the practice of the Gowan Clinic had grown to a point where they wanted another doctor to share the client load and cover when one of them was away. After we met, Gowan and Bleeker calculated that having a young surgeon fresh from working in an American base hospital during the War would provide them with a number of advantages. First, my status as a veteran would capitalize on American patriotism. Second, my experience with the newest surgical techniques that the big Eastern teaching hospitals had brought to the war effort would reflect well on their Portland clinic. For my part, hanging out my shingle with Gowan and Bleeker would make it much easier for me to get established than trying to start out in Portland on my own. So the timing of my contact with the clinic was good for all of us.

The longer I worked with Gowan, however, and observed his practice, the more I came to believe that his concern for lining his pockets outweighed his dedication to scientific medicine. During the time I'd been there, a number of tensions had arisen between us.

Before the War, a push to reform the American medical establishment had already begun. Abraham Flexner's 1910 report for the Carnegie Foundation had brought to light the uneven conditions of our medical education. At that time, the American College of Surgeons was trying to raise the level of medical instruction and hospital care. Standardization was key in their efforts to improve surgical methods. I had joined the College of Surgeons as part of my medical training. Later, my overseas experience with a number of influential surgeons in the College had introduced me to their program of reforms. My joining up with Gowan and Bleeker may have given them added prestige, but my insistence on surgical techniques that were new and unusual was a source of friction. Another sharp difference between us grew up around my resolute support for precise written records of our patients' histories so we could know which treatments worked and which didn't. My associates insisted that the traditional practice of keeping such information in the doctor's head was adequate.

As if all that weren't enough, I had been doing inspections for the College at local hospitals, starting with St. Mary's Catholic Hospital in Portland. The connection between the two institutions was no accident. The Catholic Hospital Association was founded before the War to advance the reputation of its hospitals across the country. They began working closely with the College of Surgeons so that Catholic hospitals would be recognized as leaders in promoting the most modern techniques. The inspections by the College were voluntary but they gave credibility to hospitals that chose to open themselves to its scrutiny.

The influence of these inspections put pressure on the many small proprietary hospitals like Dr. Adrian's. The guidelines for hospital organization, along with the qualifications and policies for medical staff that the inspections urged, ruffled the feathers of long-established local doctors like Gowan and Adrian. Bleeker, perhaps because he had practiced for a time in the East, seemed more open to going along with the recommendations of the College.

Another reform prohibited surgeons from dividing fees with referring physicians and discouraged unnecessary surgeries. I began to suspect Gowan of taking part in both practices. Of course, everything depended on the judgment and knowledge of the surgeon as to whether operations and treatments were necessary, which was exactly why I felt a commitment to careful medical documentation. It was necessary to judge the effectiveness of treatment based on therapeutic rather than financial results. I had seen disturbing signs that Gowan and Adrian were splitting fees, and that Gowan was carrying out needless but lucrative operations. Maybe Gowan didn't believe he was doing anything underhanded. We all have our own forms of willful blindness.

Finally, the elevator arrow swung round to 1 and the polished brass door slid open. "Goin' up," the Negro operator announced.

"Good morning, Moses," I said, stepping inside.

"Fifth floor, Dr. Holman?" I nodded and fumbled in my pocket for a coin to tip him, a ritual I practiced whenever I found myself alone in the elevator with him.

"Coming right up, Dr. Holman."

Just before the lift began to rise, I held out the coin to Moses, who was busy managing the controls. I felt the weight of my body against the upward motion of the elevator compartment. Gravity and acceleration. The coin slipped from my fingers and spiraled to a rest on the tiled floor.

There was a moment during which I thought I should pick it up and hand it to him, but before I could decide if that was appropriate, Moses bent down and retrieved the coin.

"Thank you, sir," he said, slipping it in his pocket.

"Sorry, Moses. Gravity sort of threw me off there."

"That's okay, Dr. Holman. What goes up must come down." He smiled and nodded to me and turned back to the controls.

Professor Einstein's elevator thought experiment came to mind, and I remembered Jimmy talking about music changing the shape of a room. What was Jimmy doing right now? Sitting in his sunny bay window? Shaving in the bathroom down the hall? Or had he removed his clothes and gone back to bed? I had the sudden urge to forget about medicine for the day and go back to Jimmy's. The elevator doors opened.

I thanked Moses and proceeded down the hall to the clinic.

The door was locked and I let myself in. Vivian, our receptionist didn't get in till 7, and the waiting area was dim except for a light over the transom in Gowan's office. He was often there before I arrived each day. I went directly to my office. As I hung up my hat and removed my suit coat, the mound of mail Vivian had left on my desk on Friday afternoon caught my eye. It would be a busy Monday. I reached for my white lab coat and thought of Joe Locke. I must remember to telephone him, I thought, and let him know Jimmy is coming for dinner tonight. I slipped into the coat, then began sorting through the envelopes. On top was more paperwork from the American College of Surgeons, something from the Catholic Hospital Association, a letter from the director of St. Mary's, and the latest *Journal of the American Medical Association*, just for starters. One envelope caught my eye because of its unfamiliar return address. Something from Dr. Adrian. Surely he wouldn't be writing to me. I glanced at the address and saw that it was intended for Gowan. Must have gotten sorted into the wrong stack of mail. I switched on the desk lamp and held the envelope up to the light. It looked like a letter and a check. Could it be a kickback to Gowan for referring a patient to Adrian's hospital for surgery? I set it aside to return to Vivian and sorted through the rest.

Around 7:30, I went out to the reception area. Vivian looked up from her typewriter and greeted me. She handed me a typewritten list of my appointments for the day. "I left the patient records in your examining room. Mrs. Plumley telephoned to say she won't be in till 9:30. She's your first appointment. And Dr. Gowan said he'd like to have a word with you as soon as you are free."

Was it going to be another wrangle over documenting medical procedures? I casually laid the envelope from Dr. Adrian on her desk and said, "I received this one by mistake." Judging from her taciturn response, I doubted that she attached any significance to it. Or was it just a professional habit she had carefully acquired from long practice? I thanked her and headed for Gowan's office.

"Yes," he called in response to my knock. I entered and he looked up from the papers on his desk. "Carl, my boy. Good morning. Have a seat." He set his reading aside and leaned back in his chair. "I've been wanting to have a private conversation with you. How are things going?"

"No major problems—that I know of."

"Have you given any more thought to the property at Greenwood Estates?"

"Golly, you know I've been so busy with work lately, I haven't had much of a chance to look into it."

"Keep it in mind. If you're free on Saturday, I'd be happy to show you around out there."

"I'll have to consult my calendar. Let me get back to you."

He sat forward in his chair and laid his forearms on his desk. "I'll get right to the point." He adjusted his eyeglasses. "But first let me say that I expect you will keep this in the strictest confidence."

I nodded.

"Carl, I want to privately extend to you a special opportunity." He paused for effect. "I expect you've heard about the growth of the Ku Klux Klan in our area."

I nodded and said nothing. This was unexpected.

"We'd like you to become a member of this fine organization."

His words did not sink in at first. He might have been asking if I wanted to change barbershops. But when I could make sense of it, my reaction was one of horror. I tried to keep my face from registering anything.

There had been rumors around the clinic that Gowan belonged to the Klan. He himself had dropped subtle hints that Bleeker and I should find out more about the Klan. So I shouldn't have been surprised. But this was the first time he had broached the subject with me directly so now I had to deal with the reality of it.

"Dr. Gowan, about all I know regarding the Ku Klux Klan comes from that movie *Birth of a Nation*." Like most everyone in the country, I had seen D. W. Griffith's motion picture several years back. I figured this would be a safe response.

Of course, I had heard of the Klan's reputation for lynching Negroes in the South, but since the population of colored people in Oregon was so small, there was no perceived threat to racial dominance. So it was just as Tom Harris had told me—deprived of the race issue, it appeared that the Klan was fanning the anti-Catholic sentiments in our overwhelmingly Protestant state in order to gain political advantage.

"I'm glad you mentioned this," Gowan said with a smile. "That was the old Klan. This is a whole new ballgame. You know, the name Ku Klux comes from the old Greek word for circle. And that's what the leaders of the new organization want to emphasize. We're a circle of like-minded men who are concerned about our community. Just like the Knights of the Round Table. The new Klan is a benevolent civic-oriented society, no different from the Masons."

"I see. But why should I choose the Klan rather than the Masons? Or, say, the Moose Lodge? My father belongs to the Moose."

"It hasn't escaped my attention that you don't belong to any of those fraternities. As far as I know you don't even belong to a church. Joining the Klan would be good for your standing in the community. And it would be good for our clinic."

"I've always felt that if I joined any one fraternal order, it would show some favoritism and limit my clientele. Isn't there some advantage to taking a neutral stance?"

"What you need to understand, Carl, is that by not joining up with anyone, you position yourself as an outsider. Businessmen notice this sort of thing. You stand out like a sore thumb. Just like all these foreign immigrants with their unwholesome ways and peculiar old-world ideas."

There wasn't much I could say to defend myself. I was not a joiner. I could have pointed out that I was already extraordinarily busy working with the College of Surgeons and their hospital inspections, but since that was already a sore point, I knew better than to bring that up. I tried to redirect the conversation instead. "Tell me a little more about this new Klan and their community activities."

"This is a great story, Carl. One of the most important reasons you should join the Klan now. It wasn't until the spring of '21 that the first Kleagles—our Klan organizers—came up from California and started the first Klavern in Medford. By August that year we had over a thousand members here in Portland. Our chapter leader has been so successful, the headquarters of the KKK in Georgia appointed him Grand Dragon—head of the state organization."

Tom Harris had mentioned the recruiting and organizing efforts by an ambitious local businessman, so this must be him.

"Since then," Gowan went on, "the Empire has been growing all around Oregon. We now have over a hundred Klaverns in towns all across the state. You would be getting in on the ground floor, so to speak."

"The Empire?" I asked, though I knew exactly what he meant.

Gowan laughed. "Yes, we like to call ourselves the Invisible Empire. It's just a figure of speech."

I reflected that Gowan was once again using his convenient

blindness to buy into the Klan's bogus propaganda creating a parallel between the Knights of the Round Table and the Knights of the Invisible Empire. Aside from maybe a reverence for white women and God, ironically just like the Roman Church, I didn't believe that the same high-minded chivalry prevailed in the Klan.

"But that brings up another important point. You talk about maintaining a neutral stance. Part of the beauty of the Klan is that it's a secret society. That's why we say invisible. No one outside the organization will know you belong. But those inside will know and treat you like a brother."

Why was all this secrecy necessary, I wondered. But it wasn't a question I could ask Gowan. Instead I asked, "But how is the Klan different from these other clubs?"

"The distinction is that besides doing charitable works, we're intent on cleaning up the vice that's rampant in our society and we promote vigorous, upright communities of people born here in America. 100% Americanism."

Where, then, did the Indians that I'd known growing up in eastern Oregon fit into Gowan's 100% Americanism scheme? They had been here before the white man arrived to create all these artificial boundaries of states and property lines.

"And we want to see that our children are educated in 100% American schools."

There it was, the Compulsory Education Act. Probably the most troubling aspect of my associating with the Catholic hospitals. It seemed Gwen's remarks about the fears of the nuns at St. Mary's were well-founded. It was common knowledge that the Klan was one of the strongest backers of the Compulsory Education initiative. While ensuring that every child went to school sounded noble and good on the surface, what the legislation masked was the attempt to outlaw Catholic schools outright and make certain that all children got an American education—at American public schools. My connection with St. Mary's and the College of Surgeons was becoming more of a worry by the moment.

"Why, even before we entered the War," Gowan continued,

"President Wilson was speaking out against the influence of hyphenated Americans, like all these Greek-Americans and Italian-Americans."

"What about these Night Riders I've heard about?" I asked. When I told Tom Harris about the paddling incident I had witnessed returning from Bisby Grange, he'd described these Klan vigilante groups that were harassing neighbors they thought were getting out of line.

Gowan looked surprised. "Night Riders," he said. "None of that is true. It's all propaganda spread by the Catholics to discredit our noble brotherhood."

"I'm still not convinced this is an organization I would fit in with."

"With all due respect to secrecy, I must tell you that Bleeker has just been naturalized." He looked at me directly.

I had heard this term used in reference to initiation into the Klan, but now it struck too close to home. I had believed Bleeker to be a thoughtful man who could not be cowed into conformity. I couldn't keep my surprise from registering. "You don't say." I felt it was necessary to say something and give myself time to regain my composure.

"Since we all work so closely, here, I felt you should know." Gowan paused and waited.

I glanced away, trying to think of an appropriate response, and my gaze came to rest on the family portrait on the corner of his desk.

"You would be making a big mistake not to join, Carl." He paused again. "Think it over," he insisted. "There are a number of other doctors—and lawyers—in the Klan. Besides policemen and firefighters, even city officials. Pillars of the community." He looked me in the eye. "Being a member would be a definite advantage to your career."

I felt I had to appease him somehow. I looked straight back at him and said, "I promise you I'll give it serious consideration."

"Do that, Carl." He couldn't have been more pointed.

"Was there anything else, Dr. Gowan?"

When I got back to my office, I sat at my desk for a long time. Even though I'd suspected that Gowan belonged to the Klan, having it out in the open now, straight from his mouth, seemed to change everything. Did he seriously think that I would join? Was it a test to see if I would continue to qualify to work with him and Bleeker? Was I willing to continue working with them?

The sorted stacks of mail on my desk reminded me of the letter from Adrian that I'd returned to Vivian. Was I seeing more evidence of a network of men in influential positions directing business away from St. Mary's? And Gowan had mentioned policemen and lawyers, "pillars of the community." I remembered the conversation that Charlie had overheard between Adrian and the police commissioner. What other kinds of manipulation might be at work behind the scenes?

I was relieved that I had kept our conversation away from my relationship with St. Mary's. I suspected Gowan would soon be asking me to sever my connection with them. Undoubtedly, that's what was behind his reference to Italian-Americans. Roman Catholicism. And now, because of the poverty and swarthy complexions of Sicilian and Greek immigrants, these were the most odious of the new inhabitants of America. I couldn't help thinking that the Greeks and the Romans had created the civilizations from which we had inherited much of our American culture.

The Greco-Roman statuary in the fountain at Pioneer Park came to mind. What would Gowan think if he knew about Jimmy and me? An uneasiness settled into the pit of my stomach. I didn't feel safe now. I wanted to warn Jimmy about this conversation with Gowan. I imagined Jimmy sitting down to a meal across from me at my dining table at home. I picked up the telephone and called Joe Locke to let him know that I would be bringing a guest home to dinner.

ELEVEN

Throughout the rest of the day, between patient exams and other odd moments, the image of Jimmy sitting across from me at dinner kept passing through my mind. Then I imagined us moving into the living room for conversation and, at last, the bedroom. A warm sensation spread through me.

When I finally finished up at the clinic, I walked anxiously to my car and headed toward Jimmy's boarding house. My route took me past Pioneer Park and I remembered those fleeting encounters, the heat in the blood, the hope and the disappointment. Nick with his wife and kids. All at once a nervous doubt arose. Was I just some passing fancy that Jimmy was trying on for size, a fling before he would return to Mary or someone else of the opposite sex? The prospect was too disturbing to entertain and I put the thought out of my mind.

When Jimmy's smiling face greeted me at the boarding house, I was reassured that my vague fear was only a fantasy I had allowed to torture me for a moment, perhaps a result of my unsettling encounter with Gowan.

At my house, Joe Locke had a beautifully prepared meal waiting for us. Jimmy seemed surprised and apprehensive to find another man at my house. I had mentioned numerous times that I had a Chinese housekeeper, but Jimmy had never met him, and I suspect the reality of it didn't sink in until he was confronted with it. Like my own reaction to Gowan's connection with the Klan, earlier that day.

Joe served our plates, then filled our wineglasses and withdrew. Jimmy seemed to relax once Joe was out of the room. But later as Joe served the next course, he must have observed Joe's formal reserve, clearly demonstrating that Joe was just a house servant. Jimmy's uneasiness seemed to evaporate.

A couple of times during dinner, our conversation lapsed and Jimmy's attention drifted off, as he stared into space.

"Is something wrong?" I said at last.

His attention returned to the present. "No, it's nothing." He seemed to wave something away, and after a moment he took up the conversation as if to draw attention away from his distracted state. "That crazy Larry—our banjo player—met this girl the other night and he told us she was seeing a psychoanalyst. He said that, since Freud was all about sex and being free of repression and all, he figured he wouldn't have any trouble…uh…getting her into bed. So he made a dinner date with her. You'll never guess what happened. Turns out she showed up at the restaurant with her father. And all through the meal her dad was giving Larry the third degree to see if Larry was a suitable fellow to be dating his daughter." Jimmy laughed. "Larry couldn't eat his dinner fast enough and get out of there."

I laughed along with him. His charm was infectious.

I remembered thinking earlier about Jimmy sitting across from me at my dining table. The reality was different from what I had imagined. It was better. I watched him as he looked down at his plate and returned to his meal. It was not just the shape of his features. There was something in his very nature that struck me as special. Before I could think of something to say, Jimmy spoke again.

"Tell me what happened at your clinic today. You always seem to have interesting cases to talk about." He seemed to be making an effort to keep his mind from straying off.

"Interesting is an understatement." I cleared my throat. "Not exactly a medical case, but something I wanted to discuss with you."

I paused. "This morning, Dr Gowan, the head of the clinic, asked me to join the Ku Klux Klan."

"You're kiddin' me. And he's your boss?" He was now fully present.

"In a manner of speaking."

Jimmy gave a whistle of exclamation.

"Yeah, it's disturbing," I said. "Until now it all seemed somewhat distant. Out in the country at Bisby, you know?"

"Those clowns at Bisby," he said. A cloud passed over his face, and I remembered the incident with the billy-club boys. "That was something else. One of the worst experiences of my whole music career." Jimmy shook his head, then looked up at me. "I appreciate you being so nice to me that night."

I looked at him and smiled. The moment seemed too intimate for him and he looked away. Then he spoke. "And that scene you told me about when you were driving home afterwards."

"Yes. That's something I never expected to see. Not around here anyway. And today Dr. Gowan tells me that there are pillars of the community in the Klan. Now it makes me wonder what might be going on in some of the political offices around the state."

Jimmy gave me a puzzled look.

"You remember that Compulsory Education bill? I understand that the Klan was one of its biggest supporters."

"I don't follow politics too closely," he said.

"I can't blame you for that. I don't much either, but the neighbor across the street works for one of the papers and tries to keep me informed." After a pause I added, "I worry about what this could mean for my work." I looked at Jimmy and wondered if he was piecing these implications together in his mind. "And I don't mean to scare you, but I think you and I need to be particularly discreet."

Jimmy frowned. "The other day Howard told me that…" Again that far-off look crept over his face.

"Told you what?"

"Oh…it was nothing."

"No. I'm interested."

Jimmy paused. "He told me that he…he heard Mary's uncle was in the Klan."

Of course, that was it. Mary. He was still preoccupied by all that had happened with her, while I seemed to block the subject from my mind.

"I see." Studying his downcast face, it was apparent he wasn't up to discussing her. "I expect Howard is correct. It's probably good for her uncle's insurance business. That's the same thing Gowan tried to tell me this morning." I watched Jimmy. He was staring toward the salt and pepper set without focusing. A question formed in my mind and I felt I had to ask. "Have you talked to Mary?"

"No!" It came out with more force than I expected and even Jimmy looked startled. Then his expression went blank and he looked down at his plate. He didn't say anything more.

"I'm sorry," I said. I would have added that he probably wasn't ready to talk about it yet, but even that seemed too direct. "I shouldn't have asked."

We ate in silence for a moment.

"Where does the band play next?" I tried to sound upbeat. "You told me about a speakeasy."

He came out of his silence. "Yeah, Felix Bagwell's place downtown. Wednesday through Friday. Midnight to 3 in the morning." His tone lifted. "Can you believe it?

"Pretty late hours for me."

"And Diggs nailed down that country club dance on Saturday night." His mood was brightening.

"Which country club is that?"

"It's a new one out west of town. At Greenwood Estates. Out Wilcox Road."

"Oh, yes. I know about it. Top drawer. Gowan keeps trying to interest me in buying real estate out there. He and his wife have bought one of the homes near the golf course. Your band is certainly coming up in the world."

"Small world, huh? Say, why don't you come hear us play there?" He became downright enthusiastic. "The hours are better. It starts at

8. We've added several new numbers you ought to hear."

I imagined running into Gowan out there and hesitated, but the chance of him turning up at a jazz dance for the younger set seemed unlikely. "Swell idea," I said. "I'd like that."

"Good. You'll see how much we've improved. And you'll like these new pieces we've added." He went back to his meal. I watched him a moment.

"I wanted to ask if you'd like to come back here for dinner tomorrow night. You said you don't rehearse on Tuesdays."

Jimmy seemed to flip through a mental calendar. "Oh, heck. Diggs called an extra rehearsal for tomorrow night. He wants us in top form for that speak on Wednesday night."

I felt a pang of disappointment but let it pass. Remaining hopeful, I said, "Maybe you can come back here after the dance on Saturday night."

Jimmy smiled at me with a glint in his eye. "Sure."

I allowed myself to be reassured and smiled.

Just then Joe Locke entered to clear the dishes before dessert, and Jimmy glanced nervously away.

After dinner we retired to the living room and I played some Mozart and Bach records on my Victrola, while Jimmy smoked cigarettes and pointed out parts of the music that he particularly liked. We both sensed that we were only marking time. Before long, Joe Locke came in. He'd changed from his serving jacket to his suit coat and carried his hat and a parcel of laundry. He asked if there was anything else. I told him no and thanked him.

"Excellent meal," Jimmy said. Joe gave a little bow and after saying good night, disappeared into the kitchen. A moment later we heard the back door close. Jimmy and I looked at each other and slowly stood up.

Before long we were in the bedroom stripping off each other's clothes. The bed received the weight of our bodies as I pulled Jimmy down on top of me, kissing and touching. At first his movements were tentative, but after a bit he displayed a special interest in the back of my neck and the hair on my chest. After a time, I reached down, fondling with my hand.

"I think I've found that Louisville Slugger you told me about," I said.

He laughed.

I began nuzzling my head down his torso and was about to take his penis in my mouth when I felt his body stiffen. His hands tugged gently at my head. I looked up. He sat upright and pulled me to him and began kissing me hungrily. After a moment he paused.

"Let's try that thing that my cousin Phil and I did together," Jimmy said.

I smiled at him. "Oh, the old interfemoral rub?"

"What?" Jimmy didn't understand.

"Between the thighs. Isn't that what you did with him?"

"Oh." Jimmy laughed. "Yeah. That's it."

"I can't offer you a hay loft," I said, "but I've got some Vaseline in the bathroom."

I returned from the bathroom and there was a moment of awkwardness as Jimmy showed me how he and Phil had positioned themselves. Then Jimmy used some of the lubricant and, like Phil, approached me from behind. After he was finished, I repositioned myself and showed him how we could do it facing each other and that way we could kiss at the same time. Then I took my turn.

Later we lay close together, catching our breath.

I remembered how aggressive Gerald's sexual style had been when we were getting to know each other. He suggested a number of things that I wasn't comfortable with at first, but I was so taken with Gerald that I went along with it. Over the course of our relationship, every orifice came into play. Jimmy, by contrast, seemed restrained, even bashful.

I remembered Billy Butler at Pioneer Park saying, "I'll do the other, but none of that fairy business." Maybe Jimmy had somehow adopted a similar attitude. I wanted to ask him if that was what he was thinking. I wanted to ask if I was rushing him. But there seemed to be no right way of posing these questions. The inquiry itself implied there was somewhere to rush from and somewhere to rush toward. Besides, Jimmy didn't seem inclined to talk. So I decided not to pursue it. The last thing I wanted was to make him feel uncomfortable. Jimmy seemed to be content with our sexual interactions as they were, and I was too. I was happy just to be with him. And after some of the soldiers I'd been with during the War, I was glad that Jimmy at least liked to kiss.

As a physician, the map of the body was familiar territory to me, terrain about which I felt completely clean and open. But the map of the mind and the heart was governed by overlapping fields of influence with unmarked boundaries that were forever shifting and not easily navigated. There was a no man's land between Jimmy and me that might be mined with buried explosives that I dared not risk disturbing at this delicate juncture in our acquaintance.

I lay there quietly, holding Jimmy in my arms, and let the moment pass without words.

In the future, I expected, there would be time for us to talk.

TWELVE

Friday afternoon I was at St. Mary's when one of the surgeons asked me to help with a case. In a suicide attempt, a man had done serious vascular damage to his wrists. The attending physician felt that my experience during the War might help save his hands. I followed my colleague to the operating table. When I saw the patient I stopped. I knew that face, although it took me a moment to place it. Pioneer Park. It was Nick, the mechanic. My complicated feelings resurfaced, my attraction and my reticence, my perplexity at his admitted love for his wife and kids. Be that as it may, this was a time to be professional. It took me a moment to put all that aside, and I focused in on the work at hand.

Nick had lost a dangerous amount of blood and had required a transfusion before I arrived. After assessing the lacerations with the other physician, I felt he was considering the correct surgical approach and I only suggested minor adjustments and watched as he proceeded. It seemed that Nick would come through in pretty good shape physically. I was more concerned about his mental and emotional state. After observing the other surgeon's work, I waited for the anesthesia to wear off. I was hoping to have a private word with Nick to evaluate his psychological condition.

While I waited, one of the nurses filled me in on Nick's story. He hadn't shown up for work that day, and a fellow mechanic had gone over to his house and broken in the door. He found Nick home alone, lying in a bathtub of bloody water with a straight razor on the floor beside him. So Nick had chosen the Roman bath as his way out, I thought. The nurse said they were trying to contact his family, but no one made any mention of his wife and children. I began to speculate inwardly about Nick's circumstances.

Finally, one of the nuns informed me that Mr. Riggsdale had awakened in the recovery ward. That was the first time I heard Nick's surname. Although we had been intimate, I didn't even know his full name. I went to see him at once. It was with a curious mixture of relief and apprehension that I followed the nun to his bedside. After she checked his comfort, I asked to talk to him privately. The nun pulled a folding white screen around the bed and left me alone with Nick.

Why did I feel like a priest entering a confessional? As if it was my duty to bear witness to some kind of admission? I watched his pale face for a time. Finally, he looked over at me. I didn't know if he would recognize me. I was still wearing my surgical cap and operating gown. It felt like a professional disguise. I might as well have been the priest hidden behind the screen. His expression revealed no flicker of recognition.

I examined his bandages. Then I stood silently for a moment and finally asked how he was feeling. He looked away. "I suspect you've had a rough time of it lately," I said softly. "Can you talk about it?"

He took so long to respond that I was ready to give up and come back later, but then, without turning back to me, he asked in a thin voice, "Has she called?"

I assumed that he was referring to his wife, but I felt I had to clarify it, to keep things professional.

"Your wife?" I said. From my point of view, it was unnecessary to ask, knowing what I knew.

"Did she call?"

"The hospital is trying to contact her," I said.

There was a long silence. I reflected on our first meeting and later seeing him with that stevedore after the eugenics lecture. Was it guilt that had driven him to this violence against himself? Self-loathing? I was grateful for the things that Gerald—and our friends in Germany—had taught me, all of which had helped me guard against the susceptibility to guilt and self-hatred. But unlike Nick, I did not have a wife and family.

"They won't find her," he said at last.

I moved in closer. "Can you tell us how to reach her?"

Another silence followed. Then a sob shook him.

"She's taken the kids…and gone back East to her sister's—" he paused, unable to control his voice.

I guessed at the rest of the story. Had she found out about his infidelities and left him?

"Where can we reach her? What city…?

He didn't respond to my question. After a moment he said, "How can I go on living without my family to look after?" Then he could no longer speak for the emotion that wracked his body.

I stood at his bedside for a long time. I wanted to say something encouraging about his wife coming back, but I was not at all sure that would be the best thing for him. Our society isn't kind to those caught in the middle between loving women and loving men, the territory he seemed to inhabit. Then I found myself wondering if maybe Nick had merely acquiesced in society's demand for marriage and children. Maybe he had only talked himself into believing that he wanted both worlds. Nick's sobs made me think of Jimmy, overcome with tears when we sat on that park bench in Pioneer Park while he told me about his disastrous engagement to Mary.

Gwen had said that her feeble-minded neighbor girl acquiesced to "voluntary" sterilization after she had been institutionalized. Had the pervasive societal institution of love and marriage, with its requisite childbearing, placed Nick and Jimmy in a similar position of "voluntarily" going along with the received traditions of church and government?

When Nick became calmer, I asked if he would like to see someone from the clergy or a social worker. It struck me as peculiar that, in spite of the fact that I had shared sex with Nick, I had no idea if he had a religious affiliation. In fact, I knew almost nothing about his life.

He would not turn to face me and he seemed unwilling to talk. I decided it was time for me to leave, but I felt the need to make some gesture. I gently placed my hand on his shoulder. He turned slowly to look at me, and after a moment I thought I perceived a glimmer of recognition. But he still said nothing.

Maybe I was mistaken and only imagined that he recognized me—because I wanted him to. And I wanted him to know that I had at least an inkling of what he might be feeling. I realized that I was the one who should be making the confession. Since I participated in the acts that I assumed had brought him by self-violence to this hospital bed, didn't I bear some responsibility? Didn't I owe Nick the simple honesty of confessing who I was? And that I had known him? But all this was something that I could not bring myself to volunteer. I told him I would check in on him later and I left.

THIRTEEN

I checked on Nick again Saturday morning. He was sleeping when I arrived and after I woke him, he still refused to talk. His gaze wouldn't meet my eyes and his face registered no emotion at all. On top of that, the hospital still hadn't located his family, despite various attempts. The only hopeful sign was that his surgery seemed to have been successful. Before I left, I insisted that the nurse on his ward have a social worker visit him.

Throughout the day, Nick's case haunted me. As I anticipated seeing Jimmy that evening, I continued to wonder if he was still keeping an open mind about Mary and the possibility of marriage.

After dark, as I drove out Wilcox Road to see the Diggs Monroe Jazz Orchestra at the Greenwood Country Club dance, I couldn't help smiling at how peculiar it was that Jimmy turned out to be the one to finally entice me out to Greenwood Estates. All of Gowan's attempts to show me around out there had failed, along with his efforts to sway me toward acquiring a wife and kids—accessories to the real estate I was supposed to buy. Again, I worried that tonight at this dance I might run into someone I knew, but I reminded myself that the music would only attract the younger set, not older folks in Gowan's age group. Thinking of Gowan brought my thoughts back to medicine and the Catholic hospital problem, and then Nick came to mind again.

Could it be true that Jimmy was like Nick, attracted to women as well as men? I knew that one sexual act between men did not make a person homosexual, any more than an act between a man and a woman made one a heterosexual. I thought of observing Jimmy at the dance to see if he showed any interest in the girls there. Immediately, I felt a twinge of guilt mixed with shame. Was it possible that I was jealous? Was I playing Iago to my own Othello? This was all ridiculous. I tried to put these thoughts aside and focused my attention on my driving. Still, just as with Othello, the idea had been planted.

I arrived late and hung around the periphery of the dance floor, feeling slightly uneasy as I admired the lavish new clubhouse and listened to the music. Everything Jimmy had told me about the band was true. They had added a number of new songs to their repertoire, and the music sounded better than ever. I tried not to think about Jimmy's interactions with the young women present, but my attention kept turning in that direction. His singing displayed a new polish on his natural showmanship and he seemed to play to the women in the audience. Occasionally, between songs, one or two would approach him to make a request. At one point, a flapper approached and blatantly flirted with him. I found myself weighing his every move, seeing each glance and gesture in one light and then another. Was he just being polite and ingratiating—to hide his indifference—or did he feel a real attraction?

I caught his eye at one point and he gave me a little smile and a nod. Was he holding in check a more welcoming response in order to be discreet? Or was there less warmth in his feeling for me?

There was no sorting this out, and I finally went out on the veranda to distract myself from the insoluble conundrum I had constructed. I looked out across the manicured golf course in the fading twilight of late June and tried to imagine what the homes must be like out here. I couldn't see myself fitting in with this sort of life. It amused me that Jimmy had ended up here, entertaining the society set. But suppose he had ambitions to fit in to this life. If so, he wouldn't be the first bohemian to accept the conventions of marriage and family and financial stability.

About the time I thought of making my way back indoors,

the band took a break and the crowd spilled out onto the veranda. Jimmy must have seen me slip out earlier because he quickly found me standing alone at the end of the long porch. Once I was in his presence, my jealous worries seemed completely groundless and evaporated like morning mist under his sunny smile.

I told him how much I liked the new numbers the band had added and asked how things had gone at the speakeasy. He said it had been kind of wild, and he paused to light up a cigarette. He described a fistfight that had broken out between two of the male patrons. But, he added, the music had gone over well and the crowd seemed to like the band.

As we talked, I found that I was instinctively careful not to stand too close to Jimmy or make any physical gesture that might hint at the intimacy that existed between us. And it crossed my mind that Jimmy could just as easily have interpreted this as a coolness in my affections toward him, but he didn't seem to be feeling that I was acting aloof. I was being oversensitive. Without plan, we adopted an outward appearance of off-handed good humor that any outsider would take for casual friendship. The crowd on the veranda thinned out and when no one was in earshot, I lowered my voice and asked if he still wanted to come to my place afterward.

"You bet," he said. His smile gave no hint that I should have doubted his affection. I felt guilty about having any misgivings.

"Should I plan on having you ride home with me? Or do you want me to pick you up at your boarding house?" I felt as if we were arranging an illegal liquor deal.

Jimmy thought for a moment, looking out across the greens.

"I'll tell you what. I keep thinking about what you said over dinner the other night when you were talking about the Klan. We need to be careful. I don't want the fellas in the band getting suspicious. You know?"

"I understand."

"Why don't I meet you outside my boarding house? I think it would be better that way."

"I agree. Best to play it safe. When do you finish up here?"

Jimmy told me they wound up at midnight but it would be an hour before they got their instruments packed up and went home. I said I would wait for him in my Ford across the street from his place at 1.

Jimmy went back to the bandstand and I had the feeling that our clandestine planning had bonded us together even more, like criminals living outside the law. That, too, quelled my fears about Jimmy's feelings toward women, even though it stirred up other fears about the world outside our relationship.

I listened to the band play a few more numbers while I watched the crowd and the young couples dancing. A few of the young ladies gave me the eye, but I didn't feel like asking them to dance, in spite of a nagging feeling that I had an obligation to participate in this social ritual. A handsome black-haired fellow fox-trotted gracefully past holding a girl close in his arms, their bodies touching, and I remembered Gerald dancing with the *fraulein* in Berlin. I glanced across the room at Jimmy playing piano on the bandstand. There was the only person I wanted to dance with. And I became aware of the source of my feeling of uneasiness—the same uneasiness I had felt at the Bisby Grange dance. Here were all these young men and women dancing together, and I was left out, a spectator on the outside looking in. This entire evening, the whole social encounter, was designed for them. Not for me. A ritual for the meeting of male with female, making friends, maybe making a connection that would eventually lead to marriage, and children, and a place in society. But for me, aside from the opportunity to watch Jimmy play and enjoy his music and the chance for a fleeting conversation with him, this ritual had nothing to offer me.

I decided to drive home. I felt awkward and left out, and besides, staying to watch might only give me more opportunity to torture myself with doubts about Jimmy. I preferred to pass the time at my place and drive over to the boarding house when the time came for me to pick him up.

I got to Jimmy's just before 1 and parked across the street where I could keep an eye on the front door.

I had passed Pioneer Park on my way there, and I kept remembering Nick sobbing in that hospital bed. In spite of feeling reassured about Jimmy by our bond as outlaws, I again started to worry that Jimmy might be equally attracted to women and men. Maybe it was just fatigue and the lateness of the hour. I wanted to talk to Jimmy about Mary. I knew that he must still harbor feelings for her, maybe not sexual feelings but some spiritual, platonic connection. But, I reminded myself, that did not mean his friendship with her was a threat to our relationship. I believed that Jimmy's disastrous engagement with Mary was too traumatic for him to salvage anything. And as I mulled it over, I realized that his trauma was less than two weeks old and his wounds from it were much too fresh.

But maybe, like Nick—like most people—Jimmy felt that marriage and children were inevitable. I wished there were some way I could know. But asking him was probably not the best way to find out. Most likely he wasn't sure himself.

When my watch read half past 1, I had to quiet another flurry of fantasies about Jimmy going home with a girl from the dance. I convinced myself that he and the band members had stopped off for a nightcap.

Jimmy didn't show up until nearly 2. I was nodding off when the flash of headlights woke me up, and a car pulled up in front of the boarding house. I straightened up and watched as Jimmy got out, bid good night to the band members, and went inside. When the other car had gone, I pulled up to the boarding house curb and waited. Soon Jimmy came down the steps and opened the car door.

"Gosh, Carl, I'm sorry we were so late. After the dance closed down, the country club served us a meal. And after that Larry broke out a bottle he'd gotten from some pharmacy, and there was no way to light a fire under those fellas. I hope you're not sore."

I was reassured. "No, I'm just sleepy," I said. "Climb on in." Again, being in Jimmy's presence, my doubts melted away. It seemed that all my jealousy and misgivings had been manufactured in my mind.

As we drove across town, he placed his hand on my knee. I realized that I couldn't bring up the subject of Mary. He had been touchy about the topic when I brought it up at dinner on Monday. It was still too soon and he was too vulnerable. I had to let go of it. I was no longer capable of playing out the role of Othello. But Nick's case still haunted me.

When we got inside the safety of my front door, Jimmy approached me with his arms out and we embraced and kissed. He was not acting like a man who was partial to women.

I offered him a drink, thinking that alcohol would put us at ease. He said it might help him unwind from the dance. "I kept telling Larry that I was tired and I didn't want any booze," he said. "I was hoping it would move them along, but it didn't." I was touched by his efforts to extricate himself from the band so that he could be with me, and again I felt a twinge of guilt for my doubts.

"Make yourself comfortable," I said and went to get a bottle of good brandy that I had been saving. When I returned, Jimmy was examining the framed print of the colorful Tuke painting hanging over my Victrola.

"You had it framed. Boy, they did a swell job of it."

"Yes, I'm very happy with it." He turned to look at me and we smiled at each other.

"Have a seat," I said. "You were in excellent voice tonight," I poured out shots for us in two snifters. "And your piano playing sounds better than ever."

"Thanks. Sometimes I start to think maybe we're getting too slick. But the extra rehearsals are good, I think."

"Here's to your musicianship," I said, raising my glass.

Jimmy raised his glass to me, then gave it an expert swirl to coat the inside with brandy before slowly inhaling the smell of the liquor. Finally he took a small sip and rolled it on his tongue. This act of connoisseurship took me by surprise. "Tasty," he said after swallowing.

"I see this isn't the first time you've had fine brandy."

"Yeah, ol' Diggs has been trying to teach the rest of the band a bit more refinement."

"I commend him for that."

"I think he's right. Some of these fellas in the band are a bit rough around the edges. Oh, Howard is all right. But I've known him since college—longer than the others. But that Bill, our drum player, has terrible table manners—my God—and he's liable to let out a belch anywhere, anytime. And old Larry is so forward with the ladies that I don't think he realizes how rude he comes off. He grabbed this one girl's breast right on the dance floor the other night. He'd just met her and he was going on about Freud's pleasure principle and how people needed to overcome repression and fully express their libido in order to have good health. Tell me, is that really what Freud says?"

"I'm not a psychiatrist—or a psychoanalyst—that's a whole other branch of medicine—but I've read a little bit of Freud. I'd say Larry only got part of the picture. Freud does say that from a psychological standpoint, the entire body is involved in the pursuit of pleasure, especially in childhood. All the senses can give pleasure. I know you find that's true with music."

"Of course. The ear is extremely sensitive—to a wide range of... pleasure, as you put it. Melody, rhythm, harmonies. Just like taste. And smell." Jimmy flicked the brandy snifter with his fingernail and a tiny "ping" floated in the air of the room, then faded into silence.

"Exactly," I said. "The way I understand it, Freud suggests that with maturity, humans learn to defer the gratification of sexual pleasure through a process called sublimation where we see that the realistic thing to do is to be reasonable and postpone pleasure to the appropriate time. But that's only a nutshell version. Freud has written volumes."

"I guess Larry needs to study up a bit more till he gets to the part about sublimation. Anyway, Diggs imagines us playing these high-class joints like private clubs and grand homes with ballrooms—places that privately serve fine liquor. He wants us to be able to fit in."

"He's ambitious, isn't he?"

"Yeah. He has some more high-tone dances lined up this summer. And he's working on plans for our trip to Chicago. He is a terrific manager, and we're all having a great time playing music together."

"I can't imagine what it must be like to make music the way you do. In front of a crowd and all."

"It's a thrill, all right. I sometimes get the feeling—I'm not sure how to put it—that there's something moving through us, through the band as a whole…"

"Like a living organism?" I said.

"It's the berries. When we're all together and with it. And the audience seems to notice, maybe without knowing exactly what it is, and the whole place begins to feel…electric. Something like that. I guess I'm not expressing it too well."

"No. I understand what you're saying. I felt some of that going on tonight."

"Yeah? I'm glad you have some idea what I'm talking about then. That's why music is more important to me than anything else."

"I understand." I looked at Jimmy and wondered how important to him I was.

"You must feel that way about doctoring," he said. "Saving lives and doing surgery. That's some heavyweight activity."

I thought about Nick again. "Yes, that's true. I take it seriously. Maybe too seriously." I glanced at Jimmy as he took a sip. "I had a case today—well, yesterday—that I wanted to tell you about. There was…a man at the hospital—on Friday. He tried to commit suicide. But we were able to save him."

"Holy cow!"

"It was a sad story." I paused. "You know, I keep remembering some of the things you said that night you came over here when you were so drunk."

He looked down and toyed with his brandy glass.

"Jimmy, promise me you won't ever hurt yourself."

"I still feel bad about that night." He looked up at me. "But, you know, I don't remember much about it. What did I say to you?"

I took a deep breath and began, "You said that you wished you were dead. You said you should borrow Howard's gun and go off in the woods. And you said you should jump off a bridge."

Jimmy stared at me with dismay, then looked down at his brandy. "I don't remember any of that." He set the glass down. "I must have been drunk out of my mind."

"You didn't think about killing yourself?"

"I was drunk. No, not just that. I was upset."

"Yes. I know. Drunk and upset. Sometimes people do foolish things when they are drunk—and upset."

"I told you what happened, Carl."

I watched him and waited.

He didn't look up. "It was all because..." He paused.

"Because...?" I said softly.

He seemed to stiffen. He was silent for a long time, looking off into space as if he were revisiting something from the past and trying to gather his thoughts into something he could express in words. "...because of what happened with Mary. And because Diggs and I had that argument and he said he could get another piano player. I'm not sure which one hurt more." I realized I had completely overlooked this second trauma.

"Oh, Jimmy. I'm sorry. I know you've been through a lot lately." It was obvious he was still sorting out his feelings. I was silent a moment collecting my own thoughts and feelings. "I guess what I need to know, Jimmy, is if you are feeling bad about me. About having sexual relations with me."

"Carl, you're about the best friend I've got. Even Howard—there are things I can't even begin to talk about with him."

"I'm relieved to hear that." He hadn't answered my question, but I let it go.

Jimmy looked over at me.

I took a deep breath and said quietly, "You know, I care about you, Jimmy. A whole lot. And I just hope that you haven't got it stuck in the back of your mind that you can't be happy if you are not married and raising a family." I watched him closely.

He looked away and sat quietly for a moment with downcast eyes. "No. I've pretty well given up on the idea of marriage."

"Because, you see…it's just that this fellow who tried to commit suicide—in the hospital the other day—I think he preferred to be with men, but he was married and had kids. I don't think he was able to reconcile that with the rest of his life."

I searched what I could see of Jimmy's face.

Finally he looked up at me and said, "Maybe you're getting me confused with this fella who tried to kill himself." He looked me in the eye for a moment. "I sure don't intend to commit suicide—no matter what I said when I was drunk. I wouldn't have said any of that stuff unless I was soused. And I wouldn't have said it to anyone but you. I sure wouldn't want any of the fellas in the band to know that I was thinking about killing myself. They'd think I was crazy. I must have trusted you, you see—to actually come right out and say those things to you."

We looked at each other for a moment and I knew he was sincere. And I knew he was right. He had trusted me. Now I had to trust him.

"Forgive me, Jimmy. You're right. I guess I owe you an apology. Maybe I just let my imagination get a little carried away. After what happened to…what that fellow at the hospital did to himself."

"How did he do it, anyway? Did he try to blow his brains out? How did you ever put him back together?"

"I…I don't want to give you any ideas."

"Aw, come on, Carl. Honest. I'm not gonna kill myself."

"Okay. Okay." I paused. "He cut his wrists."

Jimmy winced. "I promise you, I won't ever do that." He reached out his hand.

I leaned forward and took his hand in mine. "Thank you. I'm counting on that."

"Besides," he said, "I get sick at the sight of blood." That made us both laugh.

We finished our brandies, saying little and exchanging glances. I had the feeling that we had worked through some misunderstandings to a new equilibrium. Without a signal we leaned into each other and began kissing.

Finally, Jimmy reminded me that he had to play the organ at church in the morning. "Come on," he said reaching for my hand. "Let's take off our clothes and see about this pleasure principle of Dr. Freud's."

We went off to bed and repeated some of the acts we had tried before, then nestled together and slipped into a deep sleep.

FOURTEEN

On Sunday morning, before Jimmy dragged himself out of bed to go off to the church, I asked why he kept his job as church organist all this time.

"I don't know," he said. "It keeps me flexible. Remember how I told you I used to play at the church in Watney Junction? Playing church organ was the first job I got when I moved to Portland. Come to think of it, I guess music and religion have always been bound up together in my mind. I like the feeling it gives me—all the people and the singing and the sound reverberating all around in that space inside the church."

"Like that feeling you talked about last night, when you are playing with the band?"

"Something like that. There's a little of that—with the congregation and all—especially when they are singing along with the hymns. And I guess the people at a dance are like a congregation. But playing with the band is different. More of a team effort. More parts. More balancing. And we make part of it up as we go along. It's unpredictable. It makes a bigger kind of electricity."

"Do you believe in God?" I asked.

He shrugged. "I guess so."

"Will you stick with the church job?"

"I suppose." Jimmy paused a moment. "It isn't that I feel some great religious devotion. But I love some of the music." Then he smiled at me and said, "Say, why don't you come hear me play? You've heard me play Mozart and you've heard me play jazz. Come to the church and hear me play the organ."

"Oh, I don't know, Jimmy. I've never felt comfortable in a church."

"Don't you believe in God?"

"No. I don't."

Jimmy laughed. Then seeing that I was serious, he said, "I'm sorry. I don't mean to cast judgment. I guess I just thought everyone believed in God."

I wanted to say, just like everyone believes in marriage? but I restrained myself. Instead, I said, "Well, I don't. Not like that."

"I bet you're just afraid you'll be converted if you go to church." Jimmy was making a joke and he laughed.

Something hardened inside and kept me from laughing along with him, even though I knew it was only good-natured teasing. Wasn't it the church that converted the masses into believing that they all had to marry? That I was an abomination?

"No," I said, my voice so adamant it startled me. "I don't expect that's going to happen any time soon. I'm sorry, Jimmy. I can't take this lightly."

"Didn't you go to Sunday school when you were a kid?" His tone remained light and open-hearted.

"No, I didn't," I said firmly. "My parents were never partial to religion and so I never went to church, even as a kid. Once—only once—I went to a Baptist Church with a school friend, when I was in grade school. It was a Wednesday night, not on Sunday, which I thought was strange. And all that talk of burning in hell scared me to death. I had nightmares about it. That was enough to drive me away for good. Later, when I was old enough to think about it rationally, it all seemed to me like a racket designed to make everyone feel guilty so that they would give in to the power of the church and give them their money."

"Boy, no wonder you're so against the church and marriage and all."

I pondered for a moment. "I've never made that connection

before. You may have something there. I guess I was pretty traumatized by that early experience."

Jimmy considered a bit. "But tell me, don't you believe in some kind of life after death?"

"No. I don't think we can know about that. As a physician, I try to stick to what I can observe in the material world."

"Then do you think that life has no meaning?" he asked. "No purpose?"

"Who can say? I tend to think there's no way to know for sure when it comes to questions like that."

"What do you believe in then?"

"Oh…I believe in the way the body heals itself. That's pretty miraculous. It's something I can see happen. I believe in the way that plants grow. We can observe that. But I can't see an old man with a beard sitting up on a cloud laying down the law and tossing thunderbolts. As far as I can tell, that kind of religious belief has caused more pain and misery for the human race than non-belief. That's partly what I was trying to say last night about marriage and that fellow who tried to commit suicide."

Jimmy was silent for a moment. "But surely, as a doctor, you've seen some miraculous cures, haven't you? I've heard that those things happen. Sometimes people seem to pull through in what look like hopeless situations. Isn't that true?"

"Yes. Those things do happen. And I can't explain them. But I refuse to explain them as some divine magic. Can't we just think of them as human will in action? A powerful will to live."

"What about the stars? Whenever I take the time to look at the night sky, I get the feeling that there is something pretty grand going on there. That can't just be human will, can it?"

"No. I agree that the universe is vast. Bigger and older and more complicated than we can comprehend. I just can't say that I believe some being created it."

"Don't you find that leaves you feeling hopeless though? As if all this…this life is just bleak and meaningless?"

"I'll tell you a story I heard during the War that I think about when I look for some kind of hope in this world. There were rumors in the trenches that in No Man's Land a whole regiment existed, another army made up of deserters from both sides, soldiers who refused to fight in the War. The myth was that they had wandered off to inhabit the region between the enemy lines and were surviving in secret bunkers in a community of mutual respect and cooperation, independent from all the combatants. I don't think there was any evidence that such a thing ever existed, but that's how the story went.

"If I were going to believe in anything that I can't observe, I guess I would believe in that army, between the trenches, between the boundaries. Now there is an act of the human will. Human hope. Those who refuse to fight, who refuse to cause harm. Refuse to take sides. Those who choose to remain open-minded in a world gone mad. The ones who choose not to accept the world as it was carved up by national governments or religious belief systems. That is something I can believe in."

"That's an inspiring story," Jimmy said. We were both quiet for some time. After a while he said, "But you don't have to believe in God, or even a phantom army, to come hear me play."

"Oh, don't get me wrong. I may not believe in God, but I do believe in music. As a man of science, I believe in vibrations—and music is all just vibrations, like light, and color. They say vibrations continue to linger in the universe, perhaps for eternity. Like the conservation of energy that they taught us about in chemistry classes—how nothing is ever created or destroyed but simply changes form. Maybe your music continues on, out into the universe. Maybe it has an effect we will never know, something we can't even imagine."

"Boy, that sounds like religion to me," Jimmy said. "So why don't you come to church with me? You can just sit quietly in the back."

Something made me hesitate.

"Just to listen to the music," Jimmy said.

"Okay, Jimmy." I put my arms around him and rocked him

back and forth. "For you I would go to church. I'll come hear you play the organ. You know, I always get pleasure hearing you make music. I just wish it was in some other setting."

We drove to the east side Episcopal church where Jimmy played, but we entered the big stone building separately. I took a seat next to the aisle in a back pew and listened. Jimmy was right about the reverberations inside the church. That organ had a magnificent sound. While the church filled up, I listened to Jimmy play several pieces, ending with one that I guessed to be a Bach composition. It seemed to have roots like a tree, reaching deep into the ground and then soaring into the heavens.

As the service began, I followed along in the church program since this was all new to me. The Introit sounded and the pastor entered to begin the formal service. At its appointed time there was the Reading of the Scripture.

"Today our reading is from the Book of Leviticus, Chapter 20, verses 7 through 13," the lector said and then he began.

"Sanctify yourselves therefore, and be ye holy: for I am the Lord your God.

And ye shall keep my statutes, and do them: I am the Lord which sanctify you.

For every one that curseth his father or his mother shall be surely put to death: he hath cursed his father or his mother; his blood shall be upon him.

And the man that committeth adultery with another man's wife, even he that committeth adultery with his neighbor's wife, the adulterer and the adulteress shall surely be put to death.

And the man that lieth with his father's wife hath uncovered his father's nakedness: both of them shall surely be put to death; their blood shall be upon them.

And if a man lie with his daughter in law, both of them shall surely be put to death: they have wrought confusion; their blood shall be upon them.

If a man also lie with mankind, as he lieth with a woman, both of them have committed an abomination: they shall surely be put to death; their blood shall be upon them."

This was worse than I could have imagined. Leviticus. My German friends had insisted that I read some of these passages. No wonder I had given up on religion. After the scripture reading, the pastor took the pulpit and began his sermon.

"Today's sermon is titled Following the Rules. That's why I chose our reading from the Book of Leviticus. This book lays out the rules for us: If you curse your father or your mother, you will be put to death. If you have an adulterous relationship, you will be put to death, along with the woman who joined you in the act of adultery. If you commit incest, you will be put to death, along with the victim of your incestuous act.

"That is what the scripture says. These are the rules we are told to follow.

"But is this the way we actually live our lives? No. Should we live our lives this way? This is the question before us. Is this the way God intends for us to live? Even in these modern times?

"We hear a lot of talk these days about religious fundamentals. And I don't mean to disparage any of our Christian brethren, but our Church—the Christian Church as a whole and the Episcopal Church in particular—has a long history and a long tradition. And it behooves us to study these traditions and this history, as the Episcopal clergy has long done, in a full seminary curriculum, going all the way back to the Church of England. Many great men in our history have a seminary background, even when they did not go on to become clergymen. Even Charles Darwin studied for the ministry—after he left the study of medicine because he could not stomach the sight of blood.

"The unschooled Fundamentalist pastors—who come to the ministry from a personal calling, lacking in rigorous study—these church leaders would readily answer 'Yes. This is the way we should live.' Let us examine this question: Would the Fundamentalists honestly put to death any man or woman who curses his parents?

Would they be willing to put to death all adulterers, along with their partners in crime? The scriptures say, 'their blood shall be upon them.'"

My mind drifted back to the soapbox preacher I heard after the eugenics lecture, and the sight of Nick and his stevedore friend being hauled off in the police wagon afterward. Nick's pale face in the hospital and the white bandages around his wrists. His blood was surely upon him. A whole bathtub full of it. Was that what good Christians should be hoping for?

A commotion toward the front of the church brought me out of my thoughts. A man and woman had risen to their feet and were making their way out of the long pew to the aisle. They turned and walked quickly toward the back of the church. I recognized Mr. and Mrs. Hamlin, proprietors at the local grocery where I shopped. As they passed by me, I heard Mr. Hamlin saying in a loud whisper, "You should at least wait till they start communion." And Mrs. Hamlin shot back at him in a hiss, "I will not sit here and be insulted by this blasphemy." They disappeared into the church foyer.

The pastor had moved on to another argument. "The Fundamentalists would have us believe that the world was created in six days, just as it says in the book of Genesis. But going back a century or more, some enlightened Christians, following the advances of science, have looked at the six days in the Genesis story as a reflection of six ages, during which the Lord created this world and the varieties of life within it, each age lasting over the vast stretches of geologic time."

This was something I never expected to hear from a pulpit. I wondered how closely Jimmy was paying attention to the sermon, as I remembered him asking me if the night sky didn't make me tend to believe in a god. And I remembered that lecture in Berlin where Professor Einstein talked about one clock traveling at the speed of light to a distant galaxy, while another clock stayed behind on Earth. How far away was that galaxy, and was it created by the same God that this pastor was talking about? And how did the creation of that distant galaxy fit into the six ages? Going one step further, I wondered how you could have six ages when Professor Einstein had called into question the very notion of time itself by positing something called "space-time," which I couldn't even begin to comprehend.

The pastor was winding up his sermon. "...but I hope I have demonstrated to you that the Bible reveals an evolution, too. We can see the progress in the Hebrew concept of God from the earlier books of the Old Testament to the later writings, just as we Christians can see a more merciful God evolving in the New Testament.

"All around us the world is progressing. We as Christians must progress with the modern world. We must look at the world we live in and follow more up-to-date rules as our thinking evolves. What should be fundamental for us is the evolution of our understanding of moral and ethical principles, rather than clinging to laws that governed the Jewish people thousands of years ago. As we go forward, may the spirit of Christ's mercy guide our ever-evolving understanding of the will of God."

This was progressive indeed. Was it possible that a church could actually evolve to the point where it would accept men like Jimmy and me?

I watched the rest of the service with new, more open eyes.

When it seemed that things were about to conclude, I slipped out of the church and waited for Jimmy in the Ford. As we drove back to my place, I asked how much he paid attention to the sermons and all the ritual. He said it had all become pretty routine for him, and he mostly concentrated on the music cues and timing, and making sure he was ready with the next piece of music. He said he only listened to the sermons with half an ear. I told him I found the pastor's ideas refreshingly progressive.

"Yes," Jimmy said, "I like this new pastor. He's only been here a few months. I hear a lot of people call him a modernist."

"I liked him too. Not at all the sin and hellfire I expected."

"The church has started printing his sermons in a monthly bulletin. I can bring you a copy if you are interested."

"I'd be curious to read what else he has to say. Do you suppose the church might someday accept the human body as more than just a vehicle for vice?"

"That reminds me of something I thought of during the service," Jimmy said. "One of my music profs in college told us some old writer way back said that music was the only sensual pleasure that is without vice. I wonder what Dr. Freud would say to that."

"That's very pretty. Maybe that's what Freud was trying to say with his pleasure principle—that all our sensual pleasures are without vice." I glanced over at Jimmy. He smiled at me, and as I turned my gaze back out the windshield, I felt his hand come to rest on my thigh.

Once we got home, it wasn't long before we began removing each other's clothes, and then we found ourselves back in bed. I was careful to begin slowly and follow Jimmy's lead. He seemed more open than he had been before. After a time, he aligned our bodies with our cocks together, and then he began rubbing his body against mine in a progression of slow movements that left us lost in the pleasures of the senses.

Afterward, Jimmy dozed off and I watched him sleep for a long time in the half-light of the curtained bedroom. I never tired of looking at the shape of his face and observing the quality of his pale skin, the way the length of his slender torso molded into his hips and buttocks. His hands fascinated me, with his long, sturdy fingers, which made such beautiful music—those peculiar *Homo sapiens* hands with their opposable thumb, so richly innervated and so intimately connected with the brain—at times, almost at one with the mind.

How did his brain make those fingers move over the keyboard in that exact manner to make that certain quality of sound? I understood the mechanics of the muscles and bones that moved the hand, and I understood that messages traveled along the nerves to set the muscles in motion. But what sent those signals from the brain? Was the mind just some psychological result of electro-chemical reactions in the brain that set those hands in motion? Or was there some non-material force that came into play? From what region of our enlarged human cranium did Jimmy's quick laughter and wild enthusiasms arise? And why did his particular combination of physical and mental traits happen to attract me?

My thoughts went back to our conversation about God earlier that day, and I thought about the sermon and the church service. In Berlin, Detlef and Heinz made me read those passages in Leviticus, and other Bible passages that condemned me, and I couldn't understand the appeal of Christianity. Maybe this priest today saw something I had missed. But why, I wondered, was it necessary to invent heavens and hells and gods? Why was it necessary to think in terms of a God at all? Wasn't the fact of living enough? Wasn't it miraculous enough simply to be aware that I existed? And to be aware that the person lying asleep next to me existed? To have the power of will to simply raise a finger, as Jimmy did to play an organ key. To cause your hand to reach out to touch the flesh of another and feel the warmth. Wasn't that religion enough?

I extended my hand and stroked that demarcating epidermis of Jimmy's inner forearm, bringing my hand to rest upon his.

Jimmy's fingers twitched beneath mine on the white sheet and he made a small murmur in his sleep. Was Jimmy dreaming of playing the piano? I was reminded of a Chinese story about an emperor and a butterfly. Perhaps Jimmy was dreaming about me lying there watching him sleep, dreaming of me wondering about the existence of a God and wondering if Jimmy was dreaming about playing the piano. Perhaps I only existed in Jimmy's dream. And what if he should wake—would I still exist?

I let Jimmy sleep for a long time. When at last he woke, I continued to exist, and we got up and played Halma and listened to the phonograph until it was time for dinner.

fifTEEN

It seemed Jimmy and I couldn't see enough of each other. Throughout July, we began spending all our free time together. That wasn't easy. I had regular hours at the clinic and irregular hours at one hospital or another, plus assorted professional meetings in the evenings. Jimmy was up late at rehearsals and playing with the band at private parties, speakeasies, and dances. And no matter how late he might have been up on Saturday night, he always dragged himself out of bed on Sunday mornings to play the church organ. On the week nights when he could stay over, we took pains to leave the house early in the morning if Joe Locke was scheduled to be at my house.

I went to see the band play when I could, and eventually Jimmy introduced me to them as an acquaintance. One night I stayed till the dance was over, and as the band was packing up, I openly offered to give Jimmy a ride to his boarding house. In a voice calculated for the others to hear, he said, "Oh, no, don't bother. I'll catch a ride home with Howard."

It was clear to me that he was saying that so the band members wouldn't think there was anything remarkable about my offer. We couldn't have planned it better. I jumped in, insisting it was no trouble. "It's on my way."

Then we drove to my house where we tumbled into bed together. Other nights when I wasn't there to hear Jimmy play, one of the band members would give him a lift to the boarding house, and he'd take a taxicab to my place.

Usually, though, we saw each other on Saturday or Sunday afternoons, if there wasn't an afternoon tea dance. And we normally spent Monday and Tuesday nights together—as long as I didn't get called away by a patient or Jimmy didn't get called away by the band. I gave him a key to my house for when I was gone attending to a patient after dark. Those nights when I would find Jimmy waiting up for me, my heart would nearly burst. It was like coming home to a warm hearth rather than a cold, lifeless morgue.

About a month after Jimmy and I began sleeping together, I mentioned that I had some friends I wanted him to meet. We never know how new and old friends will react to each another, so I was feeling some apprehension about introducing Jimmy to Gwen and Charlie. So I tried to minimize the occasion by not telling Jimmy a lot about my friends, hoping he'd see it as just a casual get-together. I wanted to avoid building up the event, so I didn't tell him that Gwen and Charlie were two of my closest friends.

My plan was for us to meet them for drinks at their apartment, then go out to dinner. Jimmy agreed, but Diggs had booked the band every Friday and Saturday into August, so we settled on meeting Gwen and Charlie on a Tuesday night when the band wasn't scheduled to rehearse.

Toward the end of July, I set things up with Gwen by phone, only telling her that I was bringing along a friend. When she tried to wheedle more information out of me, I brought our conversation to a close, saying I had a patient waiting. I told her we would swing round to their place about 7 and hung up.

"Hello, Gwen." She was dressed in a dark blue gown that flattered her full figure. She was looking over my shoulder at Jimmy but then turned her eyes on me and that smile of long friendship spread across her face.

"Good evening, Carl. Good to see you, honey." She kissed my cheek and gave me a hug.

"Gwen, this is Jimmy Harper," I said. Yes, maybe it was even with a sense of pride.

Driving over, Jimmy seemed nervous, and he now seemed unsure, hesitating before he extended his hand, as if trying to decide what level of formality to adopt.

"Jimmy, sweetheart, it's so good to meet you." Gwen took his hand in both of hers and welcomed him with a warm smile as she explored his face for a moment. "Do come in."

As she led us through the small entry hall, something sparkled in her auburn hair. It was done up more elaborately than usual and held in place by a rhinestone clip. We entered the comfortable and stylish living room. It had something feminine in its feel, without being frilly. "Charlie is still getting ready. Have a seat. Let me fix us something to drink."

She went to a china cabinet against the wall. I crossed to stand by the sofa and Jimmy hesitated again, taking in the room.

"This is a special occasion so let me get out my bottle of Scotch," Gwen said. The occasion's specialness was just what I wanted to downplay and I tried to catch her eye, but she was opening a lower cupboard. I glanced at Jimmy and saw that he had seen my frustration. He covered the uneasiness of the moment by stepping over to the wall to examine a framed print of two women having tea.

"Is Scotch all right with you fellows?"

"Sure," I said.

Jimmy turned toward Gwen. "Of course," he said, then added, "Is this picture by Mary Cassatt?"

"Oh, I couldn't tell you, Jimmy. Charlie would know." The glasses clinked as she brought them out of the cabinet. "Please make yourselves comfortable."

I took a seat on the sofa, and Jimmy sat in one of the matching armchairs upholstered in a geometric pattern with rose-colored hues that picked up those in the picture.

"This has been quite a week," Gwen said, "what with the death of President Harding and all." She handed out our drinks.

"A national tragedy," I said. "It's been a shock to everyone."

"It sure has," Jimmy said. "Our band got a cancellation on a dance that we were scheduled to play last Friday."

"Carl told me you play piano." She went back to get her glass. "What's the name of your band?"

Jimmy told her.

Gwen repeated the name to herself as she took a seat at the other end of the sofa. "Tell me about Diggs Monroe. A local fellow?"

"Yeah, I met him through my friend Howard Henderson. Howard and I studied music together at college. He was a year ahead of me. Then, when I moved here, Howard introduced me to Diggs. They had already started playing together with this crazy banjo player named Larry. Diggs grew up here but he went to school in Los Angeles for a couple of years. He heard some New Orleans jazz musicians down in California—Jelly Roll Morton and Kid Ory—and became a died-in-the-wool devotee. When he flunked out of school, he came back here and decided to start a band. He's mostly self-taught, but he's pretty good. And he's—"

Charlie entered the room.

"There's our lovely lady," Gwen said.

Jimmy and I stood up. Charlie looked beautiful as ever, in a maroon evening dress. I had only seen her a couple of times since the Iverson wedding reception, and then only briefly. Tonight, without a hat, her bobbed hair showed off her features to better advantage.

Gwen went and took Charlie's hand and led her over to Jimmy.

"Charlie, this is Jimmy Harper. Jimmy, Charlie Devereaux."

Jimmy hesitated and a look of befuddlement came over his face. Then he burst out with a laugh.

"All this time I thought Charlie was a man," Jimmy explained. Gwen and I laughed. Charlie smiled and gave a little laugh but she seemed slightly irritated. Jimmy stood there awkwardly, not sure what to do or say. A blush colored his cheeks.

To me she had always just been Charlie, and I hadn't considered that her nickname could easily belong to a male. Now I saw that I had been remiss in not making it clear to Jimmy beforehand, but the possibility of this confusion hadn't occurred to me. I immediately felt guilty that I had put Jimmy in this uncomfortable position.

Besides his embarrassment over her name and gender, I sensed that Jimmy was dumbstruck by her beauty. I watched him floundering in confusion, and I was surprised. To see someone so fluid in performance before an audience now become all thumbs socially was painful. At the same time, this endeared me to him all over again.

I felt the need to say something. "I've been looking forward to us all finally getting together," I said hoping to give Jimmy a moment to collect himself.

"We've been looking forward to it too," Gwen said.

Finally, Jimmy extended his hand. "I'm enchanted to meet you…Charlie."

"Hello," she replied, shaking his hand. I had the momentary impression that she felt his reaction to her was exaggerated and uncalled-for, an ostentatious attempt to flatter her.

There was a brief silence. Then Jimmy added, "So you two are roommates?"

Charlie gave him a look, and then she exchanged glances with Gwen. "No. We're lesbians."

Jimmy was speechless. So was I for a moment, as Charlie regarded Jimmy.

I hadn't wanted to scare Jimmy off or somehow prejudice him by bringing up the nature of their relationship. As Charlie well knew, this was not a topic that came up in ordinary conversation. I was aware that Jimmy already felt sensitive about the sexual nature of our own friendship. At the least, he was reticent to talk about it. I didn't want him to be further intimidated by the knowledge he would be entering a nest of "sexual deviants"—and lesbians besides. I hoped Jimmy wasn't feeling the way I had when Nick took me to that fairy party at Dixon Calder's.

I finally found my voice. "You look lovely this evening, Charlie," I said hoping to gloss over all the awkwardness.

She came over to me and gave me a peck on the cheek. "Hello, Carl."

"That dress becomes you," I said, taking her hand.

"Why, thank you. I would have been here to greet you when you arrived, but I just started my menstrual period." Charlie glanced from me to Jimmy.

I knew Charlie could be outspoken, but she seemed to direct this challenge at Jimmy. Had she taken a dislike to him? Since I was fond of Jimmy, I automatically assumed that everyone else would like him too.

Jimmy stared on in shocked silence, and I sensed his discomfort. I was uncomfortable, too, but it was for his chagrin, not for anything that I was feeling. He must have felt in over his head. My jazz Argonaut did not seem to know what to make of this dangerous island of women. He did not possess maps that charted the unfamiliar feminine seacoast. How could he possibly navigate these shoals and tides with which sea creatures were so intimate that they moved by intuition?

I never knew what Charlie might come out with next. She was often surprising, even abrupt, though I always found her fascinating.

"Oh, Charlie," I said and forced a laugh. "You do like to get a rise out of us."

"But Carl, you're a doctor," Charlie said. "What are we supposed to do? Pretend that nature doesn't affect us?"

Gwen chuckled and said, "Maybe Jimmy isn't used to such frank talk. Will you have a drink, darling?"

"I'll wait till later," Charlie replied. "Please sit down. I've interrupted your conversation." With feline grace she crossed to the other armchair and gracefully settled into it. All eyes were on her, but there was no telling if, from long habit of attracting stares, she simply didn't notice or if she chose to ignore it. Jimmy and I took our seats. Charlie drew a cigarette from a box on the table next to her and lit up. It was no longer shocking to see women smoking, and I was certain that Jimmy was used to seeing this at dances. But the fact that Charlie was smoking now felt to me like she was throwing down another gauntlet.

Jimmy seemed to find his footing and attempted a recovery. Offhandedly, he said, "Larry, the banjo player in our band, says that women have to stay away from work during that time of month." I sensed that Jimmy was only trying to appear nonchalant and conversational, but I winced inwardly.

Charlie blew out a plume of smoke. "Why, that's completely silly."

Gwen came to his rescue. "That's a common misconception, Jimmy. When I was in nursing school, I read a scientific study, written by a woman PhD, that showed conclusively that a woman's manual dexterity and mental concentration are not adversely affected by the menstrual cycle."

Jimmy was still blushing. "I guess Larry can kind of run off at the mouth sometimes," he said. He fumbled in his coat pocket and brought out a pack of cigarettes.

"I think you had it right earlier when you referred to Larry as the crazy banjo player," I said. "From what you've told me, Larry sounds like he has a lot of half-baked ideas. You tell me he's always talking about Freud, but he doesn't seem to understand much about Freud's thought."

Charlie said, "That's not surprising. Even Freud doesn't seem to understand much about Freud's thought. He doesn't even seem to understand the symbolism of that cigar he's always smoking."

I had to laugh. I looked over at Jimmy but couldn't catch his eye as he put away his cigarette package without taking one out. He took a long drink from his Scotch.

"I must agree with you," I said. "Some of Freud's ideas seem farfetched."

"He certainly seems to be unconscious of how wrong he is about women," she added and again I couldn't help laughing.

"One good thing," I said, "is that his writings have made us all more open to talking about sex."

"Yes, I guess we have to give him credit for that," Charlie said. "I'm sure I would not have mentioned lesbianism if he hadn't paved the way. Why, not long ago the very thought of women having sex together was unimaginable. Women were not even thought of as having any sexual feeling."

"But maybe," Gwen said, "this new openness is a double-edged sword. In my grandmother's time, even while I was growing up, romantic friendships were common among girls—and women. That kind of friendship was looked on as noble and uplifting. Of course, back then no one guessed that there might be anything sexual to it. And, I suppose, in many cases there wasn't. I think it's Freud's doing that nearly everything these days is seen in the light of sex."

Charlie spoke up again. "A lot of the spinsters that I knew growing up were not old maids because they couldn't find husbands. They knew perfectly well they had more freedom and opportunity—in a man's world—if they made a career for themselves and took up housekeeping with another woman. Boston marriages, they were called. I remember a number of women couples when I was a girl, and that's how they were referred to. They certainly didn't spend their time taking care of husbands and children. And that's why so many men are terrified of suffragists and lesbians. They are afraid that we women can get along just fine without them, thank you very much. The idea that a female erotic desire doesn't require a man to satisfy it makes men unnecessary—and that threatens them."

"But in recent years," Gwen said, "I've seen the attitude develop that there is something suspicious about close women friendships. You've seen that, too, haven't you, Charlie?"

"Suspicious isn't the word," Charlie said. "They consider it pathological. Remember Krafft-Ebing's ideas. Since women are no longer so submissive, they have to be controlled. So now we are considered sick."

"It seems mighty odd to me," Gwen said, "that these men are so quick to name the illnesses of others, but are completely blind to their own."

I said, "You sound like you're talking about Dr. Gowan." I glanced at Jimmy and he caught my look, gave a soft laugh, and then took another drink of Scotch.

"I guess that's the way the world works," Gwen said. "The mote in the other fellow's eye and the log in your own. I know you don't agree with the Bible, Carl, but there are some bits of wisdom in it. I wonder what flaws we are blind to in ourselves."

"I'm a surgeon, not a scholar, but I've read some of Krafft-Ebing, and he seems to say that the only legitimate sex is that which leads to reproduction—anything that doesn't is pathological. But I've never understood that thinking. Does that mean that every ovulation must lead to pregnancy?"

"No more menstruation," Charlie said with a laugh. "Keep them pregnant and in the kitchen."

"Compared to Krafft-Ebing," I continued, "Freud is much more even-handed. He has, at least, freed our thinking about sex from the act of procreation."

"I've always maintained," Gwen said, "that women can get pregnant without an orgasm, but a man can't reproduce without it. So obviously there are aspects of sex that have nothing to do with making babies."

"I believe," Charlie said, "that the trouble with Freud is that he pretends to be scientific but his ideas are philosophy, or maybe poetic imagination, not science. There is never any way to prove them."

Jimmy had been listening to all this talk in silence with his brow knitted. At Charlie's mention of poetic imagination, he turned toward her with an attentive half-smile.

"Exactly," I said. "Freud has some good ideas, like the unconscious—which is a valuable insight. But much of it is pure conjecture. For example, his theory of the Oedipal complex and castration anxiety. It may be true for him, through his own self-analysis, but not necessarily for everybody else."

Jimmy stepped in. "I haven't read any of his writing, but it sounds to me like you two have just castrated Dr. Freud."

Charlie turned to Jimmy with a surprised look as she seemed to go through a mental reassessment. Then she gave a peel of laughter. It was infectious and we all laughed. "Touché," she said.

I smiled at Jimmy. He smiled back and then turned to look at

Charlie.

"I haven't read all that much of Freud's work either," Charlie said, "but I suspect that somewhere in his writing he associates castration with female menstruation. And menstruation is just one more thing that is wrong with being a woman in our society."

"Good point," I said. "Isn't that one reason why sex between two men is so scandalous in this society? Because it seems to turn at least one of them into a woman. And as you say, in the eyes of our society, there's something wrong with being a woman."

Jimmy looked at me with the astonishment of revelation. "Yes," he said. "That's it." His response came out with such force that we all turned toward him. He kept his eyes fastened on me. Some connection seemed to have flashed through his mind triggering a series of small adjustments like a key moving tumblers in a lock.

I smiled at him wondering if he had come to some understanding of his own reticence about specific sexual acts.

Jimmy smiled back at me and then became self-conscious as his attention slowly shifted to an awareness that the two women were looking at him with curiosity. He turned to Charlie. "I think you're right about that," he said to her. "It makes a lot of sense to me."

I glanced at Charlie and saw that she must have observed that dawn of insight cross Jimmy's face and she was regarding him with renewed interest.

Gwen said, "My guess is that if Freud had been female, his ideas would have come out a lot differently."

"Yes," Charlie said, "women are accused of attacking the natural order of things by wanting to live fuller lives—in other words, to have the opportunities men take for granted. Everyone's heard the arguments. If women are allowed to vote, it will mean an end to marriage and the family and civilization itself. Now we have the vote, and none of that has happened. But we are still considered the weaker sex." She tilted her head back in her chair and placed the back of her hand against her forehead in a mock gesture of fainting.

Gwen said, "I'd like to see a man carry a child to term."

"The rooster crows, but the hen delivers," Jimmy said.

Charlie laughed out loud. "Very good, Jimmy."

"Yes," I said, "woman gives birth. What poor powers we men have compared to that."

"And isn't it peculiar that today men—doctors—are taking over what midwives used to do?" Charlie said.

I looked at Gwen, then turned to Jimmy. "Jimmy, you should hear about Gwen's work with newborns at the hospital. She's doing remarkable things. Tell us how you got started with that, Gwen."

"I was helping a doctor deliver a baby a couple of years ago and this little one was completely blue when it came into the world. The doctor just assumed the baby was beyond help and threw it aside and concentrated on attending to the mother. The infant was showing signs of life and I began massaging it and working with it and before long it began to breathe on its own, and then it let out a wail that startled everyone. The baby made a full recovery and she's now a strong, healthy 2-year-old. But the poor thing would have died if it had been ignored."

I added, "None of the male doctors ever took the initiative that Gwen did. It's just like you said, Charlie. If women are given opportunities, they can do things that the men have never thought of. Jimmy, Gwen is now on a committee responsible for initiating a whole re-examination of the treatment of marginal births. They are starting a new program at the hospital specializing in distressed newborns."

"And premature babies too," Gwen added. "Remember that baby you and I helped deliver just recently? Remember how tiny that little fellow was? I think it's one of the smallest I've ever seen. But it survived somehow. It's something to see the fight for survival in these little ones."

"That's inspiring." Jimmy said. "It sounds like you love your work, Gwen."

"Oh, yes, I do, Jimmy. Why, every time I walk through that nursery at St. Mary's and see all those little tikes I just want to pick each one up and hug it."

"That's terrific," Jimmy said.

"She's a marvel," Charlie said.

"Are you a nurse, too?" Jimmy asked

Charlie laughed. "Heavens no. No Florence Nightingale here. I've never much liked babies or dealing with any of that blood and vomit Gwen has to face." She smiled at Gwen. "I work as a telephone operator." She made an imaginary telephone headset with her thumb and little finger. "Number, please."

Jimmy's fascination with Charlie seemed to be sparked with this new piece of information. "Gosh, what's that like?" he asked.

"Oh, it's pretty routine. We never have a real conversation with our customers, like a lot of people imagine."

"How do you keep all those plug cords and sockets sorted out?" he asked.

"How do you keep all those piano keys sorted out?" she replied.

"Touché," he said, and they both laughed.

"If you do anything long enough, you get pretty good at it," Charlie said. "Besides it's all very well organized."

"How's your work going, Charlie?" I asked.

"Don't ask. We have a new overlord. Horrid little man. He wants to bring in what he calls industrial efficiency experts. But let's not go into that."

Jimmy watched Charlie and must have sensed her distaste for the subject. He glanced at the picture on the wall and quickly said, "I've been wanting to ask you, Charlie. Gwen said you could tell me who painted that picture. Is it Mary Cassatt?"

"Why, yes," Charlie said looking at Jimmy with an expression of evolving respect. "You obviously know something about art."

"I have...I had a friend who was a painter. She liked Mary Cassatt."

"A woman painter? Your friend, I mean."

"Yes." Jimmy didn't say anything more but looked over at the picture.

Charlie studied him for a moment. At last she said, "It has a nice feeling about it, don't you think? It reminds me of Gwen. Look. She's sitting there now with her hand against her jaw and that same thoughtful look on her face. Just like the painting."

We all turned to look at Gwen, who put her hand down in her lap and chuckled. "Charlie, before you came in, Jimmy was telling us about his jazz band."

"I heard you play at the Iverson wedding reception," Charlie said. "You play beautifully."

"Why, thank you. So you were there, too. That was some do, huh?"

"Perhaps a bit overdone. You play jazz also?"

"That's right."

"Jimmy was telling us about the Diggs Monroe Jazz Band," Gwen said, "the group he plays with. What were you saying about Diggs Monroe?"

"He prefers to call us the Diggs Monroe Jazz *Orchestra*. He thinks it sounds more high class."

"I see," Gwen said.

"He's a real whiz-bang booking agent. We're booked through the end of the month and now Diggs is trying to line up some dates between here and Chicago—in college towns—for this fall. Homecoming dances and such. He wants us to work our way back to Chicago so we can hear some Chicago jazz and play some dates back there."

"My, that's ambitious," Gwen said and glanced over at me. "What do you think about all that, Carl?"

She must have had an inkling about our relationship and what Jimmy's departure might mean for me.

"Jimmy's a musician and a musician's got to make music. I think it would be good for him to go to Chicago. It sounds to me like that's the place to hear jazz. Besides, a fellow has to go out and explore the world. Have an adventure."

Charlie laughed. "And if it were a woman you were talking about, people would say she was neglecting her duties to her husband and her children."

"A lot of men would probably say that," I said, "but you wouldn't hear me saying it."

"I'm sorry, Carl. I'm being hard on you fellows tonight, aren't I?" She looked at Jimmy. He shrugged as if to say he hadn't taken offense.

"You've been to Chicago haven't you, Charlie?" Gwen said.

"It's been years and years. I never liked it much. I don't like big cities."

"Charlie grew up in San Francisco," Gwen said to Jimmy.

Charlie remained silent.

Gwen went on, "I went to Chicago when I was a little girl. We went on the train—my whole family. I remember seeing a cat get hit by a truck on a Chicago street. I was walking down the sidewalk with my mother. That poor little animal. I wanted to stay and take care of it, but Mother told me I mustn't touch it because it probably had mange. That spoiled my whole memory of the trip."

"You always were tender-hearted," I said.

"Tell us more about your band," Charlie said. "How long have you been together?"

"About six months. We're still learning a lot of new material so we rehearse most nights. And we're getting busier all the time. We'll be playing at Felix Bagwell's speakeasy next Friday and Saturday night. Say, you two should come on down and hear us there."

"That sounds like fun," Gwen said.

"It must be hard for you and Carl to find time to see each other," Charlie said, looking at Gwen.

Jimmy and I exchanged glances.

"Oh, we manage to get together from time to time," I said.

"Yes, the band doesn't rehearse *every* night," Jimmy said looking at Charlie. Then he glanced at me and quickly looked down at the carpet. I sensed that he felt he had revealed too much.

Charlie regarded him for moment. "Music is a severe muse," she said at last. "Pray that you don't end up like Mozart and die in poverty at 36."

"Yes, but I'm not a composer," Jimmy said.

"You're not?" Charlie said. "I thought that's what jazz is all about. You compose every time you play, don't you? When you improvise."

"Yes, but that's different," Jimmy said.

"Is it?" Charlie asked. "Beethoven and Mozart and many of those old masters left room for improvised cadenzas in their concertos."

"That's true." Jimmy sat quietly for a moment, then added, "Maybe men give birth through the arts." He glanced at Gwen. "But, of course, women can do both." Jimmy gestured toward the picture on the wall, then turned to Charlie. "Look at Mary Cassatt."

She smiled at him.

"How did you ladies meet?" Jimmy asked.

Gwen and Charlie looked at each other and laughed. "I work such a busy schedule at the hospital that I frequently take my day off during the week. So I was downtown buying new stockings one Wednesday and stopped at a little lunch place. And here next to me at the counter was this striking young woman. We chatted a bit during lunch and after she left, I saw that her gloves had fallen under the counter. So I ran after her. Didn't I, Charlie?"

"She invited me over for dinner. Right there on the sidewalk," Charlie said.

"After we'd gotten to know each other, we decided to share an apartment—to save money. But that didn't help you out much, dear, did it? You were living with your aunt for free."

"Nothing is for free with Aunt Inez," Charlie said. "I love her dearly, goodness knows, but she can be rather demanding. She's never married, and after living alone so many years, she's used to having everything her way."

"You certainly see her often enough," Gwen said.

"There is some family obligation there. And the poor dear is getting on in years and she needs help with things. *Without a man around.*" She glanced at Gwen and they both laughed. "I help her keep her finances in order. And she has generously insisted on paying for our maid here. We would have a hard time managing financially without her help. Besides, I usually visit her while you are working, Gwen."

"That's true, dear."

There was a lull in the conversation.

"While you're working on the telephones, do you have men asking you for dates all the time?" Jimmy asked. "I've heard that happens."

"Usually drunks," Charlie said. "But we are supposed to keep talk with customers to a minimum. The supervisors randomly listen in to our calls. Still, the other day some fellow asked me to go to Paris with him."

"You didn't tell me about that," Gwen said. "You should have taken him up on it. Maybe he would have taken both of us. You were in Paris during the War, weren't you, Carl."

"Paris, City of Lights," I said. "Yes, but I was only there briefly—on my way to the front. There was such a strange sense of chaos with war activity everywhere. But it's a beautiful city—what little I was able to see. Maybe that's why it seemed so strange—the contrast between the charm and refinement of the place and all the military presence. I'd like to see it in peacetime. It must be singularly romantic." I glanced over at Jimmy.

Charlie must have been observing me.

"You two *are* in love then," she said with relish, eyeing us both, like a detective who had just caught a suspect revealing a secret.

"Oh, I'm afraid I'm to blame," Gwen apologized. "I've been making conjectures with Charlie for weeks."

"But love has many different meanings," Jimmy said quickly, as if he was embarrassed to be the subject of such a discussion. He avoided my eyes.

"Oh, don't take offense," Charlie said. "It's just that I see it in your eyes. Besides, it's okay. Gwen and I are in love." She looked at Gwen, and Gwen raised her glass. Jimmy looked away. At first I thought maybe he was uncomfortable to think of Gwen and Charlie being intimate. Then I realized that he and I had never actually used the word "love" between us. We had never openly defined our feelings for each other. Was that what was making him uncomfortable?

He looked down at the carpet and said, "But what does love mean? Song lyrics are full of it, but—" he glanced at Charlie, "they don't tell you much."

"There is maternal love, of course," Gwen said, "and familial love."

"And platonic love," Charlie said, "like with Carl and me." She grinned.

"And the love of God," Jimmy said.

"If you believe in God," I added.

"Love of music and art," Jimmy said.

"Love for our fellow human beings," Gwen put in.

"But being *in* love means something different from all of those," Charlie said, trying to lead the conversation back where she began.

"What does being in love mean to you then?" Jimmy asked.

"Oh," Charlie's voice brightened. "To be in love is to be caught in the web of an enigma. Love is a cipher, a riddling sphinx." Her eyes shined. "It is precisely love's mystery that draws us to her."

We were silent a moment pondering Charlie's words.

"What does being in love mean to you, Jimmy?" Gwen asked.

"Being in love…" Jimmy considered. "It's even more difficult to put into words than it is to put into music. And so much music deals with being in love. Let me think." He paused a moment and then a smile crept over his face. "Love is the tonic pull of a chord progression longing to resolve itself."

I watched Jimmy with surprise. He was regarding Charlie, and I saw at once that he was in competition to top her formulation.

"I shall pray that you aren't an Arnold Schoenberg," Charlie said.

Jimmy caught her joke and laughed. "You obviously know something about music," he parroted Charlie's earlier remark to him. She laughed with him.

I didn't get the joke and looked over at Gwen, who had a puzzled look on her face. Jimmy must have noticed and said, "Schoenberg writes what they call atonal music. It sounds disconnected—doesn't seem to move forward like what we're used to hearing."

"Maybe you can play some of it for us one day," I said.

"Carl," Gwen said, "what does being in love mean to you?"

"Oh, I've always liked Aristophanes' story—from the ancient Greeks," I said. "Long, long ago, human beings had four arms and four legs, and two heads, and two sets of genitals. Some of these creatures had two male parts, some two female parts, and some, the hermaphrodites, had male and female genitals. The gods decided this was an awkward arrangement and split all the humans in two so that we came to look like we do today. But the two halves of the original beings longed to be reunited. So those who had once had two sets of male genitals became today's homosexuals searching for their other male half. Lesbians long for their lost female half. And the rest, the hermaphrodites, are heterosexuals searching for their other half of the opposite sex. So I would say that being in love describes the experience we feel upon finding our long-lost other half." I looked at Jimmy and he gave me a quizzical smile.

"Where did you get that tale?" he asked.

"It's in Plato's *Symposium*," I said. "Freud refers to it in his writing, but he doesn't give the whole story. He leaves out the part about two men or two women getting back together. So essentially, he only talks about the hermaphrodites."

Charlie looked at me and laughed. I turned to Gwen and said, "You haven't given us your thoughts yet."

"Yes," Charlie said, "what do *you* think it means to be in love?"

"You poets all make me feel pretty simple-minded," Gwen said. "To me it is a comfort and a joy—simple domestic bliss. For me, it means cooking soup together."

Charlie smiled at her.

We were all silent again for a moment, considering and weighing. I took out my watch to check the time.

"How did we ever get off on that?" Gwen broke the silence.

"We were talking about how romantic the city of Paris is," Charlie laughed.

"And it's a city of excellent food," I added. "Speaking of which, we have a dinner reservation. Is anybody else as hungry as I am?"

While the women went to freshen up and get their wraps, Jimmy and I stood in the living room waiting. He turned to me and said, "I like your friends."

I felt pleased and surprised. "I hope Charlie hasn't put you off," I said, placing my hand on his shoulder.

"No. I find with most folks that I can either charm them or find some way to put up with them. I think that with Charlie, I got her to like me."

"I think you're handling things like a champ."

I felt the urge to kiss him and Jimmy must have felt the same because we both leaned in until our lips touched. At that moment Gwen and Charlie returned, and we felt a moment of embarrassment until Gwen said, "Affection is infectious," and she leaned over and kissed Charlie on the cheek.

The ladies were holding their coats over their arms and I took Gwen's coat to help her on with it while Jimmy did the same for Charlie. Charlie slipped her right arm into her coat, and Jimmy held the cuff of the sleeve closed. A look of irritation came over her face as she struggled to work her hand out through the armhole. With a frown she glanced around at Jimmy just as he released his grip and laughed. Her frown dissolved into laughter. "Oh, Jimmy," she said as all her resistance to his charm seemed to melt away. "You tease." She took hold of the arm he offered and leaned into his shoulder as if to say all is forgiven, we will be friends from now on. I held the front door open as they walked out ahead with Gwen and me following, all of us laughing.

We rather automatically took on the roles of two heterosexual couples. I helped Gwen into the passenger seat, and Jimmy sat with Charlie in the back. It happened by wordless agreement—an implicit understanding that didn't require discussion. Our dinner reservations were at a well-known restaurant downtown, and during dinner I sat next to Gwen, opposite Jimmy and Charlie. We appeared for all the world to be two couples out on the town. Conformity was a comfortable disguise. Then, too, Jimmy and Charlie made such a handsome couple that they turned heads all through the meal.

Besides, we were all getting on well together. Conversation came naturally and we shared stories about ourselves and cracked jokes.

The menu featured trout so Jimmy and I told stories about our fishing expedition. Gwen told Jimmy about growing up on the banks of the Columbia River where she fished for salmon with her dad. Charlie told us that she had been trout fishing a couple of times with Gwen, but they felt uncomfortable as two women out fishing alone. We decided we should all go fishing together sometime.

On Friday evening, Gwen and Charlie went with me to the speakeasy to hear Jimmy play. The band sounded superb, and, hearing them for the first time, the ladies were both impressed. Now it was Charlie's turn to be dumbstruck by the beauty of Jimmy's creation. She sat with her gaze fixed on the band as Jimmy sang and played the piano with them, and the whole world of that saloon moved with the life force of the vibrating music. Jimmy joined us at our table when the band took a break. He told the girls the story about the man who lost his coat, and when Jimmy got to the part about the pockets, Gwen and Charlie and I all laughed until we cried. We had a grand time.

Later, while Charlie sat with her attention glued to the bandstand, Gwen pointed out that we were all tapping our toes to the music. So Gwen and I decided to dance, and I became aware that I felt none of the uneasiness I'd experienced at the Bisby Grange or the country club. Having someone there to dance with, to have easy conversation with, to share the music with—in the guise of coupledom—made the evening new and different, a comfortable pleasure.

After midnight Gwen and Charlie wanted to go home because they both had to work the next day, but they insisted on coming back the next evening since they didn't have to work on Sunday. I took them to their apartment and then came on home. Later, Jimmy showed up at my place in a taxi, as we'd planned.

SIXTEEN

I declined to go to church with Jimmy when he pulled himself out of bed on Sunday morning. Gwen and Charlie and I had taken him to an all-night diner after the band finished up the night before, and we hadn't gotten home until the wee hours. Still I got up and made breakfast for him before dropping him off at the church.

When he got back, he said he was tired and wanted to go back to bed. So I joined him.

Jimmy awoke around 4 in the afternoon, and I was lying awake watching him. He looked at me through his sleep-bleary eyes and said, "Hello, lover man." Then he rolled over to embrace me with one arm and snuggled up against my side. I kissed him gently on the top of his head. He began running his hand along my body, and I reached under the covers and found that he had an erection. We began kissing and I waited to let him initiate, then followed his lead. After mutual masturbation, we lay there quietly for a long time. The weather was hot and we had thrown off all the bedcovers.

Jimmy reached down and said, "What is this called?"

"Which?" I said. "Oh, you mean the foreskin? Prepuce is the medical term."

I was pleased to see Jimmy's curiosity but surprised at his innocence in such matters of anatomy, until it struck me that outside the medical profession these details were seldom discussed. Then it occurred to me that this was an opportunity to help Jimmy understand that his ideas about masculinity and femininity were limiting his sexual expression.

"Prepuce?" he said.

"That's right. There is an analogous prepuce covering the female clitoris. And there is an analog on the clitoris, of this part here—both called the glans." I retracted my foreskin to reveal the helmet-like protuberance with its flared corona. "The name comes from the Latin word for acorn. But ever since I was a kid, I thought it looked like the head of some prehistoric dinosaur."

"Hmm. I can see why," he said. "I've always thought mine looked like an old man with a bald head."

"No two look exactly the same. As a physician, I can vouch for that. And this part right here, this little line of tissue in the back, is called the frenulum. It also has an analogous part below the female clitoris. It's the same name they use for the seam of skin under the tongue." I opened my mouth so Jimmy could look under my tongue. "Some say that the frenulum is the most sensitive part of the penis."

He stroked the area gently with a finger. The sensation made my penis jump.

"So you're saying that the male and female parts are similar?"

"That's right. I've always been fascinated by the way medical books show the embryo developing in the womb. There is a time early on when there is no difference between a female body and a male—before sexual differentiation begins. The illustrations show remarkable parallels when you compare the early stages of growth in the male and female genitals."

"Hmm," Jimmy said again. "The frenulum?"

"Yes. It represents the midline of the body. The centerline of our bilateral symmetry. You know, two arms, two legs, two testicles. I believe that's why we humans have this tendency to think in terms of stark dichotomies, like good and evil, black and white, male and female. We conceive of the world in pairs of opposites. But I believe there is an endless range of grays between the two poles."

"You mean that you think there is no hard and fast difference between male and female?"

"I think the way most of society sees things, the male and female are as different as day and night, but I don't believe that's the way things are in reality."

"I guess I can see what you mean," he said. "In terms of music anyway. I think that's what music is all about. Getting in between words—like love and hate—or beauty and ugliness. Music can express things that are so much more subtle."

"That's it exactly."

"One of the best things about jazz is trying to get in between two notes on the scale—Howard calls them blue notes. Of course, it's more difficult on the piano than on a violin or a trombone."

"I'll bet it is."

"I have to keep trying to find ways to suggest it."

"Yes, there has to be room for something in between. But don't take my word for it. All you have to do is look at nature. Occasionally, she tries an experiment and alters the development of a fetus in the womb, and a person is born with six fingers on one hand—Gwen saw a case like that a while back. Or maybe a boy is born with three testicles."

"Really?" Jimmy said.

"That actually happens sometimes. Or sometimes a female is born with an extra uterus—an extra womb. And I've read about cases where babies are born with ambiguous genitalia—with some male features and some female features. There is a whole array of these midline variations."

"Hmm. Once, I remember my cousin told me they had a mare that gave birth to a foal and they couldn't tell whether it was male or female. Maybe that's what happened there."

"Probably so," I said. "It's not that uncommon."

"So at Gwen and Charlie's place when you said that certain sex acts between men turn one of them into a woman, were you saying that everyone is already part male and part female?"

"Something like that."

Jimmy seemed to be unfolding the realization he'd made the other night. I didn't say anything more, sensing that he needed time to let this discovery grow.

Jimmy examined my penis. "The frenulum," he said. "And the prepuce? Funny words."

"That's the medical Latin. In German they have a funny slang expression for the penis. Sometimes it is called der Schwanz. Literally, it means the tail."

"The tail?" Jimmy laughed and he wagged my Schwanz back and forth. "Is the foreskin sensitive?" He touched it with his fingertips.

"Very sensitive," I replied.

"I guess that's something I'll never know about," Jimmy said, turning from mine to study his own. "So they just cut it off?"

"They usually circumcise males a few days after they're born."

"I've always wondered why my cousin's cock looked so different from mine—the time we did that thing in the hay loft. Why do they do it?"

"Oh, cultural tradition, superstition, ideas about hygiene. Puritanism. Stupidity." We laughed.

"Why do you say Puritanism?"

"They say circumcision diminishes sexual pleasure. And some say sexual pleasure leads man astray from his spiritual nature. I've never understood that. People spend too much time cutting up the universe into the material and the spiritual, the physical and the emotional. A couple more dichotomies there for you. Any good doctor knows the physical and the emotional are all bound up together. Freud acknowledges that. Even Einstein says that matter and energy are different forms of the same thing."

"Hmm." He reflected for a moment. "Do you circumcise babies?"

"No, I refer them to Gowan and Bleeker."

"But why do you still have your prepuce?"

"I guess my father didn't believe in circumcision. I'm not sure. Or maybe he just couldn't bring himself to cut his own son. He was the only doctor in town, so it was him or no one. You know, I've never talked to him about it."

"Is your father's cock like mine? Circumcised?"

"As a matter of fact, he isn't. It's only become widely practiced in America and England in the past generation or so. I've read that it's less common out west here than on the East Coast. Certainly not practiced among American Indians. And in Europe it's seldom done outside the Jewish community. Of course, circumcision is at the heart of Judaism. It was meant to distinguish between God's chosen people and the rest of humankind, the Jewish us and them— another dichotomy. It seems odd to me to base a religion on cutting off part of your cock."

Jimmy cringed and placed his hand over his genitals.

"But as you know, I don't think much of religion."

I reached down and gently pulled Jimmy's hands away from his penis. I took it in my hand and studied it.

"The books say that the Egyptians practiced circumcision long before the Jews. Maybe that's where they picked it up. From the pharaohs. And then, too, in the Islamic world circumcision is common."

I let go and moved my hand slowly across his pelvic girdle and up his flank to his chest. "But the ancient Greeks didn't practice circumcision. As a matter of fact, the Greeks barred Hebrews from competing in their sports because they thought it was indecent to show the glans in public."

"Boy, you sure know a lot about the history of it."

"When I told Gowan that I didn't do circumcisions, he was less than happy with me. He insisted that I should. I had to look up the medical history so I could make my case to him. That was one of our first big disagreements."

"Circumcision," Jimmy said and re-examined his own. "What a strange idea. How did human beings ever think up such a thing?"

"Barbaric, isn't it?" I said. "When you think about it? The human family has not evolved too far from the primordial mud and slime. After all these centuries we are still pretty primitive. Take the War, for example."

We were both quiet for a time.

"Tell me this," he said after a while. "Remember that French champagne we drank that day? When we went fishing. How did you get that bottle back here after the War—to Oregon? With prohibition and all."

"I carried it with me. Smuggled it in my duffel bag wrapped up in clothing. With so many troops coming home from the service, no one checked through all those duffel bags."

"And you saved it all that time?"

"I guess I was saving it for something special." I raised my head to look at him. "Someone special."

Jimmy caught my eye and we looked at each other for a moment before he looked away.

Later we got up and played a game of Halma. Then I made dinner for us. As we ate, Jimmy sat staring off into space, lost in thought.

"What are you thinking about?"

"Oh, nothing in particular." He took a bite.

I watched him for a moment, then asked, "What did you think of Gwen and Charlie?"

He laughed and said, "That Gwen is a real angel, isn't she?"

"I couldn't agree more."

He became thoughtful.

"And Charlie?" I said.

He stared out the window into the back garden.

"You seemed to be fascinated by her."

"Well…"

I waited a moment. "It's okay," I said. "It's all right if you didn't take to her."

"No. It isn't that." He paused.

"You know she is seeing a psychoanalyst?"

Jimmy looked at me with interest. "I've never known anyone who…was doing that."

"Gwen and I convinced her to see an analyst here in town. Charlie had a difficult childhood. Maybe when you get to know her better, she will share her story with you."

"Is that how she knows so much about Freud?"

"That's right." I felt there was something else he wanted to say. "I know she can be outspoken."

"No, I liked that about her." Jimmy paused as if he were struggling to force his feelings into words. "It's just that…She reminded me a little of…of Mary."

"Is that so?" I said, surprised to hear the comparison but even more surprised to hear him mention Mary. I'd been wanting to talk to Jimmy about her for some time, but I'd hesitated to broach the subject. "I mean, never having met Mary…" I left the remark hanging.

Jimmy continued to stare off into another space and time.

"You've been thinking of her a lot lately, haven't you?"

He took a deep breath. "I guess so."

"Have you tried to contact her? Since that night?"

He shook his head no, without looking my way.

"Do you…miss her?"

He glanced at me and looked away. "Oh…I suppose I do…somehow."

I watched him for a moment, trying to make out his thoughts. He took a sip of his coffee and didn't look at me.

My old doubts and fears rose up. "You're not having second thoughts, are you? About us?"

Jimmy looked over at me with surprise. "It's not like that at all." That put my mind at ease and I felt a twinge of shame for asking. "It's just that…Mary was such an interesting person—and we knew each other…we were friends for a long time. I'm just sad that things ended the way they did."

I remember him assuring me that he had given up on the idea of marriage. Have faith in him, I told myself, and a notion emerged from my misgivings. "Maybe you need to look her up."

He looked at me in disbelief. "Why?" He had a troubled expression. "What is there for us to talk about?"

"Just to…lay things to rest. So you don't have bad feelings… lingering."

He remained silent.

"For your own peace of mind." We looked at each other for a moment. Then he turned back to the window.

"I may not believe in religion, Jimmy, but I do believe in human forgiveness."

I was betting that if he talked to her again he would see there was nothing substantial between them. After all the time Jimmy and I had spent together, I wanted to believe that was true. I had to go on trusting him.

Finally, he heaved a sigh and without looking at me he said, "You may have a point there."

"You're not angry with me for bringing it up, are you?"

Jimmy turned to me. "Not a chance. You're the best friend I've got. I just have to think things through."

After dinner, Jimmy suggested we take in a movie and we dressed and went out to a Chaplin film.

A few days later he told me that he had tried to telephone Mary and her cousin told him that she had gone back to live with her family in Chicago.

SEVENTEEN

As August passed, Jimmy's plans to go to Chicago with the band began to firm up. Diggs had been a fraternity man when he was in school in southern California and he was working his fraternity connections for all they were worth. They would drive back to Minneapolis for a homecoming dance in October, stopping at college fraternity houses to play for dances along the way. Then they would go on to Chicago where Diggs thought he had a fancy sorority dance in line.

The more time Jimmy and I spent together, the more inconvenient it became getting Jimmy to and from my house and trying to keep his comings and goings from notice by the band or by Joe Locke. Finally, one Sunday afternoon I asked if he wanted to move in with me. There was a single large bedroom upstairs that I only used for storage—more than enough room for Jimmy's belongings. I offered to let him have the room for free—which, of course, was less than he was paying Mrs. Burroughs. That way he could save up money for his trip to Chicago and when he left town, he could just leave all his gear stored upstairs. And he would have somewhere to come home to when he returned. At least, I hoped that Jimmy would be coming back—would want to come back—in spite of his dreams of a musical career in the East.

Jimmy hesitated. He liked his room at the boarding house, he said, and the independence and solitude it afforded him. He insisted that he needed to be alone after playing with the band. I pointed out that he would have the whole house to himself while I was at work. Jimmy countered that my place was out of the way and the trolley out here took too long.

"Think about it during the next few weeks," I told him and we left it at that.

Early in September, Gowan said he needed to speak to me privately. My first thought was that he wanted to press me on joining the Klan, but there was a seriousness in his tone that concerned me. I followed him into his office and he closed the door.

"Have a seat," he said as he walked around behind his desk and sat down.

"Carl, you've done good work over the past couple of years since you've been here with us. You know we appreciate your contributions to the clinic. And you've earned an impressive reputation in the community—why, I've had numerous people tell me what a good job you did on that vascular case a while back—that fellow who tried to commit suicide." He paused and leaned back in his chair. "So I thought it was a little peculiar when I got a call late yesterday from a lady named Minnie Mitchell. I believe she is a neighbor of yours."

"Yes, around the corner," I said. "I hire her son to mow my lawn. He's also been a patient of mine."

"That's what she telephoned me about, Carl. It seems she doesn't want you examining her son." He looked at me squarely.

A dozen thoughts began racing through my mind.

"She had an strange story to relate. Seems her boy saw two men kissing through a window at your house—you and another man, the boy claims—passionate kissing, I gather. It sounds to me like a case of overheated imagination on Mrs. Mitchell's part—or the boy's. But she was pretty irate and I thought you should know about it."

At first I was so surprised that I couldn't put the words in any perspective. It was as if the boundary between the private world of dreams and world of everyday life had been breached. My mind reeled. But Gowan's comments demanded a response. I tried to maintain a flat exterior to cover my confusion. My rational mind, meanwhile, searched for something that would sound reasonable and calm. I grasped at the first response that came to mind.

"There must have been some misunderstanding," I said. "I've had a friend staying with me. He's renting my upstairs room." It was not strictly true that Jimmy was renting a room—not yet, anyway— still I felt I was not bending the facts by much. "But I don't know what Clark could have seen that gave him such an impression." I immediately experienced a twinge of guilt at the implication that the Mitchell boy might be lying. I quickly added, "Maybe he simply misinterpreted something quite innocent."

"What sort of boy is this kid? Clark is his name?"

"He seems like a nice enough boy to me. He does a good job mowing the lawn."

"He's not an artistic type, is he?" Gowan's suggestion was clear to me.

"I don't think so. He wanted to play football at his school last year so I gave him a physical exam. He seemed like a pretty regular kid to me."

"What about Mrs. Mitchell? How well do you know her?"

"I don't know her well. Just a nodding acquaintance. I've heard from neighbors that she's a bit of a neighborhood busybody."

"Can you talk to her? Maybe just a little neighborly chat would clear things up. It's just that this doesn't look good for the clinic if rumors about you are going around."

"Sure, I understand. I'll talk to her."

"Meanwhile, I'll take the appointment for Clark's physical exam—just to avoid any problems. I think this should be the end of it."

"Okay." I got up to leave but when I got to the door, Gowan stopped me with a question.

"Oh, Carl. Tell me, are you dating anyone these days?"

His question caught me off guard. Since I had been dancing

with Gwen at that speakeasy a while back, she was the first woman who came to mind.

"I've been seeing a nurse who works…" I was about to say "at St. Mary's," but caught myself just in time and said, "…here in town."

"It's nice to keep things in the profession. I'm sure being a bachelor has both its advantages and its disadvantages." His remark made its point.

"Yes, Dr. Gowan, you're right about that." I laughed as if he had made a joke. Then I looked at my watch. "I have an appointment at 11. Was there anything further?"

"That's all. Just remember: marriage and family are the foundation of our great American civilization. Would you ask Vivian to send in my next patient? Thanks, Carl."

I left his office with a bad feeling in my stomach.

EIGHTEEN

That evening Jimmy and I ate dinner at a favorite cafe and then he went off to rehearsal. As much as I wanted to, I was careful not to say anything to Jimmy about my talk with Gowan. I felt it needed to percolate through my mind for a while so I could suggest some course of action to Jimmy when I did bring it up.

Back home, I sat on my front porch trying to read a medical book, but my mind kept drifting off to Gowan's remarks. It was a pleasant evening, and I would have been enjoying the breeze that was stirring away the heat of the day, had I not been preoccupied by worries about Minnie and Clark Mitchell and how to deal with them.

"Hey, Carl," a voice brought me out of my thoughts. It was Tom Harris. He was coming up the front walk, dressed in his shirtsleeves with his vest unbuttoned.

I was glad to see Tom. We hadn't had much opportunity to talk lately and then only briefly. I greeted him as he mounted the steps to the porch. "Have a seat." I indicated the other wicker chair as I laid my book down.

"Don't mind if I do. I came over to ask if I could borrow your edger. My grass is getting a bit scruffy along the sidewalk."

"Sure. The edger's out in the garage. But sit a spell first. Tell me what news I've been missing."

He settled into the chair.

"Gosh, Carl, if you would read the paper once in a while instead of keeping your nose in a book all the time…. You're going to put us out of business." He straightened his thick glasses, and let out a sigh. "It looks like Vice President-, I mean, President Coolidge is planning to keep on with Harding's policies. And I suppose you haven't heard about the inflation in Germany."

I indicated that I hadn't.

"Since the French reoccupied the Ruhr early this year, the German mark has continued to plummet. Today it takes about 200,000 marks to buy one US dollar."

"My word," I said. I thought of Heinrich and Detlef and wondered how a person could possibly manage in such an economy. "I have some friends over there. I must write them a letter and see how they're doing."

"Then there was this odd story about the new prime minister of Italy—let me see, what's his name?—Mussolini. It seems he ordered an invasion of the Greek island of Corfu after an Italian general was killed on Greek soil. The general had been working with an international commission on a boundary dispute. The scandal of it was that a number of Armenian refugees were killed in the bombardment, a large number of them children."

"What a pity," I said, shaking my head. "Don't we ever learn?" We sat in silence for a moment. "Say, anything new about the Ku Klux Klan?"

"They sure are attracting a lot of interest. Personally, I think a few people are just using the Klan organization and some sensitive local issues to get themselves into positions of power with a comfortable salary. Since the Compulsory Education Act passed, the Klan leaders seem to be making hay with the Catholic school issue."

"My friend Gwen told me that the Catholic bishops were fighting the new law in court."

"Yes, that seems to be the plan. The bishops met in Seattle a while back to discuss the issue and now they are raising funds for a legal challenge. So now the Klan is spreading a lot of nonsense about Papists and Jesuits. They've been bringing some well-known speakers in from out of town, and they've been drawing big crowds to their lectures."

"But I've never understood. What do they have against Catholics?"

"You know there's no explaining irrational hatreds," Tom said. "The Klan is just playing on the fears of foreign influence by making everyone think that all children have to go to American public schools or they will end up becoming Papists—or Bolsheviks. You know yourself from working with the College of Surgeons and that Catholic Hospital Association how riled up the locals have gotten about outside influence. In my opinion, it's all absurd, but you know how easily people are taken in."

"That's the truth," I said.

"The thing is that since the Klan operates as a secret society, it's hard to get an accurate accounting of how many people have actually joined up. I've been doing some investigating for a possible news story and I can tell you that some important members of the business community are members. I wouldn't tell just anybody, but I thought I should let you know—from a professional standpoint— about a druggist named Haskell, Lloyd Haskell, who is an active member. And a number of city officials, including a number of policemen, especially one named Bateson, a plainclothes vice officer. I wouldn't go around making disparaging remarks lightly."

"You know, Gowan asked me to join the Klan a while back. He told me the same thing, that a lot of prominent men—pillars of the community—are joining up, so I should too. That's worrisome."

"Yes, it is. Why, in Oklahoma the governor went so far as to declare martial law in parts of the state in order to clamp down on Klan violence and investigate their corruption. Boy, these are some crazy times we live in."

"I'll go along with that."

Tom and I were quiet for a moment. He glanced about the porch as if making an assessment. "This is a great front porch you've got here, Carl." He looked up and examined the porch ceiling and the broad arch across the front. "I keep thinking we should enlarge ours."

A couple of pedestrians strolled past on the sidewalk. A breeze stirred the pages of my book and I reached down and folded it closed.

"Nice weather we're having," he remarked.

"It sure is," I said. "How's your family?"

"Oh, fine. We're all fine. Young Will starts kindergarten this fall and he's excited about that. Rachel's full of mischief. What a handful. She keeps Polly on the run."

"They're sure swell kids, Tom."

"Yes. How about you? How's your work?"

"To tell you the truth, things have been better." I let out a sigh and tried to decide how much I could say to him. "We've been awfully busy…but that's nothing new." I paused. "Tell me, how well do you know the Mitchells around the corner? Clarence and Minnie?"

"I'm glad you asked. Polly told me an odd story recently. I guess there's been some neighborhood gossip. You must have heard something, too, or you wouldn't be asking, huh?" Tom looked at me, his eyes searching me out.

I looked away and gazed out across the street where the shadows were growing longer as the sun descended. "Christ, are all the neighbors talking about this?" I sighed. "Let me tell you what happened at work today. Gowan told me privately that he'd gotten a phone call from Minnie Mitchell. She doesn't want me to give her son Clark his sports physical this year. Apparently, Clark saw something over here while he was mowing my lawn…." I glanced over at Tom. "Tell me what you heard."

He looked concerned. "Maude Williams, next door, stopped Polly while she was walking the kids to the park. Apparently, Maude was irate with Minnie Mitchell. Took Polly aside and told her that busybody Minnie Mitchell came over and knocked on her door to spread a story that Clark saw two men kissing through a window at your house here—one day while he was mowing the lawn. I don't think there is any love lost between Maude and Minnie Mitchell."

I kept my eyes on the cumulus clouds near the horizon. "That's pretty much the same story Bob Gowan told me." I paused to collect my thoughts. "Tom, we've known each other for a long time. May I be candid with you?"

"Of course. You know I've always had the utmost respect for you."

"You've been around the block. I'm sure you've seen all manner of things in the newspaper business. Goodness knows, I do as a doctor. Weren't you in the Navy before the War? You must have known men who developed some close friendships during that time."

"I did."

"I'm sure it's no surprise to you that there are some men who prefer the company of men to the company of women. I don't mean just drinking and sports—men's clubs and that sort of thing." This made me feel supremely uncomfortable. How would Tom react? The consequences mattered to me. I valued his friendship. I paused and remembered Charlie casually mentioning lesbianism and her menstrual period when she first met Jimmy. Her brashness was not my style. Sharing secret knowledge in polite society. The private parts of our lives that should be kept private. I forced myself to continue. "I mean sexually."

"I know what you're saying, Carl." His voice was calm and matter of fact.

"You know I'm not married…"

"The fact that you are still single has not escaped my notice. I believe I understand what you're trying to say. You needn't go any further." Tom glanced at me and then turned his gaze back onto Elgin Street. "Yes, I knew all kinds of fellas in the Navy. I knew lots of yahoos who took their pleasure anywhere they could get it…from anyone who would give it to them, male or female. Then, too, I knew one fellow in the Navy—a fine sailor—he was like you're saying. He had a buddy, another sailor, that he was close friends with. I'd always see them together whenever they weren't on duty. He was a real decent fellow and he always did good work. It took me a while to get used to the fact that he was different, but we got to know each other and we got along well. Even got to be pretty good friends. And I respected him for being a good sailor. I decided it didn't matter what he did in private."

We sat quietly for a moment. I was relieved, and at the same time I felt a touch of guilt in doubting Tom's loyalty to our friendship.

He continued, "It's nothing to me what another man does for his pleasure. As long as he doesn't hurt anyone." I sensed Tom turning to look at me, but I couldn't turn my eyes to face him.

I kept watching the light change in the evening sky. "Thanks, Tom…You see…I've gotten to know this fellow, Jimmy…he's a musician. We've been getting to know each other for a few months now. For the first time in a long while, I've started to believe that it's possible for me to be truly happy. You know what I mean? Maybe it was like that when you first got to know Polly. I feel this enormous sense of relief…. And now all of a sudden there is all this gossip….I don't know how to respond."

"I've noticed the taxicabs coming by late at night. And I've seen you leaving in the morning sometimes with someone in your car. People notice things like that, and if they can't explain them, their imaginations get carried away."

"I told Bob Gowan today that Jimmy was renting a room from me. Jimmy and I have talked about that as a possibility, but he hasn't agreed on anything definite. Today with Gowan, it just popped into my mind as an explanation on the spur of the moment. Maybe if I made that clear to the neighbors…if it was understood that he was renting a room from me, this would all die down."

"That's possible, Carl. Sometimes if you give people something else to believe, they will accept the new explanation rather than some boogieman they've created in their minds. I've seen that sort of thing work in the newspaper business."

"Yes, and sometimes if you confront someone, come face to face with them, they will back down. Gossiping behind your back is one thing. But when they are forced to look you in the eye, their house of cards falls apart. Maybe…. Hmm." I began to feel a little less agitated. I glanced over at Tom.

He looked at me and said, "That's certainly better than sitting back and letting the tongues wag."

I considered this for a moment. Maybe my predicament was not hopeless.

Then Tom broke the silence. "You know, Carl, if I can be frank with you, the best way to protect yourself would be to arrange a marriage for yourself."

I shifted my weight in the chair and the wicker creaked.

"A marriage of convenience," Tom said.

"Hmm." I didn't know how to respond to this suggestion.

"Mull it over for a while. Meanwhile, I can tell you this about the Mitchells. Minnie Mitchell is a devout Baptist. I'm sure she believes marriage is the be all and end all. Clarence isn't religious. I don't know if he's seen the inside of a church since I've known him. So he probably doesn't give a whit one way or the other."

"Did I tell you that my friend Gwen thinks Minnie Mitchell has friends in the women's auxiliary of the Klan?"

He gave a whistle of surprise. "No, you didn't." He shook his head. "That's not good." He considered this for a time. "Let me add one more thought about marriage. If the neighbor women are gossiping, there's nothing like a wedding engagement to change the subject of the gossip. Everyone loves a scoop, huh? And you know, some engagements can go on for years." Tom gave a little chuckle, then winked at me. We sat in silence for a few moments looking out on the neighborhood. At last he said, "I'd better get back." He got up from his chair.

"Let me get that lawn edger for you," I said and led him to the garage. I thanked him for his advice and for being so open with me. "My mind is a little more at ease now."

After he left though, I sat on the porch for a long time watching the gathering dusk and the passing flight of a flock of crows.

NINETEEN

The next day I arranged to see Jimmy for coffee when I got off work. We met at a small cafe downtown where we took a table by ourselves at the back of the room. I listened while Jimmy raved about the dance they had played the night before. I waited for his excitement to unwind. But then he wanted to tell me the news that Diggs had confirmed a date to play in Madison, Wisconsin, in October on their way to Chicago.

Finally, I told him there was something we had to discuss. I described my encounter with Gowan and his story about Clark Mitchell seeing something while he was mowing the lawn. "He claims he saw two men kissing."

Jimmy was so focused on his plans for the trip to Chicago that he didn't seem to understand the seriousness of the matter until I told him that Clark's mother didn't want me to give her son a medical exam ever again.

"She's told some of the neighbors. I don't know how far this could go, but the way people gossip, it's possible this could hurt my medical practice." I gave Jimmy a moment to absorb the impact. He must have experienced some confusion trying to put all the pieces together. What had been a tender, intimate sharing between the two of us was now twisted into a malignant concern by others who had no business ever knowing about our private lives. And being newly in love, Jimmy could not reconcile his personal joy with the disgust that the outside world saw in what to us was perfectly natural and beautiful. All these conflicting feelings played out across Jimmy's face as I watched him. He sat there and slowly shook his head and then heaved a sigh.

"Oh, boy," he said and looked at me squarely. "So what are we gonna do?"

I was relieved to hear that there was still a "we" in Jimmy's mind as the situation began to sink in.

"I talked to my neighbor Tom Harris and he says we should resort to diversionary tactics."

"You talked to him about us?" Jimmy said.

"It's okay. Calm down. Tom is an old friend. I delivered one of his kids. Besides, he's a newsman and he's not easily shocked like a lot of people. Anyway, he'd already heard the story from his wife. She heard it from Mrs. Williams next door. We can't stop people from gossiping, but we can give them something different to talk about."

I paused to let Jimmy take this in. He was still shaking his head slowly.

"Damn, what if this gets back to the band?" he muttered to himself. The depth of Jimmy's concern was apparent now. I knew he saw the difficulties of our predicament and I had his full attention.

"Here's what I think we should do: Remember how we talked about you moving your stuff into my place? I hope you'll reconsider. We'll go over and pay a visit to the Mitchells, you and me together. I'll introduce you as my boarder and tell them that you have been renting the upstairs room, but just until you leave for Chicago. I'm betting that will explain to them why you are always at my house. Then I'll announce that I am engaged to be married."

"What?"

Jimmy's surprise startled me. Then I laughed.

"Oh, no, don't get the wrong idea. I'll just put out the story. Like Tom Harris said, some people are engaged for years before they get married. I can ask Gwen if she'll pose as my fiancée. I thought I'd try to contact her this evening."

That idea brought a laugh from Jimmy. Then we were both

quiet for a moment, Jimmy thinking it through while I watched his expression.

A smile crept across his face. "And you've been telling me all along that I should give up on the idea of marriage."

"I'm not blind to the irony there."

"But do you think this will work? Are they going to stop thinking about...about you and me..." he looked around to be sure no one could hear, "kissing...just like that?"

"I don't know," I said. "But maybe if we surprise them by confronting them face to face, we'll at least make them recognize that we're just people—not some kind of monsters. And I believe Tom Harris is right. If we give people something else to talk about, we can at least change the subject. Besides, I think Minnie Mitchell is the only one we need to worry about. Tom says she's on the religious side. And I know she has some connections with the Klan. But not Clarence—on both those counts. He's pretty easygoing, according to Tom, and that's been my experience, as little as I've gotten to know the man. And I've known Clark for a couple of years and I think he is a fairly decent kid."

Jimmy didn't seem convinced.

"I'm thinking you should move your things into my house as soon as possible. What do you think?"

"I have been thinking over your offer. I've got to do something with all my stuff before I leave."

"That way the neighbors will know our story is true. How soon could you make arrangements to move? Is this Saturday too soon? I know it's short notice, but.... Say, maybe I could even ask Clark Mitchell to help us out—that way Minnie Mitchell will know all about it."

Jimmy seemed to be mulling over the possibilities. "Yeah, the band is thinking of leaving for Chicago at the beginning of October. So I need to make some plans soon. I'll talk to Mrs. Burroughs tonight." He looked concerned and doubtful.

"Jimmy, I think this all might work. At any rate, we can't just sit back and let the neighbors gossip. Like Tom Harris said to me, there is nothing better to change the gossip than rumors of a wedding."

Jimmy still appeared troubled. "I don't feel too keen on the idea of talking to your neighbors."

"But Jimmy, you're a performer. You can charm the socks off them."

He looked up at me and put on a brave smile, but I had the feeling that he was not completely convinced that the plan was feasible.

TWENTY

Jimmy moved into my house as planned on Saturday. We decided that he would have some of the band members help him move his belongings. That way, we calculated, when he had them drop him off after the band played, they would know the situation.

I also talked to the Mitchells about hiring Clark to help us move in "my renter" on Saturday. Clarence Mitchell met me with a cheerful greeting at their front door, and after I made my request, he asked me to wait there on the porch while he talked with Mrs. Mitchell. Subdued but intense voices came through the screen door from the back of the house, but I couldn't make out what was being said. A moment later Clarence returned and told me that Clark was busy that day. I suspected it was an excuse, but I was relieved to have gotten my message out there.

Jimmy engaged a professional piano mover to bring the piano on the following Monday. I suggested that when it arrived Jimmy should leave the piano in my living room so he would feel more like he had the run of the house. I didn't want him feeling that he could only use the bedroom upstairs. Besides, we were not sure the piano would fit up the stairway.

Howard offered to drive his car, and Larry volunteered to help Jimmy make the move. We met at the boarding house Saturday morning. I drove my Ford to provide a second vehicle for hauling, and we all helped carry things down from Jimmy's room. Between the two autos, it took a couple of trips across town. I made sure my route took me past the Mitchells' house each time.

After we finished moving everything, I offered the musicians root beer and sandwiches that Joe Locke had left in the refrigerator for the occasion. We sat around the living room and ate while we listened to phonograph records on Jimmy's recently transported Victrola, which we decided to leave in the living room next to mine. Larry seemed to linger over the Tuke picture hanging over the Victrolas. Was that a hint of a smirk?

Howard was full of talk about the impending trip to Chicago. Larry thought it would be much easier to get alcohol there. He told us to keep it under our hats, but he'd found a druggist here in town—a fellow named Lloyd Haskell—who would sell him bottled liquor on the sly. I remembered hearing that name from Tom Harris and others. Howard had a cousin who lived in Chicago and knew the territory. "You're probably right about Chicago booze, Larry. I hear it's a pretty wild town."

Larry said he'd never been there, but he had big plans. "The first thing I want to do when we get to Chicago," Larry said, "is go to one of those high-toned whorehouses. Like you were saying the other night, Howard."

"Take it easy," Howard said with a laugh.

"Aw, I can handle myself," Larry said. "But I hear you've gotta be careful. You gotta get those whores when they're nice and young, you know, or they aren't any good. And especially if you get an old whore who's real loose in the pussy." I wondered if Larry was trying to impress me because I had an MD after my name. "Then you have to use her butthole because it's tighter. Isn't that so, Howard? That's what I heard. Do they charge extra to let you fuck their butt?"

Jimmy and I glanced at each other, while Larry, as if to get affirmation for his four-flushing, turned from Howard to Jimmy to me. Larry noticed me watching him notice our exchange. Then Jimmy quickly looked away and down at the carpet, fearing, I suspected, that Larry or Howard might catch us trading glances. Larry stared at me for a moment and I sensed in that instant he had intuited something of the relationship between Jimmy and me.

Then Howard, who had been gazing out the window, as if to discount Larry's talk, gave Larry a cool, sidelong glance and said, "I wouldn't know, Larry. And I don't think you know what you're talking about either." There was a brief and awkward silence. Howard took a long drink from his root beer.

"I understand that there is some outstanding architecture to see in Chicago," I said. No one seemed to know how to respond to my comment—maybe the awkward tension made everyone reluctant to speak. Jimmy jumped in quickly to say he was looking forward to seeing all of the great Negro bands in Chicago. The other two agreed. They began to name bands they had heard on records and specific performances by different players. Jimmy got up and put on one of the records. Soon, the brief rift was forgotten, and they were all excited and full of anticipation again.

Twenty One

I phoned Gwen and we ended up getting together Monday afternoon for coffee. After letting her know about Jimmy moving in with me, I told her about Gowan and the rumors, and then about the plans for diverting attention. While she was amused at the prospect of posing as my fiancée, she expressed grave concern about my career, since this was such a small community. She had other concerns, as well, which had to do with the etiquette of engagements. First of all, there was the engagement ring—usually a diamond, she laughed. She said she didn't care about having a ring, but it was customary. Then there was the protocol of contacting the parents and sending out announcements and notifying the newspaper.

"Couldn't I just tell the neighbors and leave it at that?" I asked.

"Aren't you going to tell Dr. Gowan, too?" she said. "And he knows your father."

"Holy smoke. I hadn't considered any of that." This was, indeed, a hornets' nest that I hadn't anticipated stirring up.

Gwen said she would discuss the matter with Charlie, because with her society background and sense of etiquette, Charlie would be better qualified to advise us on how best to handle the details of such a delicate social situation. I was anxious to devise a plan of action soon, so I invited Gwen and Charlie to join Jimmy and me at my place for dinner the next evening to discuss the whole situation.

The next evening, over another one of Joe Locke's splendid meals, Jimmy and I expressed our anxiety about our prospects and our impatience to work out a plan. Charlie, somewhat amused at our calamity, had brought her etiquette book and throughout dinner we went over the standard protocols for a wedding engagement.

"It says here," Charlie began, "that the first thing you need to do, Carl, is to ask the consent of Gwen's father."

Gwen and I exchanged glances.

Charlie continued, "Then, once the father of the bride accepts the engagement, the groom's parents are supposed to call on the parents of the bride-to-be within twenty-four hours."

"Oh, goodness," Gwen exclaimed.

"With both parents living in different parts of the state, I suppose allowances could be made," Charlie said.

"My word, no wonder I detest social conventions," I said.

Charlie continued reading silently. Then she said, "The announcement of the engagement should be made by the parents of the bride in your hometown, Gwen. The couple should contact relatives and friends to let them know about the engagement. You're supposed to ask them not to tell anyone until the date for the announcement. That's not likely." She laughed. "In my experience by the time of the formal announcement, most everybody close to the couple already knows. But the parents must be informed first. That only makes sense."

"Yes, that sounds right to me," Gwen said.

I couldn't imagine telling my parents that Gwen and I were going to be married. "Hmm," I said. I was beginning to understand just how involved this was.

Charlie continued to peruse the text. "Oh, here, listen to this," she said with a smile. "'The celebration of an engagement must not take place if a death has recently befallen one of the families. In such cases a discrete announcement may be made to family members and close friends.'"

"No," I said, "we cannot kill off one of the parents in order to keep this little masquerade under our hats."

Everyone laughed.

Charlie went on to summarize customs for contacting the newspapers and sending formal announcements.

Gwen said, "We could tell a few close friends informally, but there doesn't seem to be any way around consulting our parents."

"I guess not," I said. "Hmm." I thought of my father and then of Gowan and I became uncomfortable imagining the fuss at my office.

Charlie looked up from the book. "What about a long engagement? You could say that you want to wait till you can buy a larger house—because you want to have a big family." Charlie gave us a sly look.

Again, Gwen and I exchanged glances and then we both laughed.

Then Gwen looked at me seriously. "Carl, if you want to go through with this, here is my suggestion. We will have to visit my parents first so you can talk to Daddy. We could leave early some morning and be back by evening, so that part needn't be much trouble."

"That sounds reasonable," I said.

"Oh, you know, Mama will just be thrilled," Gwen said. "What about telling your parents?"

"How about just writing them a letter?" I said.

"I believe you two must go visit Carl's family too," Charlie said. "But maybe that can be put off till a convenient time, since they live so far away. I think a phone call or letter will be acceptable. Sometime after that, the parents can all arrange to meet. Besides, it's not like your families are in the social register."

"Gosh, this is a lot of bother," Jimmy said. He had been observing from the end of the table.

"You're telling me," I said.

He looked troubled.

I sensed that he was beginning to feel like a fifth wheel. In an effort to reassure him, I said, "Look at it this way. You're not losing a boyfriend, you're gaining some in-laws. We're lucky to have such good friends as Gwenyfred and Charlene."

A tentative smile crept over Jimmy's face.

Charlie chuckled.

"Carl, you rat," Gwen said. "You weren't supposed to tell anyone my full name."

"Gwenyfred?" Jimmy said and laughed.

Gwen leaned over and gave Jimmy a little swat on the arm. "See what you've started, Carl?" she said, looking at me.

"Oh my," Charlie said. "It's their first lovers' quarrel."

"To get back to the subject at hand," I said, "my main concern is for Jimmy and me to talk to the Mitchells as soon as possible. This coming Sunday is our plan. Is there any reason we can't tell them that Gwen and I plan to marry? Nothing in the book seems to indicate that the engagement has to be kept in strict secrecy until a formal announcement."

Charlie agreed but thought it would be best to telephone both parents right away and tell them.

Gwen said, "If Minnie Mitchell knows Lotie members out near the farm, word will get around."

"Maybe we could telephone our parents on Sunday afternoon," I suggested.

"Yes, I think that's a good plan," Gwen said. "And then we can drive out to visit my folks on my next day off." Then she turned to me with a coy smile and said, "Now, about the engagement ring…"

"I thought you said you didn't care about a ring," I protested.

"I'm just joking," Gwen said. "But that *is* important to other women, having a ring to show off."

"That's true, Carl," Charlie said. "I can't tell you what a fuss girls make about the ring with their friends and the people they work with."

"So is it settled?" I asked. "Are we going to go through with this?" I looked around the table. "And tell our parents…and the Mitchells, and Gowan, and everybody? Is this all right with all of you?" We all looked from one to another, with a sudden solemn understanding that we were on the verge of a serious decision. "Do we agree that Gwen and I will each telephone our parents on Sunday?"

"Carl, you're one of my best and oldest friends," Gwen said, "and I'm concerned for your career. I'm happy to do anything I can to help you out."

"I'm with Gwenyfred," Charlie proclaimed.

Gwen turned to Charlie and made a gruff face. "Charlene. Please."

"I'm sorry, Gwen, dear," Charlie said. "I guess I'm just jealous."

Jimmy laughed and jumped up from the table and began to sing,

"Dun tah-dah daah. Dun tah-dah *daah*…

Dun tah-dah daaah dah,

De dum dum dum dum…"

As I recognized Mendelssohn's "Wedding March," I groaned, and Gwen and Charlie both laughed.

"Let me propose a toast to the betrothed couple," Jimmy said and raised his glass. We all drank. "And to Fred and Charlie," he added, raising his glass again.

"Jimmy. Not you, too," Gwen protested. "Please, honey, it's Gwen."

"Furthermore," Jimmy said, "I propose that we seal the engagement by teaching you ladies to play Halma."

"That's a grand idea," I said.

"This gathering has gotten entirely too serious," Jimmy said. "We need some levity around here. This is an engagement celebration, not a funeral." He went to the living room and put on a phonograph record.

Gwen and Charlie danced together while I took Jimmy in my arms and danced, too. Then we set up a card table and got out the Halma set. As he began arranging the playing pieces, Jimmy said to himself, "I keep feeling like I'm forgetting something." I laughed and looked at him with a knowing smile. When he looked up at me, the same smile slowly spread across his face. We both laughed. Gwen and Charlie noticed this exchange but must have sensed its intimate nature and said nothing.

Charlie said she vaguely remembered playing Halma from childhood. Gwen had never seen it before. So we showed them how to play and the Halma game took our minds off the tangle of engagement plans for a short while. Then a wedding-related question arose. Charlie proposed that the only real solution to the whole thing was for Gwen and me to simply go ahead and marry. We all looked at each other and there was a shocked silence.

"Otherwise," she said, "your lives will become nothing but a series of lies and deceptions."

Then Jimmy cracked a joke to keep us all from becoming serious again. But by then we had forgotten whose turn it was.

When Jimmy and I drove the ladies home around 10, a hundred questions still hung in the air. Jimmy seemed disinclined to talk as we drove home. As we were getting ready for bed, he was still quiet. I could sense his uneasiness.

"What is it, Jimmy?"

"I've become a big problem for you, haven't I?"

"It isn't you that's the problem, Jimmy. It's everyone else that's the problem. The neighbors. The society."

I put my arms around him and held him close to me. "Do you know how much you mean to me, Jimmy? More than I can say. Remember that. Somehow this will all work out." We relaxed our embrace and I sat on the bed and began taking my shoes off. Jimmy began loosening his tie.

Trying to stay upbeat, I said, "Maybe this will all blow over while you are in Chicago with the band."

"And what about Chicago?" Jimmy asked. We looked at each other. This was the first time we had directly spoken of our impending separation.

"That's a question we don't know the answer to, do we?" I said.

Jimmy removed his tie and sat down on the bed next to me with a sigh.

"Look, Jimmy," I said, taking his hand in mine. "I would follow you to the ends of the earth. Even to Chicago. Let's wait and see what happens. I don't know what I'll do without you when you head off with the band. But I feel deep down in my bones that we will stick together somehow."

Then I put an arm around his shoulder and said, "Come on. Cheer up. Let's try to look on the bright side."

Jimmy sighed and looked at me with a little smile. I leaned over and kissed him and then pushed him back onto the bed. I propped my head up on my hand and said, "Besides, for right now," I began slowly unbuttoning his shirt, "we've got right now."

Jimmy forced a smile and reached up to stroke my cheek. "Now," he repeated.

TWENTY TWO

The weather had been hot for the past few weeks. My garden was flourishing and many of the tomatoes had fully ripened. Jimmy and I agreed to give each of the neighbors some tomatoes fresh off the vine when we made the rounds to announce my engagement.

When Sunday arrived, I dressed in my best business suit, paying close attention to my grooming. Joe Locke had shined my shoes earlier, and I retied my tie three times to make sure it was just right. Jimmy returned from church, already well dressed.

Looking him over, I said, "You look just as pretty as a picture." Then I gave him a hug to reassure him. "You aren't nervous are you?"

"No, it's just a routine Sunday afternoon performance for the neighbors."

Jimmy carried the paper bag of tomatoes, and we walked around past the empty lot on the corner to the Mitchells'. In the brilliant afternoon sun, the young street trees cast small pools of shade on the sidewalk.

I led the way up the walk to the small covered porch and rang the doorbell. Jimmy stood a little behind me holding the tomatoes. In a moment, Clarence Mitchell answered the door, a newspaper in one hand. Watching him through the screen door, I thought a brief expression of surprise passed over his face, but he immediately smiled and said, "Hello, Dr. Holman."

"Good afternoon, Clarence," I began. "As you know I've been

renting my upstairs room, and I want to introduce you to the new renter." I made the introductions. Clarence did not open the screen.

"How do you do, Mr. Mitchell," Jimmy said with a smile and a small wave of his hand. Clarence stood there dumbly, unsure how to respond.

"Say, are Minnie and Clark around?" I asked. "I'd like to have all of you folks meet Jimmy. That way you won't think there is some stranger around the neighborhood trying to break into my house."

Clarence still said nothing, and I added, "I want to introduce Jimmy to all the neighbors who live close by."

Clarence hesitated, "I guess Minnie is around here somewhere." He turned and walked inside a couple of steps. "Minnie," he called. "Clark. Come on out here a minute." He half-turned back toward the front door.

We waited in awkward silence for a moment. Then I said, "You see, Mr. Mitchell, Jimmy works in the evenings a lot so I don't want you to be concerned if you hear him coming home late at night."

Clark appeared at the screen door tossing a baseball up and down. He halted when he saw me, looking confused. "Oh…uh…hi, Dr. Holman," he said. It was not a warm greeting.

Minnie Mitchell appeared behind them wearing an apron and drying her hands on a kitchen towel. She stopped short when she saw us and stood frozen for a moment. I felt a sudden coldness in the air. Minnie's hostility was palpable. No one spoke for a moment.

"Hello, Clark. Hello, Mrs. Mitchell," I said. "I wanted all of you to meet my new renter. This is Jimmy Harper. He'll be staying at my place until October when he leaves for Chicago. I was just telling Mr. Mitchell that Jimmy works evenings playing music so you may hear him coming home late at night sometimes. I didn't want you folks to be alarmed."

"I also play the organ at the Episcopal Church on Sunday mornings," Jimmy spoke up. "So I keep pretty busy. I won't be any trouble."

The Mitchells all stood in silence. Since no one seemed ready to take up the greeting, I proceeded. "Say, Clark, I wanted to ask if you plan to keep up mowing my grass on into the school year. I know you'll be busy with football—Dr. Gowan told me he'll be giving you your sports exam this year—but maybe you'll be able to find time on the weekends."

Now Minnie Mitchell would know that I had talked with Dr. Gowan. Still, no one in the Mitchell family broke the silence.

"I'm willing to double your pay if you can find the time," I offered. "You do such a great job. I'd hate to lose such a good worker."

"I don't..." Minnie started, but Clark broke in, "Gee, Dad, remember that old Model T I talked to you about, down at Garrison's garage? Dave and Tony agreed to go in with me on it. We want to buy it before school starts so we can start fixin' her up. Earning a little extra money would sure help."

"Clarence, I do not approve of the boy having an automobile."

"Now, Minnie, we've been all through this. Clark wants to learn about automobile engines and he needs to have a car of his own if he's going to pursue that."

Minnie shot a hard glance at Clarence, which he either didn't see or chose to ignore.

"Clark? It's up to you," Clarence said. "Do you think you'll have time for yard work this fall? I don't want you slacking on your schoolwork."

"Sure, I'll work it in," Clark said. "The lawn doesn't take that long."

Mrs. Mitchell, with no attempt to restrain the anger on her face, let out a loud sigh.

"Okay, son, it's your decision," Clarence said.

I thanked Clark for agreeing to keep at the job.

"I have to get back to the kitchen," Minnie said and turned to leave.

"Oh, Mrs. Mitchell," I jumped in, "I have one other piece of news for you all. I wanted you all to know that I am engaged to be married." There was another awkward silence as Minnie turned and looked sharply at Clarence again. Clarence glanced at her, catching her look, and turning back to me he broke the silence. "That is a surprise. Congratulations. Who is the lucky lady?"

"She's a nurse that I've known for several years. A real swell girl named Gwen Cook. I introduced her to Mrs. Mitchell at that lecture back in May."

Minnie folded the towel in her hands and said coldly, "I have to get bet back to the Sunday dinner."

"Oh, Mrs. Mitchell," Jimmy called out as she turned away again. He held the paper bag out to me. Minnie stopped but didn't look back.

"I almost forgot," I said. "I brought you some tomatoes from my garden. I've had a bumper crop this year." I took the bag and held it out. "I wanted to share some with you folks."

There was another moment of clumsy silence before Clarence said, "Well, thank you. That's mighty neighborly of you," and he opened the screen door.

Minnie finally turned toward us but hung back. I handed Clarence the bag of tomatoes and extended my hand to shake his. He hesitated a moment, then shook my hand, and said, "Congratulations on your engagement."

I held out my hand to Clark. He hesitated, then transferred the baseball to his left hand and gave me a weak handshake as if he was afraid to touch me. I stood back and held the screen door so Jimmy could shake hands. Minnie looked on coldly.

"Glad to meet you all," Jimmy said and smiled as he stepped forward and shook hands with Clarence and then Clark.

"I'll start your new wages next week," I said to Clark, closing the screen door. "Good afternoon, now." I started down the front steps toward the sidewalk and paused to glance back. Jimmy waved to the Mitchells, who all stood in silence behind the screen door like a tableau of store window mannequins in domestic dress. "Nice to meet you, Mrs. Mitchell," Jimmy called in through the screen door, then turned to follow me. As we came out into the sunshine from the shade of the Mitchells' porch, I heard their front door close firmly behind us.

We stopped back at my place to get a bag of tomatoes for Maude Williams. Once we stepped inside the house and closed the door, Jimmy and I looked at each other and fell into an embrace.

"Good God, what an awful woman," Jimmy said with a slightly hysterical laugh into my shoulder.

"Yes. She's full of anger, isn't she?"

When we relaxed our embrace, my shirt stuck to my skin, damp with sweat. Nervous strain, I thought, and considered changing, but when I thought of retying my tie, I decided against it. I slipped off my suit coat and suggested a quick shot of gin before we started off for Mrs. Williams' house.

As I took out the bottle from a cupboard in the kitchen, Jimmy asked me to tell him something about Maude Williams. I mentioned that she had a passel of grown children and that I'd met one of her daughters at the Iverson wedding reception. When her husband died, Mrs. Williams' daughters talked her into selling the farm and buying the small house next door. She had lived there by herself for a few years before I moved in.

When we knocked on her door, Mrs. Williams was considerably more amiable than the Mitchells. She greeted Jimmy warmly. There was no hint that she was trying to hide some harbored aversion left over from the gossip that Tom Harris had reported. Maude congratulated me on my engagement—and she especially appreciated the tomatoes.

Finally, Jimmy and I visited the Harris house. They had not met Jimmy before, and Tom invited us in. Jimmy met the children and then Polly offered us lemonade in the backyard. We sat in the shade and chatted about the neighborhood, while watching Jimmy play with the kids.

By the time we made it home, it was after 5. Loosening his tie, Jimmy said he felt duly initiated into the Sunny Grove neighborhood.

My dress shirt had dried some, but I told Jimmy that I wanted to change clothes before the next order of business—telephoning my parents and telling them about my engagement plans. Without my saying anything, Jimmy sensed that I needed to be alone and undistracted, so he picked up the newspaper and said he would be out front. After meeting the neighbors, he must have felt that he had earned the right to sit on the front porch alone when I wasn't around. That made me happy. I realized that there had truly been an engagement, of sorts, after all, not with Gwen but between Jimmy and me.

I had been rehearsing this call in my mind, and now I mustered all my courage and lifted the receiver. As I expected, my mother and father were pleased to hear the news, and the whole conversation went smoother that I had anticipated. Then I called Gwen to see if she had made her phone call. She told me that her mother had burst into tears at the news.

I joined Jimmy on the front porch.

"It's done," I said. We looked at each other.

"Are you relieved?" Jimmy asked.

I nodded.

"Then it must be the right decision."

We sat quietly for a time looking out on Elgin Street, watching the late afternoon shadows lengthen. Jimmy looked at me with a smile. I knew what he was thinking, and I smiled back.

In unison we both said, "Halma?" and laughed.

"Let's bring the set out here on the front porch," Jimmy said. There was an impish twinkle in his eye. I nodded.

As we played the game there for all of Elgin Street to see, we felt like we were getting away with something.

TWENTY THREE

After one game, Jimmy and I ended up in the bedroom taking off our clothes. He seemed more relaxed somehow, as if moving in and settling the engagement plans had loosened some internal restraints he had been carrying.

We were kissing playfully among the rolling hills of tangled bed covers when my hand found its way into the deep ravine between the cheeks of his buttocks. My fingers lingered there as I massaged his anus. I wondered if maybe Jimmy was feeling more adventurous.

"Do you want to try something different?" I asked.

We both seemed to find our sexual contact satisfying, but I still felt that we were limiting ourselves. I had been holding back and following Jimmy's lead, being reluctant to push at a deep reticence that I still sensed in him, that no man's land, a holding back on his part that I did not fully understand. I got the feeling that he was still maintaining barriers inside himself that he didn't know were there.

"What?" Jimmy said.

"Do you want to try browning?" I asked.

"What's that?"

"Anal intercourse." I pushed against his anal sphincter with my finger.

Jimmy rolled away from me onto his back. "I don't know," he said and paused. "Won't that turn me into a woman? Like you said at Gwen and Charlie's place."

"How do you mean?"

"Well...make me different. Like a fairy. Wouldn't the fellas in the band see a change in me?"

I remembered Jimmy's story about his cousin saying something similar when they were practicing sex in the hayloft. Obviously, Jimmy still had superstitions lodged in his mind. I tried to reassure him that he was always a man, no matter what sex acts he performed, but Jimmy said he needed to think it over.

"I just want you to feel free to be adventurous if you want to," I said. "Do you want to try penetrating me?" I took his erect penis in my hand. "I would like that."

"I don't know," he said and he was quiet. "Maybe some other time."

Was it our cultural shame over the lower digestive tract? From childhood onward, we are taught to feel embarrassment at the mechanics of eliminating feces. The embryonic development of the genitals with their intimate proximity to the gut course and the urinary tract dooms them to the stigma of the lower functions.

"Don't tell me that you're afraid of getting your tallywacker dirty," I said.

Jimmy laughed.

"Where did you get that expression?" he asked, still laughing.

"From my Texas cousins. The ones who taught me how to fish."

"Well, you're a lot better lover than you are a fisherman. I like sex the way we've been doing it."

I suspect what motivated me more than anything else was the fear that Jimmy might become bored with me. I didn't know what he might experience in Chicago, but I anticipated that he would have his adventures. I wanted him to remember me as being open to all his desires.

"There are all different ways to have sex," I replied. "Some people have sex without even touching."

I repositioned myself and studied the unnatural appearance of his circumcised penis for a moment before I took his naked glans in my mouth. Jimmy's body didn't stiffen this time and he didn't resist. Had I taken him by surprise? Or maybe he had become more curious than before.

A quiet hissing sound escaped into the room as Jimmy took in a long slow gasp at this new kind of stimulation. As I continued, I looked up across his abdominal muscles and saw a look of puzzled surprise on his face. But he was obviously enjoying it. I took my time, paying close attention to his responses. I kept thinking of his description of playing a trout at the end of a fishing line being like playing jazz, and I paused each time his excitement seemed about to burst. But the trout got away. Jimmy wasn't used to that mode of arousal and he ejaculated quickly. I tasted the pungent flavor of his semen before I swallowed.

After a time, I nuzzled my way up Jimmy's smooth torso and hugged him in my arms. A shudder went through his body as he recovered. I started to kiss his lips and Jimmy turned his head away.

"If you swallow that stuff, doesn't it make you effeminate?" he said.

Another sexual superstition Jimmy was harboring.

"Do you think I'm effeminate?" I asked. "I've swallowed a certain amount of semen in my time. Has that made me into a fairy?"

Jimmy looked away and considered this for a moment. "You're no fairy," he replied at last.

I remembered Billy Butler from Pioneer Park saying "none of that fairy business." Maybe Jimmy had picked up these attitudes from listening to some itinerant orchard hand in Watney Junction.

"Jimmy, the acts you perform sexually do not make you either masculine or feminine."

"Then what is the difference between masculine and feminine? What makes a person one way or the other?"

I considered a dozen different approaches I could have taken to his question.

"This is what I can tell you for sure—God has dreamed up many different kinds of people. And people dream up many different ways to have sex."

"I thought you didn't believe in God."

"I don't. I meant it just as a figure of speech."

Jimmy didn't say anything for a while. Then finally he reached over and took my penis in his hand. I had lost my erection by then. "Shall I use my hand on you?" he asked. "I don't think I'm ready to take you in my mouth yet."

I pulled Jimmy close to me. "You don't have to do anything to service me, honey-boy. We aren't keeping score and I don't have to have an orgasm every time. I'm happy just to be with you."

Jimmy relaxed into my arms, but I had the feeling his mind was not relaxed. I knew that, in the end, no matter what words I might say to Jimmy, these were things that he had to learn for himself, in his own way, in his own time.

TWENTY FOUR

The next day at work, I told Gowan privately that I had spoken with the Mitchells and that there shouldn't be any more trouble. Incidentally, I added, I had finally popped the question and was engaged to be married.

"Why, that's great news, Carl. Great news. Congratulations. Welcome to the club. Here let me give you one of my best cigars."

I declined as graciously as I could and reminded Gowan that I did not smoke.

"Now that you are anticipating a wife and family, I hope you have been thinking over our conversation about joining up with the Klan." He straightened his glasses and looked me in the eye. "It's been some time now and you haven't gotten back to me."

To be politic, I told him I was still considering it, but I had been preoccupied with the engagement for a while and now the wedding plans. There was so much to consider and arrange.

"Yes, of course, Carl. But you must keep it in mind. It's an opportunity that you shouldn't pass up. I know you were over there fighting to save the world for democracy," he went on. "And we appreciate your sacrifice there. And the expertise you picked up over there is a great asset to our community. But now we are under threat. We are in the middle of a moral war right here at home to save the heart of America from foreign influence. Join with us. We need men like you. This country is being flooded with foreign immigrants of the lowest caliber, and it is not healthy for our democracy. Socialists, radicals, uneducated imbeciles, degenerates."

I couldn't help noticing that he had left out Catholics from his list. Was he editing his remarks for my consumption? "They will go to the polls and vote to take over our government. You must join with us to save this great country we live in. Why someday soon you will be having children, Carl. Do it for your children. For all our children." Gowan gestured to the family portrait of his wife and four boys sitting on the desk. "For our future."

As politely as I could I reminded him that we had all immigrated to America from Europe at some point in the past. That was ancient history, he said. He was talking about today's dangers.

I told him I was thinking it over and repeated that I was awfully busy right now with marriage preparations and all the social obligations that entailed. Maybe after the wedding. I looked at my watch and mentioned that I had an appointment to get to.

As he led me to his door, Gowan put an arm around my shoulder and said, "You think about this seriously, Carl. We need you to join the fight. We beat the Huns. We can win this war, too. We've gone along with your medical reforms. Now help us reform American civilization. Form it anew, in the image of our forefathers, those glorious founding fathers who gave us the Constitution."

Again, I assured Gowan that I was carefully considering it.

If this was a war and everyone had to take sides, how could I remain neutral? Where would I find that phantom army in No Man's Land where I could escape joining the conflict surrounding me?

I deeply resented Gowan invoking the rhetoric of war to enlist me in the Klan. I knew that neither he nor Bleeker had ever been to war. Neither of them had even served in the military. Old men who have never been to war are often the most eager to embrace it. Most Americans walking around in our streets had no idea what war is. I had seen it. The moonscape of No Man's Land. The German artillery barrage at Meuse-Argonne. The triage.

I knew that war was the antithesis of civilization. And yet these "civilized" people held to the conventional belief in war, contributed to it, even actively supported the idea of it. But they couldn't ever imagine what war is and what it can do to you. The imagination cannot enlighten us about the unimaginable.

I had served with soldiers who, I knew, still believed in war. Perhaps it was akin to the physical phenomenon of primary shock. The mind, unable to deal with an unacceptable reality, shuts down and refuses to recognize that the body has been profoundly injured. Perhaps these soldiers had willfully blinded themselves to the terrible reality, unable to accept the political truth that a paternal government, in which they had invested their faith to act with wisdom and benevolence, had foolishly sent them into a situation that was so horribly wrong.

The human capacity for blindness and self-deception cannot be underestimated.

By the end of the day, everyone in the clinic and a number of other people working in the building had heard the news of my engagement. Whenever I was asked about it, I said that we hadn't set a date yet. This whole ruse, which began so casually, almost as a joke, had now taken on a life of its own. I would have to learn to live with it.

TWENTY FIVE

As September passed and the weather cooled, Jimmy settled into living at my house. The trolley line that ran through the neighborhood gave him convenient access to downtown and his new location was not the constraint he thought it would be. Jimmy said he liked living in a quiet neighborhood compared to the noise and bustle of downtown. He seemed to enjoy having more space and privacy after living at the boarding house. In the afternoons he could practice piano without the worry of disturbing boarders.

For myself, I was glad to have someone besides Joe Locke at the house during the day. When I got home from work, it was a comfort to find an intimate companion there. Jimmy was often fiddling around on the piano out in the living room, and the music was an added bonus that I had not anticipated. It was a pleasure to be awakened late at night by Jimmy's body slipping quietly into bed after he got home from playing with the band. And when I woke in the mornings, I was happy to have a warm body in the bed beside me, breathing softly in sleep—even though having him there made me reluctant to get up and go to the clinic.

I had informed Joe Locke that Jimmy would be moving in with me. But there was nothing I could say about our relationship or our sleeping arrangements. Previously, we had been careful to always leave the house before Joe arrived in the morning, but now it seemed absurd to keep up any pretenses. Since Jimmy slept till past noon some days after playing music into the wee hours, we decided that I would simply tell Joe not to bother my bedroom until after Jimmy got up. There was no hiding the fact that we were sharing my bed. Joe could not have neglected to notice, and he was well aware of the unused bed upstairs and Jimmy's clothes left in my room. When another person takes care of your dirty laundry, there are no secrets between you. But if any of this struck him as peculiar, Joe maintained his decorum and never mentioned it.

Joe Locke usually did my grocery shopping at Hamlin's Grocery on a commercial street a short walk from my bungalow. One afternoon, I left the clinic early because there were no patients scheduled after 3. Since Joe Locke was not working for me that day, I decided to stop by the grocery store on my way home. Jimmy was fond of chocolate bars, but Joe wasn't in the habit of purchasing sweets, and I kept forgetting to ask him to pick some up. I thought I would buy a surprise for Jimmy and shop for a few things for myself. As I approached the Hamlin's storefront, I puzzled over a new sign in the window—a small sign, placed in the bottom corner of the glass near the front door, reading simply "100%." It couldn't be an announcement for a sale at 100% off. That would be absurd. Then I remembered Gowan's remarks about 100% Americanism.

Inside, I wandered along the aisles past several shoppers, looking at items on the shelves until I found the chocolate bars. At the meat case, I said hello to Mr. Hamlin, the butcher.

"Hello, Dr. Holman," he said, "How can I help you?"

I ordered a quarter pound of sliced turkey breast.

Moving on to the produce area, I saw Minnie Mitchell carefully examining the celery. This was the first time I had seen her since Jimmy and I dropped by their house.

"Hello, Mrs. Mitchell," I said as I approached. At the sound of my voice she looked up, and then a hardness came over her face. Our eyes met momentarily, and I was taken aback by the sudden cold fury in her face. She returned her attention to the celery with a renewed intensity. I paused for a second, but she did not return my greeting, nor did she look up again. I passed on to look at the apples.

As soon as I left her, Minnie Mitchell turned abruptly and went to the meat case and began speaking in low tones to Mr. Hamlin. I saw them glancing in my direction, but I attended to my business and picked out several apples.

A minute later, a rapid murmur of voices caught my attention as I rounded the corner of the baking supply aisle. Mrs. Hamlin was speaking with Minnie Mitchell at the cash register. They were looking in my direction but they quickly glanced away when they saw me notice them. I walked away down the aisle to the bread loaves. I heard the sound of the cash register as Mrs. Hamlin rang up Minnie Mitchell's groceries, and the bell chimed at the front door as she left the store.

When I finished my shopping, I went to the front counter where Mrs. Hamlin stood next to the ornate brass cash register helping a young lady with her purchases. After the young woman left, Mrs. Hamlin busied herself with some boxes behind the counter. I stood by patiently, and an older lady shopper approached the cash register. Mrs. Hamlin greeted her by name and began ringing up her things. As the older woman departed, Mrs. Hamlin again turned her back and busied herself behind the counter without acknowledging my presence.

I waited for a few moments, expecting that Mrs. Hamlin would finish up her business and ring up my purchases, but when there seemed to be no end to her fussing and tidying, I spoke up.

"Excuse me, Mrs. Hamlin. Could you please help me with these things?"

She paused and stiffened at the sound of my voice, then continued with her business for a time.

"Mrs. Hamlin," I repeated. Again she paused and then pulled herself up erect without turning to face me. With slow deliberate movements, she walked silently away and went over behind the meat case where she held a brief whispered conversation with her husband. I looked away from this acrimonious exchange to regard my small basket of groceries. Shortly, Mr. Hamlin approached me and said, "Dr. Holman, let me talk with you outside."

I turned to look at him, standing nearby in his blood-stained butcher's apron, and I was surprised by the seriousness of his expression. He indicated the front door. I set my shopping basket down on the counter and he ushered me out. On the sidewalk he escorted me away from the storefront over to the curb.

"So, Doctor, you're the one who sends that little Chink to shop here at my grocery?"

"Why, yes. He's done housekeeping for me for the past few years."

"Let me tell you something, Doc. This is a 100% American shop and we don't want any Chinks shopping here."

My face must have revealed my astonishment.

"Don't pretend to be so shocked, mister."

I felt my blood pounding and my stomach tightened. I mustered all my restraint as I took a deep breath and replied, "My housekeeper's name is Mr. Locke and he is a fellow of excellent character."

"From what I hear, you're not such an excellent character yourself, and I don't want you shopping at my store either."

"My character?" I said. "What do you mean by that?"

"Certain things don't bear discussing, Doc. Now listen to what I am saying to you. Take your business elsewhere. Do you understand me?"

Mr. Hamlin's face was coloring and his posture had stiffened. I sensed that he might be getting ready to throw a punch at me any moment. There was nothing more to discuss. I looked him in the eye and tipped my hat. "Good day, Mr. Hamlin." I turned and walked away.

I had walked several blocks before I regained my composure. I became aware that beneath my suit coat my white shirt was drenched. I turned a corner and headed back to my car. I sat for a long time with my hands grasping the steering wheel, going over what had just occurred. My mind couldn't take it all in. I had never been treated this way, and I had no personal point of reference for such behavior.

At last I drove around until I found another grocery less than a mile away. I had heard of the place and seen it in passing, but I had never shopped there. When I walked in, I was surprised and relieved to hear the proprietor greet me in a thick German accent similar to that of Heinrich and Detlef when they spoke English. The sound comforted me.

I introduced myself and learned that the proprietor was Klaus Dietrich. I told him I had been stationed in Koblenz and visited Berlin after the War. He was from Bonn, he said, and immigrated to America in 1913 after crossing into Holland and then on to England. He told me with obvious pride that his sister in Milwaukee was married to an American.

I bought my chocolates and other items and left the grocery store thinking of the old proverb about clouds with silver linings. I instructed Joe Locke to shop at Mr. Dietrich's grocery after that.

TWENTY SIX

I wasn't able to tell Jimmy about the Hamlins that evening. He phoned to say that he had an afternoon rehearsal with the band before going off to an evening dance, so he planned to catch dinner out with the fellows.

He returned in the early morning hours and I awoke when he slipped into bed. After we exchanged mumbled greetings and kisses, Jimmy said he was beat and drifted off to sleep.

But I couldn't sleep and I watched him for a long time, listening to the gentle inspiration of his breath. If I'd had my stethoscope, I could have heard the internal sounds.

His chest rose and fell, the air passing into and out of his ribcage, like the tides of the ocean moving in and out of some seacoast grotto. There, deep inside Jimmy's lungs, the exterior world of the atmosphere joined the dark interior passageways of his bronchial tree where oxygen from outside joined the blood inside and pumped throughout his body. Jimmy shifted and exhaled with a little sigh.

My mind drifted back to the frightening incident at Hamlin's Grocery. I still needed to warn Jimmy.

Mrs. and Mr. Hamlin breathed from an atmosphere of white Anglo-Saxon heritage, steeped in Protestantism and heterosexuality governed by customs of courtship, marriage, and child-rearing. I had to forgive them their blindness. A fish in water doesn't know what water is, just as the air we all breathe is invisible to us. Being different, I was like a fish that had leapt up and broken out of the water's surface into a different realm.

I was reminded of Einstein's courage in discarding the old habits of thought of Newton's physics. He saw that the whole problem had to be restated and so he had demolished the accepted theory of ether. By changing his frame of reference, he discovered that the familiar ideas of space and of time were not absolute. He demonstrated that we are blinded by the comfort and security of an orthodox belief system. Truth often defies conventional thinking.

Protected by the predominance of accepted attitudes, society could justify the most heinous crimes against those who are perceived as different. So how could Jimmy and I protect ourselves from the blindness that surrounded us? Could our plan to hide behind a ruse of false conventionality possibly keep us safe? I held my breath, thinking of the consequences of failure, until I was forced to exhale, and the air in my lungs passed from the boundaries of my body out into the dangerous external world.

TWENTY SEVEN

The next day the old Lutheran Hospital called me in about a man who had a bullet wound to the chest. The patient died on the operating table and afterward I was filling out paperwork in a small office next to a nursing station. The door stood open as I worked and I could hear voices from the hallway. Dr. Ferguson's thin nasal voice was familiar. He was the one who had called on my war experience to help with this case, and he had assisted me in the operation.

"I'm Vice Officer Bateson," the other voice said. "We have some concerns about this case. What can you tell me about the murder victim and his wounds?"

Dr. Ferguson gave him a description.

"I understand this Dr. Holman was involved in the surgery," the officer said.

"That's right. He was an excellent hand in trying to save this fellow's life. The War certainly taught Dr. Holman a thing or two. But in the end there was nothing we could do."

"Isn't he connected with the Catholic hospital?" Bateson asked.

"I've heard he does surgeries there from time to time. But he's a colleague of the Gowan Clinic downtown."

"Oh. Bob Gowan and Harold Bleeker? I see. Very good. I guess there's nothing to worry about then."

Their voices faded off down the hall.

I could have read much into the brief exchange, but I tried not to. At the least, my association with Gowan and Bleeker served as some protection. How far would I have to go to maintain my standing with Gowan?

TWENTY EIGHT

Jimmy came home Saturday morning just before 7 after a late night at Bagwell's place downtown. I woke up when he sat down on the edge of the bed to take off his shoes. I rolled over toward him and mumbled, "Hey, honey-boy." I could just make out his dim figure in the predawn light struggling in around the window curtains. Through bleary eyes I watched Jimmy kick off the other shoe and fall back across the bed, still wearing his tuxedo shirt and pants.

"Hello, Carl, old boy," he said and kissed me. I could smell the liquor on his breath. "We made some hot jazz tonight, let me tell you. An old friend of Diggs' was up from Los Angeles and after the speak closed, he played music with us all night. And, of course, we had to celebrate his visit. We decided to try to finish off Old Man Bagwell's supply of booze. Guess what? We weren't able to do it." He laid his head on my chest and I stroked his hair.

"It smells like you gave it a good go."

"It was like trying to drink down the level of the ocean." Jimmy laughed. He nuzzled his face against my chest, sniffed at my scent several times, and then let out a long, slow breath.

The morning songs of the neighborhood birds floated in through the wire screen of the open window behind the drawn curtains. Jimmy raised his head and cocked it to one side, listening.

"Do you want to see me make the sun come up?" he asked.

"Hmm?" I asked, sleep still hovering close about me.

He sat up and turned to face the bedroom window. "Watch. I'll make the sun rise for you." I raised my head and propped it up by rearranging my pillow. Jimmy took a deep breath and began to sing softly.

"I hate to see…that evenin' sun go down

O, I hate to see…that evenin' sun go down

It makes me feel like…I'm on my last go round."

In spite of all the liquor, that extraordinary voice sang out with dark power and emotion, even as he kept the volume low.

"If I'm feelin' tomorrow…like I feel today

Feelin' tomorrow…like I feel today

I'll pack my grip…and make my getaway.

St. Louis woman…wears a diamond ring

She pulls my man around…by her apron string…

If it weren't for powder…and this store-bought hair

That man I love…wouldn't go nowhere.

Nowhere."

As Jimmy sang, the rays of the rising sun struck the outside of the window shade turning it golden. The sunshine filtered in around the edges of the heavy curtain, lighting up the dim room with its rosy glow. Jimmy turned back to me and lay across the bed on his stomach, propping his head on his hand and looking at me with a sly smile.

"You always make the sun shine for me," I said and I reached out and touched his cheek.

He leaned forward and gave me a long kiss. Then he quickly jumped up and slipped out of his clothes, leaving them lying in a puddle on the floor. Hopping into bed, he kissed me again, and groping toward my genitals with his hand, he said, "Let's see what else I can make come up." The liquor must have loosened his tongue—and his inhibitions. Jimmy burrowed his head under the covers and licked down my torso till he found what he was looking for. He was tentative at first. Then his lips and tongue grew bolder and he finally took my organ into his mouth. He and the alcohol must have thought it over and come to a favorable conclusion.

The sun came up twice that morning.

TWENTY NINE

The date of the band's departure for Chicago was nearly upon us. Diggs planned on taking several days to drive to Minnesota, then Wisconsin, with all the musicians and instruments and luggage in two cars, his and Howard's. The fellows in the band were all working hard, playing most nights and rehearsing new material in the afternoons. Jimmy busied himself with last-minute details, tidying up his room upstairs, organizing his sheet music, buying some new clothes and a new suitcase. Joe Locke helped Jimmy make sure his small wardrobe was clean and pressed.

I asked Gwen and Charlie to join us for a farewell dinner on the Saturday before Jimmy's departure. We all pitched in and cooked a big Italian meal. Gwen and Charlie gave Jimmy a silver St. Cecelia's medal on a neck chain so that the patron saint of music could watch over him. I gave him a new leather belt with a cleverly concealed compartment for hiding cash and two hundred dollar bills tucked carefully inside. Jimmy said he was a little nervous but mostly excited and eager to get going.

Charlie was the only one of us who had spent any length of time in Chicago, and we enticed her to tell us her memories of the city but she confined herself to mentioning some sights Jimmy should take in. Before dinner was over, Gwen and Charlie had coaxed Jimmy into telling his story about the man who lost his coat again. When he got to the part about the pockets, we were all laughing so hard that our sides ached.

After dinner, Jimmy played some of the band's new material for us on the piano. Then we played records and took turns dancing with each other.

Before the evening was over, we made sure to play a couple of farewell rounds of Halma. I won the first round and as we began setting up for a second game, Jimmy took out a cigarette. As he was striking a wooden match on the matchbox, it broke in two and the flaming head flew across the table and landed on the Halma board. We were all so taken by surprise that it took a moment for anyone to respond. Finally, Gwen leaned forward and blew out the flame, but not before it had caused a small burned spot in the wood of one of the white ash playing squares.

"Oops," Jimmy said, "My fire got away from me."

"Sounds just like Mrs. O'Leary and her cow," Charlie joked. "Be careful in Chicago, Jimmy."

Charlie won the second game and she proposed a toast, wishing Jimmy the best of luck in Chicago.

"Charlie and I are sure going to miss you, honey," Gwen said. "I hope you will come back to Oregon."

I secretly made the same fervent wish.

The band was to leave on Monday morning. Jimmy had given notice at the church so we were able to sleep in on Sunday morning. Later he said he wanted to have a quiet meal at home and turn in early so he would be rested for the trip. I made a special arrangement with Joe Locke to come in for the Sunday evening meal. He poached a salmon, and I opened a bottle of white wine that I had been saving. I told Jimmy that I was going to miss him, but I wanted him to take advantage of this opportunity. I reminded him that he knew Mary, that her family lived in Chicago, and that I suspected they were pretty well-connected. Maybe they could help him make some contacts. I encouraged him to get in touch with her while he was there, just to lay things to rest. He promised he would.

As we finished our meal, Jimmy was quiet for a time. At last he said, "I didn't want to think about leaving…and the band has been so busy lately, it was easy not to think about it. But now that it is actually happening, I don't want to go. If I'd known…. Maybe I never would have planned to go to Chicago. But I can't let the fellows in the band down. And now I feel like I'm letting you down."

"I know, Jimmy. It's okay. I know you have to give this a try. I went off to war in Europe and had some adventures. Now it's your turn to have some adventures."

I handed him a package. "I brought these home from the clinic for you. I know you will probably have some sexual encounters in Chicago. Use these condoms and you can avoid contracting any venereal diseases. An ounce of prevention, you know."

Jimmy examined the package and then looked over at me with a forlorn expression.

"Hell, Carl. This makes me even more reluctant to leave."

"No, Jimmy. You have to get out and see some more of the world. Hear some jazz. Find out what's out there."

We looked at each other.

"We never know what the future has in store for us. But I believe…I know we'll end up back together again sometime." I paused. "Maybe sooner than you think." I studied his sad face for a moment and felt I had to say something to brighten the mood. "Maybe Gowan will drive me so crazy that I'll have to pack up and move to Chicago." I laughed and Jimmy finally cracked a smile.

"Carl, you've been the best friend a fella could ask for." He reached out and put his hand on mine.

We were silent for a moment. I turned my hand over so our palms met and clasped his fingers.

"You know, there is always a place here for you if things don't work out in Chicago."

Jimmy nodded.

Soon after Joe Locke cleaned up and left, Jimmy and I went to bed and repeated acts we had become accustomed to. I prayed this would not be the last time.

In the morning, before I left for the clinic, Jimmy carried his suitcase out into the living room and left it by the front door. It was time to say goodbye. We stood in the middle of the carpet and hugged each other. I remembered the first time we played Halma there on the carpet. I remembered hugging Jimmy there the midnight he came to visit, drunk and feeling so miserable. I remembered the Sunday afternoons we spent listening to the phonograph there.

We kissed one last time and I reluctantly broke our embrace.

"I'd better get to work," I said, but I hesitated. "Here, keep one of my business cards." I held one out to him.

He took the card in his hand and looked it over. "You bet I will." He looked up at me.

"Stay in touch," I said looking back at him. Then I forced myself to turn and walk to the front door. He followed me out.

I left Jimmy standing on the porch waving goodbye as I backed down the driveway and out into the street. I truly didn't know if I would ever see him again.

During my day at the office, my thoughts would not let go of the impending emptiness that threatened my existence.

Should I regret letting Jimmy go? I could have been selfish and tried to discourage him from leaving. But then he might have come to hate me for closing off his big opportunity. That would be worse than losing him to Chicago. And I had put the idea in his head that he should visit Mary. What if that should rekindle their relationship?

But I remembered when I left for the War, nothing could have dissuaded me. I was enticed by a wide open future and the anticipated career advantages. Jimmy was no different.

Still, I was not ready to go back to my old life seeing only Joe Locke at home and having only an occasional friend for companionship. I did not look forward to an empty house, a house without piano music, an empty bed.

I had lost Gerald for good. Now I had to hold on to the hope that Jimmy and I would be together again someday.

When I returned home from the clinic that night, Jimmy and his suitcase were gone.

Esteemed Reader,

This is a self-published novel. You can help make it a success:

- Tell all your friends about this book.
- Post reviews on amazon.com and goodreads.com
- Sign up for my newsletter at medicinefortheblues.com
- Share about the book on social media networks and blogs.

Thank you for reading books.

Jeff Stookey

ACKNOWLEDGEMENTS

I must thank Merilee Karr, MD, for invaluable advice about medical details, for pointing me in the right direction in areas of medical history, and for recommending numerous resources. I thank her too for her encouragement and for implanting in my mind the dangerously liberating concept of writer's intuition.

Historians George Painter, author of *The Vice Clique: Portland's Great Sex Scandal*, and Tom Cook, founding member of the Gay and Lesbian Archives of the Pacific Northwest, have both been extremely helpful. I am grateful for their generosity with their time, their resources, and their knowledge of Pacific Northwest gay history. The Archive is now housed at the Oregon Historical Society.

I have to acknowledge the memory of Jesse Bernstein (known as Stephen J. Bernstein in print). Even though he's been dead for all these years since his suicide, I have felt him watching over my shoulder as I wrote this, and I could never have done it without his example and his encouragement. I guess you won't mind, Jesse, that I used some of your ideas.

All my dear friends who read the first draft have my undying gratitude for saving me from numerous mistakes, and my writing group from The Attic contributed invaluable feedback. This book would never have emerged into public form without the help and encouragement of my editor Jill Kelly. She reined me in and prodded me to judiciously prune countless twigs and branches.

And, it goes without saying, (but those are exactly the things that must be said), that I am endlessly indebted to my partner, Ken Barker, for tolerating, and even encouraging, this peculiar obsession with writing words on paper. Thanks for your support in keeping me going, and especially for helping me to keep from losing my nerve.

THE STORY CONTINUES.

Watch for *Chicago Blues*, Book 2 of the trilogy *Medicine for the Blues*, planned for publication in Spring of 2018.

Book 3: *Dangerous Medicine*. Available Fall 2018.

Please visit the website:
www.medicinefortheblues.com

ABOUT THE AUTHOR:

Growing up in a small town in rural Washington State, Jeff Stookey enjoyed writing stories. He studied literature, history, and cinema at Occidental College, and then got a BFA in Theater from Fort Wright College. In his 40s he retrained in the medical field and worked for many years with pathologists, trauma surgeons, and emergency room reports.

Jeff lives in Portland, Oregon, with his longtime partner, Ken, and their unruly garden. *Acquaintance* is his first novel. Contact Jeff at **medicinefortheblues.com**.